To Rachel:

Merriest of Christmases to you, my friend!! Calling you "friend" is a high priviledge indeed :)

Here's to MANY more awesome conversations,

Love ya, April Arnold-Gillar

Watch for More
Novels by April Arnold
Also from Indigo Sea Press

indigoseapress.com

Ghosts & Physics

By

April Arnold

Abyss Books
Published by Indigo Sea Press, LLC.
Winston-Salem

Abyss Books
Indigo Sea Press, LLC
302 Ricks Drive
Winston-Salem, NC 27284

This book is a work of fiction. Names, characters, locations and events are either a product of the author's imagination, fictitious or used fictitiously. Any resemblance to any event, locale or person, living or dead, is purely coincidental.

Copyright 2015 by April Arnold

All rights reserved, including the right of reproduction in whole or part in any format.

First Abyss Books edition published
December, 2015
Abyss Books, Moon Sailor, and all production design are trademarks of Indigo Sea Press, used under license.

For information regarding bulk purchases of this book, digital purchase and special discounts, please contact the publisher at indigoseapress.com

Cover design by Stacy Castanedo

Manufactured in the United States of America
ISBN 978-1-63066-196-0

For Mildred "Mickey" Arnold: my all-time favorite storyteller, my inspiration to write, and an absolutely amazing Grandma. Love you much!

CHAPTER ONE

"What are you getting?" Mick asked, still absorbed in the "entrees" section of his menu as well as the giant glass of iced tea he'd been sipping for the past several minutes.

Katie dropped her own menu onto the table, scrunched her eyes closed in concentration, and waved her right hand around in circles before slamming a single finger down onto a random portion of menu print. She opened her eyes and replied, "Apparently I'm having the 'printed in USA.'"

"Of course you are. I should've known. But I'll bet the grilled salmon would work better for your stomach."

"Yeah, you're right. Printer ink always has given me indigestion. Then the salmon it is! What are you having?"

"Hamburger with extra 'burger,'" Mick said.

"They call that a 'double' now. C'mon, Mick, this is a seafood restaurant. The surf 'n turf option is the only scenario in which you're allowed to order anything that doesn't breathe underwater."

"Who says?"

Katie closed her menu and pointed at the front-page logo. "Eva does. She owns the place. She gets final say."

Mick grinned. "If she has final say, then why did she put a hamburger on the menu in the first place?"

"Well if you're gonna get nitpicky," Katie responded with a teasing pout. She removed the silverware that had been wrapped tightly and sanitarily inside her napkin then looked down just long enough to lay said napkin in her lap. When she looked back up again, Mick was staring disbelievingly at his menu. Precisely where the item "hamburger" had been printed, there was now a big, black, burned spot.

Katie frowned. "That's weird."

"Tell me about it."

"You're getting the shrimp."

*****

Long, long ago but not so far away, I, Katie Burgess, was born. Okay, so it wasn't that long ago, but considering the story I'm about to tell, it could be interpreted as such. It all depends upon your definition and perception of time: is it linear or layered? For most of my life, I assumed it was linear. You're born, you exist, you die, and there's no going backward...or forward. But the more ghost-hunting shows I watched (stop laughing), the more I started to wonder about the linearness of life. Of course, now I'm giving away the story before it even gets started and must therefore shut up about it. Where was I going with this?

Oh yes! I was born. I was born in the mid-70s to a typical Central Texas farming-and-ranching couple. We lived in a modest two-story house on the outskirts of Austin, just outskirty enough to have an open field behind our house bordered on all sides by trees of various levels of attractiveness: oak, pecan, sycamore, cottonwood, and a smattering of those annoying mesquites that are only good for flavoring barbecue sauce, or so it seems. There was a creek at one end of the field that generally had running water in it except for the summertime when rain decided not to grace us with its presence overly often. I particularly loved that spot until one afternoon when I unwittingly sat down on a piece of driftwood . . . and noticed that a four-foot rattlesnake already occupied the space. My Discman and I removed ourselves in short order. When not cavorting in the great outdoors listening to music and singing at the top of my lungs to reptilian audiences that likely wanted to bite me, I loved to read and write stories which transformed me into the biggest daydreamy English nerd ever. Add to that a penchant for all things sci-fi and fantasy, and you've got a quirky personality.

When I wasn't enjoying my favorite pastimes, my parents used me as free child labor in the cotton fields. Okay, so it wasn't that bad, but I never want to chop up another sunflower again. We always had a dog and a few cats that kept inbreeding and producing imbecile kittens which, of course, meant that they inbred themselves out of existence. The dogs fared much better (because they were big man-sluts who spread their canine seed far and wide) and provided adequate "a stranger's here" alerts over the years with their voluble barking. My Dad also kept chickens, but I'll tell you more about that nightmare later.

From little girlhood I'd always been fascinated with the supernatural. Most people seem to be, but I was one of the unusual ones (unusual for back then, anyway) who took said fascination to the next level by organizing community Halloween ghost hunts for all the local kids. There was this creepy old broken-down house a couple of neighborhoods away from ours that simply begged to be investigated, so every year I conned my best friend Mick into accompanying me as co-leader . . . well, protecting me would be more accurate. Why nobody ever tore that sagging wooden remnant of a building down was beyond my comprehension, but as things turned out, it was a darn fortuitous thing that they didn't. So now that you have a bit of backstory, we'll get to the actual story.

The eight-year-old version of myself stared dubiously out her bedroom window. The ten feet between ledge and ground were much scarier at night than they were in the daytime, and it was such sights that made me long for the real-life existence of transporter beams. Normally after a fun-filled Halloween evening of candy gathering, hoarding, and devouring I was ready for sleep, but not this Halloween evening. Tonight my friends and I were going to find ghosts. What we were going to do with them once we found them, we didn't know. We just liked the glamorous idea of looking for them because, odds were, we'd run screaming into the opposite direction should one actually appear.

Having changed out of my Lt. Commander Deanna Troi costume and into something more clandestine yet teeny-bopperishly stylish, I clutched my Hello Kitty bag crammed full of trick-or-treat chocolate bounty while intently watching the driveway leading up to our house. He was late.

"Katie!" I jumped at the sound of Mick's nine-year-old voice unexpectedly coming from the side of the house instead of the back. "Up here! Did you bring the ladder?"

Mick clunked his way to my window, dragging the modified ladder he'd just "invented" along behind him. "Yeah, I just finished it today. Do you have any extra chocolate? I didn't have time to go out and get any myself."

That was his code for "I was too busy combining uncombinable chemicals and blowing up stuff to remember today was Halloween and we were supposed to go candy-gathering and ghost-hunting tonight." Even at age eight, I had accepted this about Mick's personality. "Plenty. I got extra just in case. Where's everybody else?"

Mick quietly and carefully leaned the ladder against my outside wall as I tentatively made my way onto the ledge. It had a bizarre configuration, but even as I stepped onto the top step, I knew it would be the sturdiest ladder ever. Mick was a brilliant and nice kid like that, always making sure he didn't accidentally murder me. As I slowly descended, Mick replied to my previously asked question. "They're not coming."

I stopped mid-ladder. "What? The big sissies, are they really that scared?"

Mick stood at the base of the ladder helping to hold it steady. "No, they got caught toilet- papering Principal Dooley's house. They barely got away before he smacked 'em all with that paddle of his. Anyway, now they're hiding out."

I couldn't help but laugh at the thought of my friends being chased down Rosewood Avenue by an irate Principal Dooley armed with his monogrammed paddle. "Then I guess we'll just have to do this ourselves and make fun of them later," I said as I hopped off the final step. Together he and I dragged the ladder behind the house until it was sort of hidden in some tree shadows. "You ready?" I asked him.

Mick dug around in his pockets for several seconds then pulled out a compass, map, notebook, and a pencil whose use I could only assume was for taking notes. He spent several more seconds aligning his compass with magnetic north as I rolled my eyes. "We're only going a few blocks away. I don't think magnetic poles are going to flip in that length of time."

He looked at me, surprised. "How do you know about magnetic poles flipping?"

"I decided to read my science assignment this month. Now let's go."

"Candy, please?"

I handed him my Hello Kitty bag. He was less than pleased. "Really? You want me to carry this thing?"

"Did you want the chocolate or not?"

He finally took the girly accessory from me, his lust for candy overcoming his manly sense of shame and embarrassment. A walk that should've taken fifteen minutes wound up taking half an hour due to the "unusually bright and defined appearance" of Mick's favorite constellation at which he decided to stare for the additional fifteen minutes. And he took notes. Copious notes. They even had equations in them. Never trust someone—especially a nine-year-old—who uses words and equations on the same sheet of paper.

"Stop it with the math already! We have a mission, and it has nothing to do with the dimensions of the Snickers Galaxy."

"Milky Way."

"Whatever! Don't talk about it, just eat it!"

We spent the rest of our walk in relative silence, relative because anytime Mick ate caramel, he smacked it like a gum-chewing cow with TMJ. As we reached the front gate of our destination, Mick was excited in a scientifically intrigued sort of way. I was bloody freaking terrified.

Mick yanked out his pencil and notepad again then grabbed my hand. He was in "unparalleled discovery" mode. "C'mon, Katie! Let's see what we find!"

He may as well have been attempting to coerce an antelope to play in the lion's lair. "I can't. I, umm . . . I have to pee."

"No you don't, you're just scared."

"Scared people have to pee all the time!"

"You can hold my hand, and I promise I won't let go." He meant it. It was sweet.

Still, I continued to resist his insistent tugging at my hand. Suddenly an old white, lacy curtain wafted from one of the supposedly haunted house's front room windows and into my line of vision. The ghosts wanted my soul! "No, I really do need to pee now! I think I'll run over to Rosewood Avenue for some toilet paper."

And with those words, I ran fearfully in the direction of my house leaving a poor, bewildered Mick standing on that forlorn sidewalk all by himself.

The next morning I discovered my Hello Kitty bag situated safely on my window ledge, still half-full of candy. I felt really bad.

He was a trooper about it though. The same routine carried itself out for several more years, though why Mick continued to blindly believe I'd suddenly develop courage in the face of paranormal entities was beyond me. By the time we'd outgrown the Halloween urge to seek out ghosts and ghoulies, Mick was graduating with a Master of Physics degree, seriously contemplating a doctorate, and was being recruited by multiple higher-brain-function employers including NASA. His dark brown, buzz-cut little-boy hair had grown out nicely since childhood, not that it was a conscious decision on his part, mind you. As an adult, he simply never seemed to realize that it needed to be trimmed. I liked it longer and shaggier, though, so I neglected to share with him that a haircut might be a more professional-looking idea. Yeah, selfishness happens. He'd always been a scrawny little boy, so I was shocked to one day realize that he'd achieved an even height of six feet. It had happened so gradually, I hadn't noticed. His one incongruous vanity was a penchant for arm and tummy muscles, so he had a regular two-days-a-week workout at the local gym. Otherwise he took little pride in his physical appearance, preferring to wear ratty old t-shirts and slouchy jeans accompanied by hiking boots that were groovy circa 1994. I thought he was pretty cool anyway. He did hobo chic quite well.

Then there's me. I had finally managed to earn my Bachelor of English degree, was in no way interested in even higher education, and was contemplating how much longer I'd have to be receptionist at the local tire store. Sure, it gave me time to write, but after a while oil fumes and steel-belted radials begin losing their ability to literarily inspire. As far as looks go, most of the time I think I'm cute enough. I'm a comfortable 5'6" with a sort-of slender build. Like many women, I have days when part of my brain tells me in no uncertain terms that I'm fat, but then the other part of my brain says no you're not, go eat some chips and salsa. My eyes are chocolate brown, and my hair is usually-auburn (thank you, over-the-drugstore-counter hair dye!). At one point in life I thought it would be an awesome idea to hack my hair off a la Halle Berry and kept it super short for a few years until all the comments from family members about how I looked like I had head mange convinced me to grow it back out as soon as possible. So being the hair extremist that I apparently am, I embarked upon a years-long quest to see just how long my hair could get. It's now to the length point that, when I lean back in a chair, I'm hair-pinioned and can't turn my head. That's my physical appearance in a nutshell, unless you're allergic to nuts at which point I'll put it into a plastic Easter egg.

So yeah, despite the fact that I didn't much care for my day job, a girl had to pay the bills; and until something better came along, it's what I kept doing. One Friday night upon leaving my place of gainful employment, I decided I wanted company for that night's season premiere episode of my favorite ghost-hunting series. Smartphone in hand, I called my best friend Marianne. We'd been pals since the old ghost-hunting days, but her direction in life had solidified at a far earlier age than mine had. She impressively and forward-thinkingly earned some type of computer degree and got a job that I can't pronounce; which, of course, means she makes the big bucks. I forgave her for this financial sin, however, because she seemed to actually enjoy hanging out with my weird self and always brought the wine. Hey, she could afford it! She didn't sling steel-belted radials for a living.

Her ringback tone sang "Funky Town" at me while I waited for her to answer. When she did, I verbally hit her hard and fast. "Hey, chicky! You have any plans tonight? Groovy! Then grab a couple bottles of wine 'n come over. The season premiere is tonight! What? Oh, he's locked away in that laboratory of his. Something about Higgs boson particles and matter conversion, I don't know. Hey, we could order pizza!"

Plans that included happy pizza and fermented beverage solidified, I rushed home to my apartment—or "rushed" as much as 5:00 Austin traffic would let me—and attempted to tidy things up to the point of looking respectable. Trash needed to be taken out, but I knew my neighbor would corner me and spend a good twenty minutes describing how their toilet would randomly run during the night and that he suspected a plumbing conspiracy. So no taking the trash out right now. I'd hide it on the patio and take it to the dumpster after Marianne left and Mr. Wiggins fell asleep.

My own silent toilet really needed cleaning. Crap, no way around that one. So I cleaned it, swept the visible areas of the bathroom and kitchen floors, then closed my bedroom door because the floor desperately needed vacuuming due to all the crickets in multiple stages of dying. I always sprayed them with bleach cleaner then left them to their crickety fates.

Pizza ordered and quickly delivered, I awaited the arrival of my wannabe ghost hunter compatriot. One day we'd actually get out there and hunt again. Really, we would! For now, I blamed Marianne's reluctance on that bad toilet-papering experience all those years ago.

Knock, knock. It was Marianne. And wine! I excitedly opened the door, grabbed the wine, and beelined for the kitchen. "Great to see you too, Katie," she said as she closed the door behind her and I drilled the wine bottle opener into the cork. "Why is your neighbor staring at me like that?"

"He probably thinks you're from the plumber's association or something. But it's almost time! Here," I said and slammed a full wine glass into her hand. Thankfully it was white wine otherwise her brand new ivory sweater would've been ruined. "The pizza's in the oven. I've got paper plates and paper towels here if you'll grab the box."

"Sure thing," Marianne replied, smiling all the while. She knew how excited I got over this show. Of course I knew how excited she got over the main investigator dude's physique, and I had to admit, it was a thing of true masculine beauty. "Can't wait to see how tight his t-shirts are this season," she remarked, placing the pizza box onto the floor then sitting down next to it.

Munching hungrily on the thin crust veggie pizza, I full-mouthedly answered, "They have to be to distract viewers from all the stupid comments he makes. I actually can't wait to see what new devices they'll be using. That spirit box thing is too cool!"

"Yeah, but don't you think it's a little unscientific? I mean, the thing searches radio frequencies for voices. Human voices. How can you be certain that what's heard isn't coincidental?"

That was Marianne: always the pragmatist. I think it went with the unpronounceable computer software design gig. "Now you sound like Mick." I sighed then paused to consider her question in unbiased terms. "Okay, so I have to admit that there's a chance for contamination when such investigation tools are used, but some of the direct responses they've gotten have been amazing. The voices actually answered the investigators' very specific questions."

Marianne took a sip of her alcoholic grape juice. "Your point is also valid. I don't know, I guess I just have a harder time believing in all this stuff. I've never seen anything like it myself, and neither has anyone I know."

"Oh ye of tiny, itsy bitsy faith! Just because you haven't seen it doesn't mean it doesn't exist. Like the atom, for instance. Until we had the proper investigative tools available, we didn't know they existed either."

Marianne nodded her agreement. "But they do. Touché."

"Thanks!" I said, then clanked my glass against hers in a conciliatory toast.

The show had begun, and Marianne was well into the process of lusting after weight-lifting, fully-buffed-out investigator dude. I, despite my devoted interest in the televised haunted prison investigation now taking place, was suddenly being pulled along a new mental pathway. What if . . . oh my, the inspiration! The possibilities of such a hypothesis were endless if said hypothesis could be proven. But how could I ever hope to explain it in proper physics terms? I had no clue about physics beyond how to spell it. This called for mental reinforcements.

"You can hang out here as long as you want, Marianne, but I gotta go."

"That's cool," she mumbled, completely lost in her glass of wine and the hunky ghost hunter on T.V.

CHAPTER TWO

"I still say it would work."
"Yeah, and you did so well in that physics course you took."
"I never took physics."
"And that's my point."
I exhaled in frustrated exasperation. Conceptually, my newly-inspired theory was sound. No, of course I didn't understand the finer points of quantum physics. I could barely grasp the thicker, chunkier points of regular physics. Higher mathematics is Satan's chosen vehicle on the road to insanity. Still, did that mean I couldn't have a creative-yet-analytical inspiration? Did that mean my brain was so deficient that any idea it might produce should be immediately discounted as ludicrous?

"Katie, that you would even attempt to understand the subject is borderline ludicrous."

Damn. "You and Mulder don't see eye to eye, do you?" He mostly glared at me.

"So you don't know anyone who might be interested in working with me? Anyone with real science brains to whom I could postulate my theory?"

"The simple fact that you could put together a sentence so chock full of vocabulary candy is a sure sign that you aren't geared toward a field as number-focused as this," Mick continued. Apparently he thought all those job offers from NASA made him some kind of an expert on the subject.

In spite of a strong compulsion to pout, I persevered and pushed one last time. "You're not going to help then. That's it, the end, I'm going to have to forge ahead all by myself and create several killer headaches in the process thereby having to delve deeply into savings simply to afford the necessary pain-relieving aspirin so I can indirectly burn holes into my stomach lining in order to alleviate the agonies of . . . "

"You're not letting this go anytime soon, are you?"
"Nope."
"Fine, whatever, I'll see what I can to do help."

I grinned, inwardly and outwardly. I knew he'd cave if I used enough big words and way-too-long sentences. Lots of words all strung together like that never ceased to annoy him, especially when he was in the middle of math-related projects. "Then you'll meet me on Saturday, say around 11:00? You know the place. We've gone there every Halloween since we could walk."

"But you always stayed at the end of the sidewalk and made me go inside by myself."

"That was only for the last ten years. I ran away and left you by yourself the first time, remember?"

Mick sighed once more then conceded with a grin of surrender. "This could be fun even if it's just a 'for old time's sake' kind of thing. Besides, as much as I hate to admit it, your idea really does have some basis in reasonable theory. And who knows? Maybe such crack-inspired thought processes really will help me get a mention in a few major scientific journals."

"Or maybe The Enquirer."

"Were you wanting my help or not?"

I hugged him gratefully, slung my purse over my shoulder, and prepared to exit his makeshift, trash-strewn office that was actually just a glorified mop closet; or it would have been had he owned a mop. "Yes, I want your help. And our work might indeed help to solidify the validity of a brilliant new theory thereby launching quantum physics into a whole new realm of understanding and all thanks to you!"

"That would be nice."

I was nearly out the door before turning around to whisper, "Hey, Mick."

"What?"

"The truth is out there!"

He smacked me with a paper wad.

*****

I arrived on location at 10:30 just to make sure all was prepared. I sat down on a large tuft of dried-up-and-crunchy brown grass and leaned against the weathered, creaking gate post that was miraculously still standing and capable of supporting weight. I glanced right and left to see if maybe perchance the always-late guy would be early. No sign of him yet, but I wasn't overly shocked or even taken aback. To pass the time and help maintain a firm grip on my nerves that kept screaming, "This is still so stupid!" to my brain, I opened my super-cool black leather bag and took inventory. It was Goodbye Kitty for me now! Inside the big-girl bag were our hi-techgadgets sure to record paranormal evidence for presentation to posterity. "Flashlight . . . check. Batteries for when the ghosts drain the batteries already in the flashlight . . . check. EMF detector that I stole from that electrician I don't like . . . check. Electronic voice recorder . . . check."

"That's the mini tape recorder you've had since you were nine and have yet to use."

My head jerked upward. He was here. I looked at my watch. He was early! "Hey, it works the same as the spiffy digital stuff, at least I think it still works. Better test it right quick." I proceeded to do so, and all circuits were functioning within normal parameters.

"Hey, can you do that thing where you talk really slow into the recorder then change the tape speed during playback so it sounds like you just sucked helium? The ghosts might like that."

"Your face might like that," I muttered in response.

Mick ceased making fun of me just long enough to stare at the dilapidated pile of circa-1920, nailed-together boards looming before us. Well, maybe "looming" was a bit on the exaggerated side. What was left of the house consisted of six rooms, and one of those had already cracked and crumbled into nothing. He'd heard tell that even rattlesnakes found living there to be beneath them.

"Having thoughts?" I asked as I stuffed everything back into the bag for easy transfer.

"A few, yeah. Ya know, this would be a lot easier if we had the traditional stash of chocolate for those fear-induced low-blood-sugar moments."

I reached back into my bag and yanked out a king-size bag of Reese's Pieces. "You read my mind!" he said and grabbed the bag from me.

"No, I heard you speak." I'd already eaten half the package's contents in my panicked quest to remain calm. I would be going in this time. I would not run back home citing overflowing trash bags—or bladders—as excuse for my departure.

Mick finished off the candy in an impressive matter of seconds. "Hope you have more buried in that MIB bag of yours."

"Even if I did, I certainly wouldn't tell you . . . friggin' candy stealer," I replied, rising from my now-squashed tuft of grass and lugging the equipment bag back onto my shoulder.

Ruminating on the last few Pieces stuck in his teeth, Mick surveyed the house one more time before falling in behind my beeline for the front door that was hanging by a hinge. "We're really doing this, huh? There's no way I can talk you out of here and into someplace less condemned? The last several decades haven't exactly been kind to the foundations."

"Yes, we're doing this, and no, you can't talk me out of it," I declared. I grabbed his flashlight and slapped it into his semi-supplicating hand. "You're in charge of the EMF detector too. It should squeal if there's a spike in the electromagnetic frequencies around us."

"Oh boy," he said in monotone, taking the device from me. "At least I get stuck with the manly equipment and not a Hello Kitty bag this time."

"It had chocolate in it."

"So what's your theory on all this again? If a ghost is around then the electromagnetic field will increase?"

"That's the usual ghost-hunting theory. I'm taking it a step further and thinking that it might not be the ghost itself that causes the spike. It might actually be the shifting and bending layer of time that is the primary culprit."

"The 'primary culprit.' Geez, only you could take friendly ghost hunt banter and turn it into a display of English prowess."

"Ya know, for a math person, you have a sizeable vocabulary of your own, mister! My theory still makes sense though, doesn't it? I mean, isn't it more logical that time is layered as opposed to linear? Why couldn't there be parallel universes going on around us all the time? Isn't that part of this whole quantum theory business?"

"Yes," Mick said as he carefully stepped over a board with huge nails sticking straight up and into the path of his foot. "But you've managed to reduce it to the simplest terms possible."

I switched on my flashlight and beamed it around until we were deep enough inside the house to eliminate as much outside noise as we could. Since we were investigating inside the busy city limits of Austin and right next door to a popular Austin-area pharmacy, that was indeed a challenge. The only other distracting noise heard were my feet shuffling carefully through potentially-hazardous debris and rat droppings. When I finally encountered a space that was reasonably clean, I laid the leather bag down and proceeded to sit on top of it. "Turn off your flashlight and have a seat somewhere. It needs to be totally dark."

"And that lit-up drugstore sign a street over really contributes nicely to the ambience. Doesn't it seem odd that they haven't torn this place down yet?"

I ignored his last question. Yes, it did seem rather odd, but now wasn't the time to discuss the whys and wherefores of residential versus commercial zoning practices. "As dark as it can be, then. The ghosts are used to it. We can be too."

"No, you can be too. I can be used to a cold beer at the pub by my apartment. That's what I can be used to."

"Oh, stop whining," I ordered, reaching into the pocket of my jeans. "Here, eat some more chocolate."

"Oooo," he gasped before devouring the caloric mass.

"Shhhh! I'm going to start asking questions and see if I can get any responses on tape."

I got a grunt from Mick, but that was it. He generally had a one-track mind, and right now that track was on the Baby Ruth between his jaws. I heard him fling the wrapper somewhere in the general vicinity of "in front of us" and rolled my eyes. "Seriously, what parts of 'be quiet' don't you comprendo? On top of that, you're littering. Pick that up."

I could feel Mick staring at me as incredulously as was within his power. He was right. The ghosts most likely wouldn't mind one more tiny article of trash strewn about their happy home. "Is anybody here with us?" I asked to the relative silence.

"Did you bring any soda?"

"Dammit, Mick, would you please shut it?"

"Hey, if you don't like the way I conduct paranormal investigations then I'll just be on my way . . . ouch! What was that for?"

"What was what for? I didn't do anything, although a smack to the back of your head is definitely warranted by now."

There was nothing but measurable silence from Mick. Finally. "You kicked my leg when I asked for soda."

"It's not that I didn't want to, but I'm a paragon of restraint. Now what do you mean I kicked your . . . ?"

The EMF detector screeched, then nothing. It screeched again. More nothing. With a slightly shaky voice, Mick said, "I take it that's supposed to mean something."

I didn't answer. In between my rapidly-increasing heartbeats I managed to address thin air yet again and asked, "Is someone here? Was that you who set off the machine Mick is holding?"

Several seconds' worth of screeching.

"Dude," was all Mick could manage. He reverted to his junior high vocabulary in moments of stress. I flicked my flashlight on and pointed it toward the detector. It was quiet yet again. "Is that what you wanted to happen? Does that mean time was warping or overlapping?"

"That's the theory I need you to help me prove," I whispered in response. "I, umm . . . I think we should go now."

"Big, bad ghost hunter you are," he teased, as bravely as possible. It was obvious Mick was just as shaken.

"Well, we can't be passing out from fear or whatever. The rats might come gnaw our legs off. Besides, I actually got into the house this time. It's progress." I was rising slowly to my feet, holding tightly to what was left of the wall behind me. My leg muscles were the consistency of apricot preserves, and from the noise Mick was making simply by getting up, I could tell that his were too. "Wanna go have that beer now?"

"Thought you'd never ask. I need something to wash down the chocolate anyway," Mick replied as he weaved our way through the garbage and back out the front door.

Newly-laid asphalt and exhaust fumes aside, the night air was incredibly welcoming as we left the musty confines of the old house and made for the sidewalk. I rewound the small amount of tape used and hit "play" just to see what we might have caught: us arguing, Mick chewing, cockroaches laughing at us, me griping at him about throwing his trash on the floor . . . "Wait!" I called to Mick who was now several steps ahead of me.

He turned around, annoyed at having his forward motion impeded. "What? Can't we at least vacate the general premises first before you get all sleuthy?"

His annoyance faded as he looked at me. My face was pale (and for me, that means hotel-sheet white), my eyes were wide, and my lips were quivering. "Listen," was the only word I could force out as

I played the tape back for him.

We heard me say, "... on top of that, you're littering. Pick that up."

Immediately afterward a high-pitched someone whispered, "Pick it up!"

*****

The beer tasted extra good, and I hated beer. "This is good," I reaffirmed in case Mick couldn't read my thoughts.

"But you hate beer. And that's just a light beer anyway. It's the white bread of beers."

He read my thoughts. "And you're drinking tar in a glass. Under the circumstances, my iceberg lettuce beer tastes good. So what do you think? You heard it too, right? There's something there . . . a spirit, a living person in another time existing in the same spot as us but within a different phase differential . . ."

"Phase differential?"

"Well . . . that's what Geordi LaForge suggested."

"Oh, in that case . . . glad you haven't resorted to citing Wikipedia."

I smacked him for that one, sloshing hoppy goodness down the front of my t-shirt in the process. Dabbing away at the inconvenient dampness, I unsuccessfully resisted the urge to retort, "Those plotlines and technical scenarios are based in scientific fact, thank you very much!"

"And who told you that? Locutis of Borg?"

I just sighed and nodded. I sounded like the biggest sci-fi freak of a nerd in the whole wondrous Roddenberry universe. But we did have evidence. We did! I just had to keep Mick from embracing the sarcastic long enough to help me explain it all. With a sudden longing for a fruity, girly alcoholic beverage I admitted, "Look, Mick, I know this is quite the far-fetched notion for your creative-boneless body to comprehend, but if you'll forget it's me for just one second and address the question a bit more objectively, you can at least give me some idea closure."

"Closure, huh? Well, that's reasonable. What am I getting out of this again?"

"Besides the chocolate?"

He grinned stupidly, bits of Baby Ruth peanuts still stuck in his teeth.

"My undying love and devotion."
"And another glass of tar. I'll do it for another Guinness."
"Done."

CHAPTER THREE

It couldn't be this simple, I thought to myself as I ascended the science building steps at the local university where Mick was studying. The process was never this easy, even for the crew of Starship Enterprise. The pivotal answer always involved tachyon particles and warp nacelles being interconnected by an illegal phasing-cloak, or some sort of techno-babble along those lines. But all Mick wanted to do was set up an intensely focused and concentrated electromagnetic field around and inside a small area, namely our observation space inside the old house. I finally found him in his cramped office, knee-deep in pencil shavings, graph paper, and file folders. He was muttering out thoughts to himself when I entered the sort-of room.

"We already know something is a bit off about that house, so it's a logical place to start. We did get some EMF spikes, and maybe with a prolonged injection of extra power we can get even more activity."

"All of that stands to reason," I audibly confirmed as a way of announcing my presence. "It doesn't sound nearly as complicated as I thought it would, but . . . "

After jumping slightly at the sound of my voice, he switched right back into thinking mode. "Hey, you weren't up for the past forty-eight hours researching, working through, and reworking through the formulas necessary to create a field intense enough to break through time barriers but not kill us both in the process."

"No, I was sleeping 'n stuff."

"I even had to run our plans by one of my professor's TAs and get a second opinion. But I do think we've finally got an adequate-yet-safe equation that should sufficiently destabilize the theoretical time continuum enough for some amount of collapse to occur. We'll probably feel some dizziness during the process, but it shouldn't be too bad assuming we won't be exposed to the field for too long a period of time. How long were you thinking anyway?"

I was very much feeling my ignorance, disliked it immensely, and was suddenly irrationally suspicious of his big-word usage. I also felt an unnerving longing to respond with a, "Make it so!" "I'm thinking that 'as long as it takes' or 'as long as we can consciously stand it' will be plenty good enough. I don't particularly want to be passing out in some unknown parallel dimension for an indeterminate amount of time if we can help it . . . especially now that Andy knows about the plan."

"He's not that bad."

"Says you."

"Still haven't forgiven him for beating you on the verbal half of the SAT, huh?"

"It was a conspiracy."

Mick scooted his rolling chair across the room—all six feet of it—and consulted yet another pile of number-covered papers. Obviously he'd been researching topics along these lines for quite some time, and the jerk never told me about it? But upon seeing his mountain of research numbers, I looked quickly away. Such sights gave me bad dreams. "I'd ask you to explain more in-depth, but I just had lunch."

He grinned in the midst of his paper perusals. "Equations still terrify you, huh?"

"I'm about to pee my pants."

He laughed harder than was anywhere nearly acceptable for a doctoral physics candidate. "Okay, the toilet's over . . . hmm. No. The toilet's actually stopped up right now. I've been kind of preoccupied and haven't had time to call the plumber."

"It's all good, sir. I'll give the plumber a call from the convenience store where I am now going to pee."

"I'll bet Mr. Wiggins knows a good one!" And he laughed yet again. "Anyway, I should have everything figured out 'n wired together by the weekend. What say we transcend time and space Saturday night?"

Urinary trauma forgotten, I kissed his forehead and said, "It's a date. I'll bring extra chocolate."

"And soda. Bring soda this time."

"What, no Guinness?"

"No, no. I never drink alcohol when ghost-hunting . . . or travelling into other dimensions of time. We might hit town during Prohibition."

In precisely two nanoseconds, Mick had forgotten my presence and was waltzing happily about in his mathematical world where no mere mortal dared to tread. With much fear and not a little trepidation, the notion that I was totally falling for him hit me like a quart of milk . . . and not the present-day quart of milk, no. This was the old-school, glass-bottled stuff that was left on people's doorsteps every morning. I was Elizabeth Brainerd, and he was Fred McMurray in The Absent-Minded Professor. We would marry and have little flubberlings.

I exited his workspace and firmly grasped reality in the shape of the door knob. I was officially lusting after my life-long best friend who was a math freak. I needed mental and emotional balance. I needed that girly alcoholic beverage!

*****

The rest of the week crept by like the last glop of ketchup that simply will not slide down the sides of the bottle and into an advantageous squeezing-out position. I wisely used this slowly-moving time to get a manicure. Upon exiting the nail salon, I wasn't outside thirty seconds when I felt the need to get a pedicure as well. Forces of nature against me and my limited bank account, I rushed back inside the salon and was plopping my feet almost immediately into the bubbling whirlpool of foot-massaging ecstasy. If I could've said "Emergency!" in Vietnamese, I would have. Surely whatever time period we discovered would be inhabited by people who could respect proper nail maintenance.

Then there was the shopping. I needed proper time-warping attire. Some strange cliché-ful voice inside my head said it should be a black outfit. Why black? We weren't going to be breaking and entering. Well, technically I guess we were . . . breaking down time barriers and entering spaces the Divine had never intended for us to go. If we weren't meant to discover, then this whole experiment wouldn't work anyway . . . right? Oh crap, I just smeared a nail!

Four hours and $400 later, I exited a particularly trendy shop near the university and deposited my designer black leather skinny jeans, black high-heeled leather boots, and black leather corset-thingy into the passenger seat of my car. What the hades had I been thinking? Apparently, "Seduction: priceless!"

The credit card company would probably go ahead and price the excursion at $400, I thought as I cruised my old Pontiac up the interstate and back to my apartment.

When Mick dropped by to go over the official game plan and saw my new duds lying atop the bed, he rolled his very practical eyes. "So what, you're thinking we'll wind up in the dominatrix dimension?"

I whimpered.

"What's wrong with a good old-fashioned t-shirt and jeans?"

I didn't know. I had wanted to do something special. I wanted to look good for him. How was I supposed to tell him I was awkwardly tripping head over stiletto heels for his left-brained, number-worshipping self? I was an English guru, for heaven's sake . . . a creative-minded gal to the core! I wrote, I sang, I daydreamed, I romped freely through waterfall-laden lands with full bottles of wine in hand to enhance the experience! What the freak was I supposed to do now that I loved a math nerd?

"I have these," I mindlessly mumbled, dragging out an old, holey t-shirt with my high school mascot emblazoned across the chest. Likewise, the jeans I bemusedly brandished possessed the structural integrity of a paper airplane. I'd look like Mick!

Upon seeing that no leather or high heels were included in the ensemble, Mick nodded his head and proclaimed, "That's perfect."

Exhaling heavily, I re-bagged my awesome-but-entirely-impractical sexy outfit and stuffed it into my closet. What did I have to do to impress the guy? Get "$\pi r2$" tattooed across my butt?

"Why are you trying so hard? I realize you have a tendency to overdress sometimes, but . . . well, this is extreme even for you. In fact, I think I'll take that stuff with me just so you won't be tempted to actually wear it in public."

After spending a few extra seconds throwing things around my closet in order to curb the tears that were so irrationally threatening to form, I exited and promptly sat myself down upon the bed, grasping my pillow tightly. "I can honestly say that I have no idea what I was thinking."

He smiled and plopped down beside me, slinging an arm around my neck and shoulders. "On that we agree. I'm guessing you're starting to feel the nervousness that could arise from the idea of warping into a different time period, huh?"

An out! "It could upset anyone's equilibrium, and seeing as how I already have tendencies leaning toward the unbalanced when it comes to clothing . . ."

"Exactly." Then he kissed my cheek before rising nonchalantly from the bed and heading for the door, my never-to-be-worn outfit in hand. He paused only a moment to add, "Plus there's the fact that you're madly in love with me." He smiled, watching intently as I stared open-mouthed from my pillow-clinging position on the bed. Without another word he winked, left my room, and departed.

The boy really knew how to make an exit . . . for a math nerd.

*****

After a slight delay caused by me finally having to take out the trash and Mr. Wiggins subsequently questioning me about why Mick (who was disguised as a plumber) had been in my apartment several evenings ago, I was now making my way to our launch site. I employed yoga-esque breathing exercises to calm my nerves. I would've used actual yoga breathing exercises if I'd known any.

Alright. Now I must behave normally, must pretend like no top secret codes of silence have been breached. If he didn't say anything about it, I wouldn't say anything about it. Breathing, just breathing . . . and popping chocolate like there was no tomorrow. If this experiment went all wrong, there might not even be a tomorrow. Theoretically there could be a "yesterday," but . . .

Dressed acceptably in the old jeans, disintegrating t-shirt, and chunky black Candie's tennis shoes that were almost as old as the t-shirt, I trudged yet again along the same semi-scary sidewalk up to the dilapidated gate swinging single-hingedly from a fence that was once whitewashed. My nifty black bag was draped over one shoulder, carefully packed so that extra candy and soda would fit along with the other necessary gear. Supposedly Mick was already on location setting up his gadgets, but I'd believe that when I saw it.

Lo and behold, I saw it. A stationary spotlight shot a single white beam through half of the paneless front window. Making my way carefully through the gate, up the concrete walkway creased with grass struggling for growing space, and onto what was left of the front porch, I heard Mick curse unabashedly as some manner of tool hit the ground.

"Hey," I called, letting my bag slide to the floor.

His head immediately shot upward. "Perfect timing. I'm in need of high-calorie salvation."

I knelt onto the rotting boards and dug a giant bag of peanut butter M&Ms from out of its depths. "They didn't have Reese's Pieces today."

Mick grabbed his salvation gratefully. "You're an angel...a

chocolate-covered angel with peanut butter for a heart. Marry me and have my miniature peanut butter cups."

I laughed as all tension dissolved from the pit of my stomach and was replaced with giddiness. "So what do you think of my outfit? Haute couture, hmm?" I spun around once before catwalking a few feet back and forth.

"Nice. Very nice . . . much better than the leather," he commented. "Soda?"

"Ah yes," I remembered and handed him one of my carefully hoarded diet sodas, still cold from sitting awhile in the freezer before bagging.

"It's diet."

"Yes, and it's a good thing considering how much chocolate you just inhaled. You know that stuff goes right to the hips."

"To your hips, maybe, but it looks good on you." And he winked again, leaving me speechless. "Now. I've gotten everything set up according to the present plan, but it may need to be tweaked as we go. I can increase the field from this handy little device."

He brandished a gadget that looked frighteningly like a garage door opener. "That looks like a garage door opener."

"It is, basically. It's a garage door opener on meth. This can harness and control more than enough power to change your world, baby."

Grinning amusedly, I perused the room and intently studied his handiwork. Sort of encircling us were five cylindrical devices that looked like those room deionizers or ionizers or air wafters or whatever. "You've been just a little busy! Dare I ask how this is going to work?"

He glanced up at me from the mad whirl of equating he was doing on his MENSA-approved scientific calculator. "You may dare, but I don't think you really want to know. Tachyon particles aren't involved, but . . . "

"Well, then I don't want to know. Nothing good can come of an experiment that doesn't include tachyon particles." I stared into his eyes, blank-faced and serious.

He covered the four feet that separated us, wrapped both arms around my waist—calculator still in hand—and kissed me smack on the lips. "That's all you really need to know anyway," he whispered before pulling reluctantly away.

The goofy, drug-addict smile that must've been on my face only increased the size of the one already on his face. "Took you long enough," I managed.

"Eh, you know us math types. We rarely see the momentous discovery right in front of us."

I watched in a state of semi-delirium as he checked wires and took readings at various points in the room. Back in Doctor of Physics mode, Mick relayed his findings to me. "The edges of the room have a slight electromagnetic reading, but there really does seem to be some sort of convergence in this central area where we're standing."

"I think it might be the limestone. It's supposed to help conduct such energies, and this whole city sits on top of limestone . . . thus the cave system running beneath us."

He stared at me like I had just announced the Death Star's destruction. "Of course. Limestone tends to store electromagnetic energy. Good call." And then he went back to his calculator.

I would never have to be jealous of another woman, just that calculator . . . which didn't matter too much since he'd have to share me with a dictionary AND a thesaurus. I dug out my own EMF detector and began my own sweeps of the room. A sudden powerful spike right around my right knee told me that Mick had turned on his machine or devices or . . . I wasn't sure what to call it. "Are we ready then?"

He analyzed each cylindrical thingy one more time before walking to the center of our hi-tech Stonehenge. "We're ready," he said, reaching a hand out to me. "Time to make history, m'dear."

"Or re-make it," I whispered, suddenly terrified by the concept of what we were about to do. It was one thing exploring a haunted house. It was another thing entirely exploring uncharted time/space continuums. Giggling nervously I continued, "Maybe I should get my head out of Starfleet and back on planet Earth, huh?"

He hugged me tightly and kissed the hair falling out of its clippy. "I like your head right where it is, thanks. Okay. I'm going to gradually increase the field's strength until we start seeing changes in our surroundings."

"Assuming that we actually do see changes."

"Hey, if it doesn't work this time, we'll just keep trying. Remember what Thomas Edison said."

"Wow, imagine how much brighter and more efficient this bulb thing could be with nuclear power?"

"1% inspiration, 99% perspiration?"

"I know, but my answer was better."

With one arm wrapped firmly around me and his other hand working the garage door opener, Mick began modulating frequencies and increasing power and all manner of sci-fi crap I couldn't believe was happening in real life. With a heart mostly full of Mick (and the rest longing for my scoffed-at diet soda), I watched carefully for any difference in the spotlit view around me. For at least a minute nothing happened, but after that minute I began to feel dizzy. "Mick . . . I think something is happening. My head is getting all spinny."

His grip tightened on my shoulder. "Mine too. Just hold onto me. Can you take another minute or two?"

"Yeah, I'm okay," I said and wrapped my own arm bracingly around his waist. As I did the room began to quiver like still water when a stone has been dropped into it. The room's rippling only increased my sense of vertigo, so I searched out one object upon which I could focus. The center of the mayhem seemed safe enough, so I stared with as much concentration as possible. The air around us was humming, buzzing with energy. It sounded like a jetliner still on approach yet not close enough to produce an eardrum-rupturing sound.

"There's something," Mick said, his voice somewhat shaky.

"You mean besides the rippling? I don't . . . no, wait. There IS something!" I thought I was excited but wasn't quite sure due to the massive disorientation of reality.

He pulled me closer as a vague shadow began to materialize. The room seemed brighter, more organized, much more intact. No cockroach would ever dare scurry across this incredibly clean floor. There were curtains appearing at windows which were no longer pane-less. Faded wallpaper was suddenly vivid and affixed onto well-defined walls delineating the boundaries of lived-in rooms. An old wood-and-metal crank-activated phone came into view on the wall just to my right. Rugs were laid neatly upon the aforementioned cleanly-swept floors as the sounds of an old radio became audible. I could see a well-used cast iron bed pushed against a wall in the little room to my right, a new fringe-edged dress with matching hat and gloves lying upon it.

"What the . . . " Mick gasped as our surroundings came into full, sharp Technicolor view.

A thirty-something-year-old lady in heels and a bright floral housedress glared at us. Her hair was tightly-knotted into a bun at the back of her head. She would have had a pleasant demeanor had she not been brandishing a broom and scowling at the severely-displaced time travelers before her. Without missing a beat she reiterated, "I told you to pick that up!"

*****

"Open the garage, Mick, open the garage!" I yelled with latent terror in each syllable.

"What the hell are you talking about?"

"Turn off the thingies! She'll beat us to death with her broom, and our corpses will be full of splinters!"

It finally dawned upon Mick that what I actually wanted was for him to discontinue our time crossover due to extreme psychological and emotional duress. "I can't just turn it off, Katie."

"That's what she said!" Extreme fear always made me grasp at humor.

"Oh good lord. I'm trying to explain to you that the process must be slowed down gradually, or the sudden electromagnetic field dispersion might do us considerable bodily harm."

Frantic, I clawed at his arm with my polish-flaking fingernails. "We're not ascending from the ocean's depths, now, just do it!"

Growing more frantic because of my own franticness, Mick began adjusting the dial on his futuristic mechanism. I watched as the woman turned her back on us and began walking away, her knuckles noticeably white from clutching the broom handle. Seconds later the sights around us rippled once again until we were securely back in our own time. We both stood motionless for several seconds, afraid to move lest we initiate an unwanted time warp.

Oddly enough, Mick was the first to speak. "Beer. Mick want beer."

CHAPTER FOUR

So this is how we found ourselves sitting on the same stools in that same pub where our brilliant time-transcending, quantumly-physical plan was hatched. My hand shook involuntarily as I raised a Tanqueray martini to my lips. Thus far I'd spilled half of it down my shirt front thanks to these rattling nerves. I'd have to drink in bibs from now on lest I ruin all my shirts. By contrast, Mick's gargantuan mug of Guinness hadn't been touched. Instead he stared intently into its depths, back rigidly straight, hands tightly clasped in his lap.

"What do you expect to see in there? Dumbledore's memories?"

"They don't serve butterbeer here."

I relaxed ever so slightly at his "lighthearted banter" attempt. "Well at least you haven't lost that rollicking sense of humor." One sip of martini finally made it successfully down my throat.

"We did it, Katie. We really, really did it. So why aren't we excited? Why do I want to lock myself in my lab and reread the scientific papers of Sir Isaac Newton while sipping warm brandy?"

I swiped a swizzle stick from the bartender's stash and sucked up the last of my martini before I could spill any more of it. Felt much better then. "Because it's your comfort zone, although I'm not sure how the brandy worked its way into the scenario. We just exited the most uncomfortable zone we've ever been in to date. I personally would like to lock myself in my apartment with my blankets, several Jane Austen movies, and my favorite thin crust veggie pizza, but we've got to accept and deal with what we've just accomplished . . . what you've just accomplished."

Mick finally calmed down enough to realize the hollow helpfulness of a swizzle stick. "Hey, it was your idea," he admitted, slurping at the beer with desperate dedication. "It's doubtful I'd have ever come up with anything so . . ."

"Insane?" I smiled at him.

Mick returned said smile. "I was going to say 'innovative,' actually. You have a fantastic mind. It just leans more toward the creative than the hard-line scientific. That's probably part of the reason we work so well together."

"Two halves of a whole?"

"Something like that."

"Nifty. Just don't make me write it as a fraction."

Mick all-out laughed at that typically-Katie remark and waved to the bartender for two more drinks. Tossing aside his swizzle stick crutch, he returned to the main subject of import. "Okay, so we just made quantum physics history. At some point I'll have to write a scientific report on the topic which means you get to edit."

"Goody!"

"Thought you'd like that. Of course Andy will have to get some of the credit for this."

"Not goody."

"Now, now, let's be fair. He was always better than you at those analogy exercises."

I threw the swizzle stick at his face.

"But for now I think we need to go back and further assess 'the other side,' if you will. Maybe we could even have a conversation with Broom Lady."

All muscle shaking having ceased, I was tackling my Tanqueray like a big girl and with renewed confidence, despite the fact Andy realized before I did that red was to apple as green was to pear. "We could bring her a dustpan as a gift!"

Deadpan expression.

"Or not. Instead we could find out what time she's in, her name because I don't think she'd appreciate 'Broom Lady' much, what her life is like, if she gets criticism from men for expressing herself with her clothing . . . "

"Good start. You make a list of interview-type questions, and I'll check out the equipment to make sure all is still well with the programming."

I could see the manic exhilaration in his eyes. It always preceded thirty-six straight hours of mathematical over-indulgence and mechanical invention. "Not tonight, Mick. Tonight I just want to crawl into bed and sleep, and you need to sleep because you've been up a lot longer than I have."

Mick winked over the top of his mug. "You want to just sleep?"

Beer generally made him frisky.

****

The following morning dawned far too brightly and early. After drinking my glass of diet instant tea and reveling in my usual makeup routine, I scoured my closet for clothing sloppy enough to warrant Mick's approval. Having achieved success, I exited the apartment with my bag of time-warping accoutrements slung over my shoulder, interview questions included. I trudged slowly down the very-familiar sidewalks and up to our launch pad for time exploration. Upon entering the house, I immediately knew that all was not well with Mick by the fact that wires were unattached and strewn about the blackened wooden boards. "This is always what happens when cockroaches attack."

Silent fuming from my new boyfriend ensued for several seconds, then, "We blew the generator. At least that's the best solution I can come up with. I've disconnected and reconnected everything in all manner of workable configurations imaginable, but nothing...well, nothing works."

My bag clunked dejectedly to the floor. "So we need a new power source. Okay, we can figure this out. Umm . . . how about the RXS Pharmacy across the street? Surely they have outlets."

Mick looked incredulously up at me from his crouched position on the splintering floor. "I'm sure they do, but it's doubtful that they'd appreciate having time and space warping their goods and customers into other dimensions. It's just rude."

"No, no, I mean outside the store. There's got to be one of those industrial looking outdoor outlets too. I'll go check!" And before Mick could offer a negative response, I was out the door and jogging to the back of the next-door pharmacy. It was still early, so the store wasn't open thereby guaranteeing minimal prying eyes. Sure enough, implanted into the back wall of the store was a super-duty outlet just perfect for our needs. Now all we needed to do was cart the equipment over here. Huh. I might not have thought this through thoroughly.

With a little less "jog" in my step, I reentered the house just in time to see Mick kick the generator across what was left of the room. "So there's a plug as predicted, but . . . "

"But how the hades are we going to get all this stuff over there? Yeah, as much as I hate admitting this, it's probably the only way we're going to get any experimentation done anytime soon. It would take several days to locate another spot with this much natural electromagnetic energy for us to manipulate."

"So let's do it! Tell me what I can carry, 'n thy will shall be done."

Mick suddenly got "that look" one didn't typically see in his eyes as he sauntered up to me. "My will, huh? This has tremendous possibilities." And he kissed me. Science aside, boys will always, ultimately, be boys.

"Keep it in your pocket protector, honey," I said, even as my cheeks flushed red-hot. "It's an intriguing thought which I'd love to explore later, but at present, we've got journeys to make."

"I know, but I love messing with you. Alright, you start carrying the cylinders over, and do please be careful. You have no idea what this stuff costs."

"No I don't, but you have all those awesome research grants that need spending. And after all of this gets announced?" I waved my arm around the room, indicating the incredible system he'd invented. "You'll have your pick of any grant out there!"

"That's likely, but for now we've got to gather more information which requires functioning, unbroken cylinders. Now hop to it." And he smacked me on the butt.

"Aye, aye, Captain!" I saluted. Then firmly grasping the first cylinder, I walked determinedly toward our new—and kind of stolen—power source. He'd have to hook everything up, but at least I could provide the cheap manual labor portion of the process. Upon reaching our new research site, I gingerly set the apparatus onto the pavement and returned to the shack for more. "Now that I think about it, we probably could've finagled something with an extension cord," I said.

"Now that you think about it?"

That lapse in mental acuity aside, everything had now been relocated and put back together rather quickly since a) we were motivated to discover new realms of existence today and b) the store opened in just over an hour. We had to make this quick. All necessary components connected, Mick plugged the mechanism into our secondary power source, grabbed my hand, kissed it for good measure, then began his attempt to shift us back into whatever time we'd occupied the previous day. "Now, it's likely we won't be arriving in the same house. It might not even be a house at all. Come to think of it, it might not even be the same time."

"Doesn't matter. We'll just ask whoever we meet if they know the Broom Lady," I giggled, this time with anticipation.

Mick continued making adjustments to his garage door opener as the familiar rippling effect happened. It only took seconds for us to start seeing our alternate surroundings, and Mick had been right: it wasn't the same house. There were more windows, and it had wall-to-wall carpeting on the floor instead of simply a rug on hardwood. There was, however, the same lady, though instead of a broom, she was carrying a coffee cup from what appeared to be a kitchen and into the living room where we were now standing.

Understandably, she dropped the coffee cup.

April Arnold
CHAPTER FIVE

A small fire blazed on the ground outside the back door of Grandpa Jimmy's implement shed. A copper pot dangled above it from an iron chain, its contents boiling in the heat. He considered the temperature level then added a few more chunks of broken tree branch to the fire. Walking back into the shed for further inspection of his undercover enterprise, Jimmy listened intently to the rhythmic drip, drip, dripping of liquid falling from looping coils and into a ceramic jug. Nodding approval, Jimmy sat down and leaned awkwardly back in a rickety wooden chair, its joints creaking painfully as he rocked all of his weight back and forth on cracked back legs. Flakes of whitewash fluttered to the dirt floor with each movement, blanketing said floor like lead-based snow.

"Bubble, bubble, toil and trouble . . . who says I ain't got class?" he spouted to no one in particular before bursting into laughter. Reaching to the ground, he picked up a second ceramic jug, this one already filled with the brewing beverage. Jimmy guzzled a couple of mouthfuls and shivered a full-body shiver. "Good stuff! This batch will sell for a pretty penny, that's for sure."

"I hope it sells for several pennies," came a female voice from behind him. "The cotton fields look pretty bad since the storm. We'll be lucky to break even after those straight-line winds hit last week."

Jimmy smiled semi-dazedly at his wife as she inspected their only source of income. "It had to be a tornado, May. No straight-line wind could've done damage like that on its own. Want a taste?"

Knowing that contradicting him was futile, May only nodded her head and accepted the pleasantly-offered "taste" from Jimmy's outstretched hand. Her initial reaction to the liquid of dubious legality was similar to that of her husband's. "Mercy! At least our corn crop was good. We might just make it through the winter thanks to your more creative ways of using it."

Jimmy rocked once more with pride, and as he did, the chair finally gave way. With a splintering of worn-out wood and ruined joints—Jimmy's and the chair's—he crashed to the ground in a moment of butt-smashing glory. After a few moments of sucking in oxygen, he muttered a, "Well now!"

Concerned, May knelt by his side. "You alright? I've warned you a hundred times about doing that, Jim. That chair was part of my mother's dining room set and made it here all the way from Boston. It's a wonder the thing put up with your beer gut for as long as it did."

"Corn gut," he corrected. Dusting himself off, Jimmy slowly rose to a standing position, testing his muscles and bones with each movement. "Yeah I know, but I like rocking in it . . . soothes me."

"Well, don't think you're going to swipe one of my good dining room chairs to destroy, I don't care how soothing it is."

"I can swap some of these jugs for a whole new dining room if all the liquor comes out as good as this batch. Hey, have you seen Sammy? He was here a while ago."

May glanced around the room, performing a cursory search for her husband's pet. "Not since this morning. You sure you didn't squash him just then?"

Now somewhat panicked, Jimmy moved quickly around the shed looking in cupboards, moving aside farm implements, crawling on the ground, and peering into cracks. No Sammy.

"Did you check the well?"

Hands on his hips and a frown creasing his face, Jimmy said with an exasperated tone, "Now why would he be in the well?"

"Because that's where he sleeps. That's where they all sleep."

"Huh," he muttered then hurried outside in search of his helpless little friend. May followed, shaking her head and hiding a grin as she watched her husband disappear into the well from the waist up. "Well, what do you know?" Jimmy's voice echoed from inside the hollow space. "Guess it got too hot for 'em out here."

"Good thing you already started digging that new well. I refuse to share my drinking water with any of your snakes, pets or not."

Jimmy pulled himself out of the well and momentarily considered his wife's sentiments. "That's fair. Now will you send Eva out to help me load the jugs? I've got to get this first delivery to Mr. Simmons by midnight."

*****

A few years later, Eva found herself staring bleakly yet determinedly at row upon row of just-blossoming cotton plants. Here and there the weed intruders would make their vile chlorophyllic presence known, staring her down from their presumed place of power, their tips reaching only a few inches higher than the cotton leaves. Her eyes continued roving further and further down the row until they struck horizon where waves of traditional Texas heat rippled into mirages. Was that an ice-cold Coca-Cola at the end of this last row?

Forcing tasty thirst-quenching thoughts aside, Eva knelt and yanked a wayward hunk of Johnson grass with delusions of survival from the drying dirt. One weed down, fourteen billion to go, she thought as she hacked up a tenacious sunflower then knelt down to retrieve what seemed like the root system of a redwood. While retrieving, she noticed an odd but unfortunately familiar glimmer refracted by the 95-degree sunlight. Carefully rising, she couldn't help but utter a quiet curse followed by, "Oh, that's just great."

She brushed an exasperated hand across her forehead for what seemed like the twentieth time that minute. The never-ending trickle of sweat dripping from scalp into eyebrows only intensified her frustrations with the suddenly-changed situation at hand. In the hand that wasn't occupied with wiping away salty moisture, Eva gripped her decades-old weed-chopping, rattlesnake-beheading hoe. Nervousness abounded since it was specifically the rattlesnake beheading that concerned her just then; for there, lolling lazily beneath the deep green leaves of a fully-grown sunflower plant, lay the reptilian granddaddy of them all. His black-onyx eyes stared unblinking and unfocused into some rattlesnake daydream, unaware of—or perhaps uncaring that—she was about to end his existence.

"No respect," she muttered, buying time to rein in her nervousness as she sized up what appeared to be about four feet of diamondback. "No respect at all. You should fear me, you know. I have a mostly-sharp implement brandished here in my hand and am only a little bit afraid to use it on that forked tongue of yours. Flee! Flee for your miserable life!"

Not so much as a rattle.

She sighed and glanced dramatically into the distance, seriously contemplating kicking a dirt clod. That would never do, of course. The snake might actually be startled enough by it to flick his tongue at her thereby flinging poison into some exposed hair follicle . . . or something. With a roll of her eyes she ditched all reluctance and raised her tool-turned-weapon high into the air.

"Hello, Eva."

She screamed and hurled the hoe across the field. The snake

looked annoyedly up at her before sighing—yes, sighing—and slithering away to find a less lively cotton plant.

"So you're just finishing up then?"

Eva "grrred" and stormed off to find her much-abused hoe. Halfway down the cotton row she changed her mind and finally kicked the previously-pondered dirt clod. "I need a new hoe."

"That's a shame. That one's been in the family since 1872, or thereabouts. You told me it forded the Mississippi with your great-granddaddy. And didn't he use it to magnetically find true north somewhere in Arkansas?"

Eva glared at him. "Timothy . . . I'm putting out poison."

"Rattlesnake poison?"

"No, hoe poison. Of course rattlesnake poison! Don't they make such a thing? Maybe I could turn loose a bunch of infected chicken eggs, and when the snakes eat them . . . "

"Infected with what, Eva?"

"Chicken pox! Can they die of chicken pox? I could make sure they eat only the infected chicken eggs . . . leave them lying around all willy nilly in the snakes' paths!"

"I think chicken pox only happens in people."

"Then why not call it people pox, dammit?"

"So are you planning on getting ready for the dance anytime soon? You now have," and after pausing to look at his pocket watch, he continued, "one hour and forty-five minutes."

Eva wasn't finished fuming over her rattlesnake condition and planned to show it with pride. "It's in the town square, for Pete's sake. The town square is precisely one hundred and fifty feet from my front door."

"Who's this Pete guy anyway?" He grinned and tapped the face of his watch. "I'll be here in precisely one hour and thirty minutes."

"I could walk a whole hundred and fifty feet by myself, you know."

"Yeah, you could . . . " he replied, already moseying past her house.

Precisely one hour and fifteen minutes later Eva exited her bedroom, dressed adorably. Both her husband and father had left relatively sizeable sums to she and her mother—now passed on, God bless her—to help ensure their comfort and security after the Great War. She and her mom had worked hard to keep the farm prosperous, and Eva was able to afford some luxuries as a result. Even so there weren't many French modistes setting up shop in the Austin area in 1920, modern age though it had been declared. No, she had to settle on Sears and Roebuck for her evening attire. She did, however, manage two fashion-savvy concessions to the day's feminine mode of dress: lots and lots of fringe and a pair of 2-inch heels.

"Why can't you just dress comfortably?" Timothy asked, walking up the wooden front steps and peering through the matching screen door. His semi-formal attire consisted of jeans that hadn't faded out or developed holes, brown boots that still looked respectable if polished, and a simple-but-furiously-starched white shirt without tie. Barn owls had more style . . . and they didn't smell like starch.

"And why can't you just appreciate the lady?"

"I do," he replied, opening the front door for her to exit. "That's my point, in fact. You don't need all those little strings hanging every which way to get appreciation."

She had forgotten her handbag and was on her way back to the bedroom to retrieve it when out of nowhere she stumbled over . . . well, thin air was what it was.

Timothy, true to laid-back form, walked casually to her side and extended his hand. "You okay? Must've been a rumple in the carpet."

Eva took his hand and slowly got up so as to avoid losing any additional pieces of fringe. What had tripped her? No, no carpet rumples. There was no deviant furniture within tripping distance of her either. "There's no obvious culprit lying around. It might be these new shoes," she guessed by way of an attempt at logic.

Timothy glanced downward, noticing her shoes for the first time. "Are those shoes or stilts?"

She whacked him with her handbag.

"Hey, what's this?" he asked, kneeling floorward for a closer look. Lying haphazardly on Eva's otherwise-spotless floor was a piece of what looked like some sort of food wrapping. "Huh. What's a 'Baby Ruth?'"

Eva was more concerned with the strange looking man suddenly sitting stiffly against the wall separating the living room from her bedroom. She had time to notice the stark terror in his eyes and that he was soundlessly saying something. How he'd gotten there she didn't know, but apparently he hadn't intended to stay long anyway since he vanished as quickly as he'd materialized. "The least he could've done was pick that up," she mumbled before reaching for Timothy and pulling him up by his shirt sleeves. She swore she heard them crackle.

"Aren't you going to throw that away?" he asked.

"No."

"You're not behaving quite like yourself."

"Yes, well, neither is the universe."

Now that did sound like "herself," Timothy thought as he allowed Eva to drag him out the door and down the steps. As Eva had earlier indicated, it took them all of five minutes to reach the festivities already in full-swing.

*****

They had danced four dances before Eva realized she was having fun and not in any way thinking about the disappearing person routine going on in her house. Timothy was a nice, respectable, responsible sort of man that most girls would one day hope to marry. For whatever reason, however, Eva was unable to think of him that way. She figured he'd ask her eventually since they'd been keeping company for nearly a year now, but what would she say when he did? As was seemingly typical, Eva always assumed she could and would love only one man . . . and that man was now lying buried somewhere in France.

Timothy, who was engaged in rapt conversation with Mr. Simmons the grocer and sometimes moonshine dealer, had ambled over to the refreshment table to get her some lemonade that she didn't particularly want anyway. Mrs. Simmons, the grocer's wife, never added enough sugar into the mix, and you had to spend your entire sipping experience with a forced smile on your face in order to disguise the grimace. Eva always found herself waking up with face cramps in the middle of the night after a glass of that stuff. So under such circumstances, any delay in Timothy's return with liquid torture in a glass was a joyful delay. The thought that she was purposely changing her own personal mental subject wandered by, but she chased it far away.

"So my husband tells me you're having rattlesnake problems."

Oh dear lord, not now! Eva screamed loudly inside her head. "Good evening, Mrs. Simmons. Yes, I'm afraid so. I've been working in the field all week and have seen at least one rattler every day."

"We had that same problem twenty-odd years ago . . . thought we'd never get rid of the rascals. You couldn't walk ten steps without seeing at least the shed skins. One of them ate my favorite cat, you know . . . the rattlesnake, not the skin, ate the cat. That cat was the sweetest thing but had a tendency to claw up the living room curtains and not feed her babies 'til they all starved to death. They were silk back then . . . the curtains, not the kittens. Of course then the cat ripped the silk to shreds, so maybe it served her right getting eaten by a rattlesnake. You know what you need to do about all this, don't you?"

No, but I'm sure you'll tell me in the most long-winded way possible.

"You need to block up that old well there behind your house. That's where the snakes are living. But be careful you don't fall in. My Aunt Lucy fell in a well once and broke both ankles and her left uvula." Eva figured she'd meant "left ulna" but wisely kept silent. "You know the old well that goes down into the cave?"

You mean the one I've been walking past every day for the past thirty years of my life?

"The one my Aunt Lucy fell into was bigger and deeper than your well though. You might only slip and twist an ankle instead of falling in and breaking something like my Aunt Lucy. Once you block it up there won't be any place for them to hide out when it gets too hot or too cold . . . the snakes, I mean."

The dickens, you say!

"Then you can just kill the ones that don't die naturally."

Damn, and I didn't even consider the supernaturally-dying ones. "Well thanks, Mrs. Simmons. I'll certainly give that some serious thought." Eva wanted to ask her if she knew how to get rid of ghosts too but thought better of it since she really hoped to get home and go to sleep at some point this month. She suspected the woman would have a lengthy answer for that problem too!

A conspiratorial grin o'erspread Mrs. Simmons's grandmotherly facial features as she added, "You should get that nice Timothy to help you. You know Timothy, the man whose farm is next to yours?"

I have no idea who you're talking about. Oh look! There's Timothy, my date!

"He's just the one to ask. I'm sure he'll get your problem cleared up right quickly!" And with a wink she was gone. Free at last.

Timothy reappeared with a brimming glass of the godforsaken lemonade. "Here you go. Sorry that took so long. Mr. Simmons was giving me some pointers on your rattlesnake problem, and . . . "

"Got any whiskey to go with this?" Eva asked, pausing only a second before downing the entire glass of sourness. She made no attempt to hide her "pain" face. A shot of Mrs. Simmons with this stuff as a chaser had her desperate for something stronger.

What a minute! Which problem had Mrs. Simmons been talking about? "So are you gonna ask me to marry you at some point?"

Timothy spewed lemonade from his nose. Eva had to admire his recovery skills when he very quickly replied, "Well, now, I don't know. Do you want me to?"

"Mrs. Simmons does, from the sound of things." Eva had a feeling that her "rattlesnake problem" was merely a euphemism for what was considered to be a much bigger problem for adult women of the area: the state of non-marriage.

Timothy seemed to be clutching his glass more tightly than normal. "I would've asked you before this, but you really didn't seem to be all that interested. I don't have a problem with waiting a while longer though."

What passion. He probably didn't mind waiting because the only other eligible girl in town had just turned five and only recently stopped wetting the bed. "Truthfully, I'm not interested at this point. I'm sorry if that sounded harsh."

"What could sound harsh about that?"

"I was just worried that I might be leading you on, and since I'm about to ask you to help me rid my property of the rattlesnake vermin, I thought it would be helpful to clarify where things stood between us."

"You're not one to beat around bushes, are you?"

"The bushes don't like it."

He couldn't help but smile. Of course he didn't mind extending bachelorhood, and of course he'd help her. He'd fall at her feet and worship if he thought he could do it without ruining the perfectly-starched creases in his shirt. He knew Eva. He'd known Eva since she was barely taller than those cotton plants, though the plants tended to make more sense to him most days. She just needed time, and Timothy figured he had plenty of it himself to go around.

CHAPTER SIX

"Just because you have a big mouth, that doesn't mean you have to open it!" Eva chided herself, glaring at her reflection in her bedroom mirror. It was 2 a.m., and sleep simply was not happening. After the evening's disastrous denouement due to her haphazard broaching of the marriage subject, she made excuses as quickly as possible to get herself back home and away from well-meaning-but-prying eyes. It was with great reluctance that she removed her brand new party dress and hung it in the hall closet. It would be out of style by the time she had another opportunity to wear it.

Her brain on overload, Eva stalked around the bedroom several times more then stalked frustratedly out into the living room. That infernal candy wrapper was still lying innocently on the otherwise-spotless floor. "And I'm just gonna leave it there too," she announced to thin air which was now appropriately unoccupied once again.

Stomping to the back door and down the back steps, she immersed herself in the peaceful, stress-relieving night air. She couldn't help but ponder what a good sport Timothy had been about everything tonight. Of course that was nothing unusual for him. A tornado could blow through uprooting his house by the foundations, and the happening would elicit no more than a passing nod from the man. Then again, considering the impetuous and impulsive aspects of her own nature, maybe marrying him would be the intelligent decision in the end . . . maintaining of balance and all that.

But only in the end when I absolutely have to make the decision, Eva thought. The moon was half-full this evening—or perhaps half-empty—but still provided plenty of light in order to see where she was going. She frequently scanned the path in front of her for snakes, though it was highly unlikely they'd be out sunning when there was no sun. She made her way barefoot through the back yard and meandered further to the edge of a cotton row. The harvest would be good this year assuming that a sudden boll weevil infestation or the aforementioned tornado didn't strike. Hail was always a possible danger as well, but she had every reason to hope for the best. She knelt to inspect the blooms on a plant and counted twelve on that one alone. Yes, the harvest would be very good this year.

Such thoughts always restored some modicum of internal balance, and after one more round of field-wide bloom estimates, Eva walked back toward the house. The dirt was cool between her toes, a natural stimulant for depressed spirits. Just before she had a chance to smile, she caught sight of the strangest thing . . . or another one of the strangest things. To the general left of her back yard an odd glow began to appear twelve or so feet off the ground, the sight rippling into view like that afternoon's heat mirages. In sharply-contrasting red lettering on a glowing white background, Eva saw "RXS Pharmacy: Open 24 Hours" come into clear view before melting away into nothing once more.

So much for modicums of balance . . . or was it modici?

It was now 10:45 a.m., and Eva still hadn't been to sleep. She had, at least, changed into more suitable clothes for daytime hours and focused her mind firmly upon the rattlesnake problem. She would go talk over snake-eradication options with Timothy immediately. Disappearing men and inexplicable glowing signs would not distract her from the necessary task to be accomplished. She slid her feet back into last night's heels because they were the most accessible shoes at the time. She had also donned her oldest, lightest summertime dress that still maintained adequate seam integrity then grabbed a broom. The old hoe was still lost somewhere in sunflower-infested lands, probably never to be seen again. Still, she had to have a defensive weapon and hoped that any rattlesnake interlopers would be more afraid of a reed bundle attached to a stick than they had been of dull iron.

She grabbed her beat-up straw hat from a peg by the front door before turning and walking toward the back door. The candy wrapper that she so illogically refused to move was still lying right where she'd left it, a bizarre and even fearful object should she contemplate it overly much. "Of course if I threw it away I wouldn't have to contemplate it at all," she reasoned even as she kept walking. Hand on the back door handle, she got firm hold of her willpower and decided to toss the paper into the garbage. With a sigh of determination she turned toward the living room just in time to see those heat wave-looking things undulating through her surroundings yet again. Around the outer edges of the undulations were futuristic cylindrical objects sitting on the floor in a nonthreatening fashion. The look of her living room—the furnishings, the telephone on the wall, the rug she'd kept clean for years through much blood, sweat, and tears—were turning dark. After a few more seconds they were gone completely until the entire inside of the circle formed by the cylinder thingies showed rotted, dislocated boards and little else . . . except for that guy! That very same guy who'd been sitting against the wall was now standing in the center of the circle with his arm around a girl. And what in the world was she wearing?

Eva's nerves were in no way calmed by the disoriented and horrified expressions on the faces of these visitors. Brandishing her broom as menacingly as she could, she approached the pair. With an obvious glance downward at the candy wrapper she said, "I told you to pick that up!"

And they were gone. Her living room was normal once again with no trace of fiendish cylindrical objects or badly-dressed women. Still wielding her broom in an offensive manner, Eva turned around and walked toward the back door once more. Her hands were starting to ache as she remembered to relax her grip long enough to open the screen door. Timothy. She needed to see Timothy. His clear-headed ways were precisely what her nerves required. His living room would never contain vanishing people. His living room was too practical for such outlandish goings-on.

She found him working diligently in his own field behind his own sensible farm house. "So . . . snakes," she announced in place of a greeting. He'd like that no-nonsense approach. She could change. Really, she could! One more disappearing act, however, and she'd change right into a crazy person.

Nonplussed as per usual, Timothy glanced toward her from his kneeling position at the base of a problematic bloodweed. "Mornin', Eva. Just let me get the rest of these roots up. They're multiplying faster than usual this year."

She watched with a surprising amount of patience as he finished the immediate task and rose, dusting black dirt from his not-danceworthy jeans. "Are we just inspecting, or do you expect to commence with the killing too?"

"Inspecting for the moment," she replied and began walking in the direction of the old well. "I've got some old boards behind the tool shed we can use to block everything up, but I just don't think that will be enough to eliminate the problem."

"Tough call," he said as the well became graspable. "I don't see any gaps in the well itself, but that doesn't mean there aren't any. We can start by boarding up the top and see if it helps."

"Or we could just blow them all to smithereens."

Timothy scratched his head and looked expressionless in her direction. For him "expressionless" was an expression. "Well, we don't even know how many are down there or even if they're down there. Let me just stick my head in and take a look. Do you have a candle handy?"

Eva went inside for the candle and grabbed a match. Once lit, she handed it helpfully to her snake-hunting knight in denim armor. He cautiously extended the candle-holding hand downward a few feet. "Nothing yet. How deep is this thing anyway?"

"The spring starts a few yards down, or at least it used to. I haven't gotten water from this well in years though. That new one Grandpa dug before he died has better water."

"The spring should be better with the limestone leaching it clean," Timothy's voice echoed. He had safely extended his head and arm further down the well.

"It should be, but it's not."

"You have odd taste buds."

"Maybe, but they know what they like. See anything?" Truth be told, Eva had known for years that snakes lived down the old well. Her Grandpa had a peculiar pet snake addiction.

Having experienced enough of subterranea, he blew out the candle and stood fully upright. "Well, they're down there alright. Dozens of 'em."

"You know what the worst part about this is, don't you?"

"What?"

"Mrs. Simmons knew about the snake den. She was actually right about something. I won't be able to buy groceries there for a month."

"At least."

"So where can I get some TNT?"

"Eva…"

"Or some other flammable substance. We could pump something that will burn down into the cave, strike a match, and let it explode!"

Timothy stared expressionlessly again. "Oh, it would explode, alright…the snakes, the house, pretty much anything above this branch of the cave system. Let me think about this for a while before you do anything Eva-like, okay?"

"Okay," she said, all the while knowing she'd do exactly as Eva would do.

****

The sun had descended almost completely behind the horizon before Eva had the guts to peek outside toward Timothy's house. As was his weekly routine, he'd already departed for a domino tournament with his buddies. She was mostly certain he wouldn't be back until late. Granted, for Timothy that meant about 8:30, but she still had some time.

Feeling her stubbornness levels rise even higher than was typical, Eva climbed into her Dad's Model T and backed it up to the well. Since she had no idea where to buy flammable gas, and since she knew Timothy wasn't nearly stupid enough to properly direct her, she figured she'd get it from the only accessible place she had available: the exhaust pipe. The concept of applying gasoline to her present problem never entered her mind.

She'd found some old rubber tubing that should work okay as long as it hadn't dry rotted too badly. It didn't look like it had, but gasses didn't require much in the way of space for seepage. Her task illuminated by the lone light bulb beaming from above the back steps, Eva fitted the tube to the end of the exhaust pipe. She hoped intently that it would reach into the well . . . or that the heat from the car wouldn't melt the rubber before it had a chance to transfer the gas. Geez. She hadn't thought about that before now. Ah well, too late! She was doing this, and nothing short of ghost people tying her to a glowing sign while inflicting lemonade torture would stop her.

She restarted the engine and quickly felt the movement of air through the tubing. It had extended several feet down into the well, so Eva felt sure that enough of the gas was arriving at its appointed destination. Now how long should she let the motor run? Half an hour, maybe? "Mrs. Simmons never would've thought of this," she declared aloud. And for good reason, her common-sensical side responded. She tried hard to breathe as little as possible lest she be poisoned herself by the fumes. After thirty minutes had passed, she climbed into the car and drove it to what she considered a safe distance. Nervously approaching the well with legs prepared for a rapid retreat, Eva lit a match. A fleeting image of Aunt Lucy wafted through her brain as she let the portable flame go.

Not a cotton-pickin' thing happened. "Well poop and the word I'd rather be saying in its place!" she yelled. At the moment yelling felt better than covertly-whispered curses, and the yelling of said curses would never do with such a straight-laced populace within earshot.

She needed a drink. Surely there was something lying around the house someplace. Intending to make her way to the backdoor, Eva had a sudden revelation. "Grandpa's stash!" she yelled, this time much more joyfully. She instead trotted to the shed, rummaged around in an old cabinet, and finally pulled out a crusty, dusty old bottle of the strongest, most illegal moonshine ever to sneak across a border. Uncorking it with much gusto, Eva threw her head back and guzzled a mouthful. Wow. They really should bottle this stuff.

When the world stopped spinning and her breathing returned to normal, she ambled a little less trot-like from the shed back to the well. "Stupid snakes," she slurred, slamming back another shot from the filthy bottle. She didn't care if it was filthy. This stuff was capable of killing any deadly organism within a hundred miles. Hmm . . . that was a thought! She peered into the well at her slithering nemeses before dumping half the remaining liquid contents onto their unsuspecting heads. "Ha, HA! I have you now!" she cried. Tearing off a chunk of her dress at the hemline, she stuffed it into the bottle. When most but not all of the material was inside, she shook it up until the inside portion was thoroughly doused in flammable liquid. She ran back to the truck and pulled another matchbook from the glove box. With slightly blurred vision, Eva lit the dry end of the material before letting the bottle go.

And then everything went. There was no logical reason she shouldn't have gone with it, but apparently the cave didn't extend overly far. The cave, the well, and the house's foundations shuddered in an instant. Shouts of alarm could be heard just down the street as a fire brigade began mobilizing. This isn't going to be very easy to live down, she thought belatedly as flames worked their way through the floorboards of her home. In what seemed like seconds men were frantically dumping water onto the site, Timothy among them. Once the fire was under control and the house semi-salvaged, he approached Eva who was still standing next to the exploded well. "So . . . you killed the snakes."

"Snakes go boom."

"I probably should've told you there was a natural gas pocket down there."

She nodded, marveling at the lack of temper. "Told you the other well water was better," she replied. Within a moment she was stuck by the stark realization that there weren't two Timothies out there and that she really needed this one. She would be an idiot to delay the inevitable any longer. "Let's get married," she said.

"You need a place to live, huh?"

"Exactly."

He smiled contentedly and kissed her on the cheek.

CHAPTER SEVEN

One month later, Eva was happily situated in her new living room with Timothy sitting comfortably in his chair across from her. All of the windows were open, a cool evening breeze wafting in through lacy white curtains: a decidedly feminine addition to which Timothy had conceded with an air of masculine indulgence. The leaves of tall trees surrounding the house bent themselves to the wind's will while bees buzzed lazily among the blossoms of a Mustang grape bush sprawling next to the front porch. Eva was very much hoping to make a giant batch of grape jelly before the winter . . . and, in keeping with family's alcoholic tradition, an equally giant batch of wine.

Timothy slowly smoked a pipe and perused that day's newspaper, relishing the fact that he would finally be updated on global events after a long day's work in the fields. Eva thumbed through her latest mail-order catalog in an attempt to update herself on this season's global fashions. Parisian style it wasn't, but a girl did the best she could. Her husband's voice interrupted her longing for the red silk shoulder cape showcased on the very first page. "It's too harsh, this treaty."

Eva allowed herself to be drawn from clothing reverie. "Hmm? What treaty?"

"Versailles. If Germany is forced to pay out these 'monetary reparations' to all of Europe, how will it have enough money to take care of its own?"

"Maybe it shouldn't. They tried to take over the entire world, you remember. Some punishment is warranted."

"To a point. But warranted or not, if the common people can't take care of their families and communities in the long run, they might get desperate and do something . . . well, desperate. I have a bad feeling we're making a whole new set of problems for ourselves here."

Eva pondered Timothy's simple wisdom as she laid down her catalog and prepared to go wash that evening's dinner dishes. "Or a repeat of the same problems. The human race seems to have a hard time actually applying history's lessons."

Timothy smiled. She talked kind of high-fallutin' sometimes, but

Eva's points were always well-founded. "Do we have any coffee left?"

Eva feigned shock. "What? Coffee after 6:00 p.m.? Why Timothy, what a wildman you've turned out to be!"

Timothy chuckled. "Just a cup. I'll go back to being predictable tomorrow."

Chuckling herself, Eva headed to the kitchen and set a pot atop the wood-burning stove. She washed a few dishes as it heated then prepared Timothy's coffee just as he liked it: black as tar. Glopping it into a cup, she turned to take his beverage into the living room. Upon focusing her attention room-ward, she immediately dropped the cup. Right there in the middle of her level-headed, practical husband's living room, the same two male and female interlopers were materializing.

The pipe fell from Timothy's lips. "There's something you don't see every day. Eva! Two more cups of coffee."

"But I don't like coffee," was the first completely unnecessary string of coherent words that came into my head. In retrospect, it was a very rude thing to say to the poor, frightened woman whose home we'd been randomly invading.

Eva never missed a beat. "And I don't like strange women who arrive unannounced from out of nowhere!"

"She's got you there," Mick managed. He was fumbling with the magic garage door opener trying his hardest to avoid eye contact. While this is what was supposed to happen, this wasn't supposed to happen. And what do you say to someone whose personal time/space continuum you just violated? He couldn't help but wonder if there was an inter-dimensional version of INTERPOL charged with handling such occurrences.

"Well now," Timothy said again. He had managed to retrieve his fallen pipe since starting another house fire wasn't at the top of his priority list, but once he'd reflexively announced the need for extra coffee, thought processes mostly ceased. This sort of thing simply didn't take place in his well-ordered world. In such instances, he usually shoved his hands into his pants pockets and deferred to Eva.

Eva, true to form, was rapidly assessing each performer on this oddly transcendent stage. She had already noticed multiple similarities between Timothy and the new guy simply by watching the way they handled the inherent peculiarities of this present circumstance. They both clammed up and became voiceless, for one.

I elbowed Mick. "Talk much? Geez. Why is it always up to me to break the proverbial ice?"

"Because you talk easily . . . and a lot," he unwisely replied.

"You too?" Eva suddenly said to me, deciding that it was safe to extend a hand of introduction. I took it and shook it firmly. "My husband here would remain happily silent for the rest of his life if he could. Honestly, I think the main reason he married me was so he'd never have to talk in public again." Eva winked good-naturedly at Timothy before continuing, "I'm Eva Reed, and this is my husband Timothy."

Since I was apparently the designated spokesperson for the Delegation from the 21st Century, I responded with, "I'm Katie Burgess, and this is my friend Mick McClaren. We're . . .we're time travelers." The second I said that, I felt like a total moron.

The coffee Timothy had finally received and managed to sip spewed from his mouth.

"Nothing seems to want to stay in there tonight, does it, Timothy?" Eva remarked while handing him a towel. He knelt down onto his brand new store-bought carpet and dabbed furiously at the stains

"At least he gave you fair warning," I heard myself saying with a smile.

Eva laughed. It was a musical, from-the-gut sound that I immediately loved. This was a woman who took her laughing seriously. "Too true, Katie! He may wind up on the couch tonight yet."

"Oh, does he misbehave often?"

"No, I snore, apparently. Actually, I think he's just afraid I'll accidentally rumple his starched nightshirt in my sleep. The man spends a small fortune on starch, but I'm not allowed to buy the dress I want even though it's a quarter of the price of that confounded starch supply."

"No way! I just bought this killer black leather outfit, but I'm not allowed to wear it. Mick here says it's impractical. Since when does clothing have to be practical all the friggin' time? It's about personal expression!"

Eva stared for a split second then recovered and said, "I don't know about all that black leather or why you'd want to wear it in the middle of summer, but I agree with your main point: it's about expressing yourself."

Mick and Timothy had involuntarily migrated toward each other until they were standing protectively side by side, their mouths hanging dumbfoundedly open. There were two of them, they jointly thought. In the same room. This called for some serious male solidarity. In an attempt to redirect a conversation that was pushing the menfolk further and further into a bad light, Timothy finally spoke up. "So whereabouts are you two from?"

"Austin, TX," I automatically replied as Eva motioned for us to be seated. This woman, this couple, this place was quickly growing on me. It almost felt like home, even. Almost.

If he could've stared with even more disbelief, Timothy did. "Must be South Austin," he muttered.

Mick finally rediscovered his vocal cords and made a valiant attempt at explaining what was a relatively inexplicable situation. "She's right. We are from Austin, but it's not the Austin you know, obviously."

"I heard there's an Austin in Minnesota. Is this how all the Yankees dress?" Eva asked, genuinely curious without any hint of insult intended.

"Well yes," I slowly and thoughtfully began, "but it's not just Yankees. It's the entire country. You see, we're from Austin, TX in the 21st century. Didn't we already cover this?"

It was Eva's turn to be speechless.

I picked up where her speechlessness left off. "See, I had this idea that ghosts—I love the whole ghost-hunting thing, see—are not always spirits trapped in a certain time or place. They could also be living, breathing people whose times are simply overlapping with other peoples' times, and since that overlapping occurs based on the strength of any given electromagnetic field, the people from one time might not appear clearly to the people in the other time thereby making both sets of people look like ghosts . . . kind of fuzzy and stuff. Does that make sense?"

Poor Timothy and Eva could only gape in astonished confusion.

"It's a whole quantum physics thing. Mick can explain it much better than I can."

In perfect concert, Timothy and Eva turned their dazed faces to Mick.

He looked at me in terrified anxiety.

"Sorry, honey, this is your department," I said. "You love this scientific stuff, remember? And besides, we all just heard my best attempt at an intelligible explanation, and I think it would come across a bit better if a few theory-supporting numbers and equations were included."

Eva shivered. "Equations give me the hives."

That confirmed it. I'd found a kindred spirit.

With a sudden need to pace, Mick took a deep breath and proceeded to explain as best he could in simpler terms. "I don't know if there's a necessity for numbers and equations, but some background information might be helpful. First of all, I need to know what year we're in right now."

"It's the summer of 1920 . . . good cotton crop this year if the boll weevils don't get it," Timothy answered.

"Wow," Mick whispered. "So the war just ended."

"Yes, my daddy and late husband were both killed in France," Eva remarked sadly. Timothy tenderly grasped her hand and squeezed.

Having strangely bonded with our "ghost" woman/broom lady, I felt tears immediately rising. "Oh, I'm so sorry, Eva!"

She nodded and allowed herself a tiny smile. "Thank you. I've come to terms with it now, of course, but doubt I'll ever come to terms with how many others had to die too. It really must be the War to End all Wars."

I cautiously looked at Mick and bit my lower lip to keep from speaking. He made eye contact and nodded his approval of my decision to remain silent. We'd both seen *Back to the Future* innumerable times. We knew what would happen if we screwed with any aspect of the historical record . . . more than we already had, that is. I shoved that thought into a distant corner of my brain.

"We can hope," was Mick's vague response. He then paused for a respectful moment of silence before continuing his attempt at clarifying precisely why we were sitting here out of proper time. "So you've probably heard of Albert Einstein, yes?"

They both nodded. "I believe so. He's a scientist, isn't he?" Eva asked.

"Yes, he is. More precisely he's a physicist and mathematician who helped pioneer the more specific field of quantum physics. Now, simply put, quantum physics is the branch of physics that studies quantum theory."

"I thought he said this was going to be simple," Eva loudly whispered to me. "I'm already getting itchy."

"Yeah, he told me the same thing my freshman year of college, right? 'Oh, you'll love it!' he said. 'Oh, you'll make an A easy in that class!' he said. Yeah, I dropped physics after the first hour of lecturing because it gave me the only migraine I've ever had in my life. Signed up for creative writing instead."

"Smart move," Eva commented.

"As I was saying," Mick continued with a glare in my direction, "Quantum physics studies quantum theory. Quantum theory describes and predicts the properties of a physical system."

"You mean like borders and property lines on a map?" Timothy asked, trying distraughtly to sound competent.

In full math geek mode, Mick enthusiastically continued. "No, this is on a much smaller scale than the land and boundaries we can see in our various environments. This theory explains the nature and behavior of matter and energy on an atomic and subatomic, level. While another scientist, Max Planck, introduced the foundations of this theory, it was Albert Einstein who really helped it take off practically in the scientific world. Other scientists came along, of course, and built upon the work of these two men . . . or they will come along, rather."

Eva nodded in at least partial understanding. "I remember my husband talking some about this with one of his cousins back before the war. His cousin was such a know-it-all. I always wanted to understand more about the subject myself but figured the math would do me in."

"Math is Satan expressed in numeric form," I declared.

"Amen, sister," Eva agreed. "But if there was a way I could learn more about it without having to delve into the equation side of science, I'd really like to."

Mick was overjoyed by her expressed interest in his adored subject and proceeded to behave in a downright giddy fashion. "I'm sure I could explain more to you without the use of the complicated equations, but unfortunately there are aspects of the theory that haven't been discovered yet in your time . . . in 1920, I mean. I don't want to educate this society before it's technically ready to be educated."

He was so thrilled to have an eager listener to absorb his obsession that I was afraid he'd get too carried away with the premature tossing around of knowledge. There were simply concepts they weren't prepared to deal with, intelligent though I knew they were. Still, it was with much reluctance that I forced myself to interrupt what had become a fascinating discussion for our new acquaintances. "And speaking of our presence in 1920, we really should be getting back to our own time. I honestly hate to cut this visit short, but the pharmacy will be opening any minute now, and how are we going to explain all the cylinders out back disrupting business functions with an excess of electromagnetic energy?"

Mick looked like I'd just slapped him in the face. Rapidly deflating as physics talk ceased, he sensibly agreed. "You're right. Yes, we do need to be returning."

Eva's brow furrowed with concentration as she asked a question that should've been beyond her comprehension. "Returning, you say? Did you ever actually leave?"

I was somewhat shocked. "Good observation. We actually haven't left that space, we've only jumped times."

Mick re-inflated slightly when she spoke. "Exactly, and since the energy produced by the cylinders is still in this space—past and present—it can still be manipulated to return us to our own time."

"I thought you really were ghosts," Timothy remarked, otherwise at a loss. We'd unintentionally left him behind several explanations ago.

Mick felt badly for him. "Then I guess you successfully proved Katie's theory," Mick said as a way of offering consolation.

"You really did," I confirmed. "We appreciate it very much too."

Timothy could, at least, completely understand sincere appreciation and smiled broadly. "My pleasure . . . anything for science. Maybe during your next visit you can tell me how farming and ranching will change. It would be a hoot to use ideas from, say, thirty years in the future. Are they still using horses?"

Mick was already beginning adjustments on his garage door opener, so I had to respond quickly yet judiciously to Timothy's eager question. "I think it's safe to simply tell you no, they're not."

"Bet they still use hoes though," Eva interjected glumly.

"I knew it!" Timothy said, finally enthused by the conversation. "Fully-automated, I'll bet. Think of that! And what about the weather?" Now that he'd found his voice, he couldn't seem to stop asking questions. "Can they control weather? Back in May we had two twisters hit at the same time. Good thing we were between crops, or it would've meant a rough time makin' it this winter."

"No, I'm afraid we haven't achieved weather control yet," I replied, "but it's much easier to predict the formation and path of tornadoes in our time. The warning time is, what, like fifteen minutes? It's enough time to find a safe place to hide anyway."

"Think of that," Timothy marveled, apparently in some sort of dream state. We had officially made the man's day.

I waved a quick good-bye to Eva, but she was having none of it and hugged me tightly instead. "You should know this is the way we do it in Texas!"

I giggled and hugged her back. Timothy moved forward and laid a manly good-bye hand on Mick's shoulder. He wasn't a hugger. Texas men didn't traditionally "do it that way."

"Come back for a visit sometime. If we're not here, just make yourselves at home anyway," he said.

"Thanks," Mick and I said in unison as the ripples began forming again, skewing our view of the super-awesome couple smiling at us in the past present tense. Though sad to see them disappearing before my eyes, there was a sense of something even darker lurking on the outskirts of my suspicious consciousness. As we got "closer" to the 21st century version of this place, I saw the outlines of several different people coming gradually into focus but never completely forming. Something was going very, very wrong.

"Mick!" I yelled in horror, the warped sound of my own once-familiar voice scaring me even further.

"Just hang onto me," he reassured, holding me tightly in his bear-hugging arms, as a small explosion popped blurrily into our limited view of home. One of the cylinders had just ascended into electronics heaven. That one down, the other four immediately overloaded then expired. I screamed as time and space rushed and pulled us into an unscheduled "sometime."

CHAPTER EIGHT

"There's that red and white sign again," Eva remarked numbly.

Bewildered, bemused, and completely beside themselves, Eva and Timothy gawked at the store's new pharmacist charging toward them. With an instinctive need to protect, Timothy moved determinedly in front of his wife. "What is all this junk?" the pharmacist demanded. "This is a fire hazard, and I will be holding you responsible for any property damages!"

Eva peeked nervously from behind Timothy's shoulder and observed, "Quantum theory is stupid."

*****

My arms had lost all feeling, and my hands were in deep REM sleep. If Mick didn't let go soon, I was very much afraid he'd impede blood flow to my brain. "Umm, sweetie?" I managed between gasps of air. "Maybe you can let go now?"

Slowly he unwrapped me and took a step back. In another moment his hands grasped my face and firmly pressed his lips to mine. After several seconds of we're-not-dead-or-in-the-middle-of-a-tyrannosaur-nest kissing, he let me go and spoke. "You okay, Katie? Any bruises or concussions or pains that aren't supposed to be there?"

"Is any pain actually supposed to be there? Anyway, I don't know yet since the feeling is just now coming back into 80% of my body. You do know how to hug a girl though. I look forward to enjoying that under different circumstances." I was assessing my internal organs and happily concluded that nothing was wrong beyond a time warp-related headache. "Yeah, I think I'm good. You? Need me to play nurse?"

He grinned and winked. "I'm fine too, but that doesn't mean I don't still need a thorough examination later. Do I need to make an appointment?"

"My schedule is always open for you, babe," I replied and winked back. "Now where do you think they keep the aspirin?"

Mick and I walked into the kitchen and started opening cabinet doors. We had immediately known where we'd been stranded the second we smelled burned coffee and Timothy's lingering pipe smoke, so acclimation was happening more quickly than might be typical. I was pretty psyched about that "absence of tyrannosaur nest" thing. While Mick opened more cabinets, I removed the coffee pot from the stove and set it in the sink for future washing. "I'm not finding anything yet," Mick said, still searching.

"Maybe they keep it in the bathroom then."

He paused and looked amusedly at me. "Oh, do outhouses have medicine cabinets?"

Oh my gravy. That's right. This was rural Texas situated within the openly-spaced Austin area, not within Austin proper. "Oh no!" I cried, a sinking feeling turning my stomach to mush. "This house doesn't even exist in our time, so I have no clue about the bathroom situation! Did Eva's house have a bathroom?"

Mick finally found an old-school bottle of aspirin, though right now it was still technically "new-school." "Not one that was recognizable as a bathroom, but there was too much damage to know for sure."

Forgetting about my tension headache that was rapidly escalating to "throbbing" status, I raced through the tiny house in search of that precious space designated as the place to bathe and poop. The closest I found to it was a screened-in back porch with a giant washtub pushed into one of the corners. Mick found me staring disconsolately at our bath-only room and rapturously said, "Calgon, take me away!"

I elbowed him in the stomach. He laughed. "Hey, if you'd like, I could find a straw and turn it into a Jacuzzi for you!"

"So not helpful," I whined then collapsed to the floor in an Indian-style sitting position. My chin rested pathetically against my chest.

Repentant and attempting to understand my emotional upheaval at the sudden loss of indoor plumbing, Mick sat down on the floor next to me. He draped an arm over my shoulders and pulled me closer. "Please don't cut off circulation again," I begged.

"I won't, Lady Smells-So-Sweet," he said, kissing the top of my head. "We'll figure it all out, Katie. I promise, we'll get it figured out. And remember, there won't be an ongoing supply of my chocolate to get rid of stress here either. I'm just sayin', we can both find ways to cope."

"But how?" I logically asked. "Nobody knows who we are, I have no idea how to cook on a wood-burning stove, what in the crazy world am I going to wear, and what if there are snakes in the outhouse? I can't go pee in the middle of the night if I think there's even a miniscule chance of stepping on a rattlesnake! Mick, I'm an indoor girl. You know that. And I'm sorry about your state of non-chocolate too."

Mick smiled as his eyes took in the night sky outside "our" back porch. A gorgeous, silvery full moon glimmered from behind numerous leaf-laden tree branches as he offered as much reassurance as possible. "I believe it was customary to drag wash tubs into the kitchen where it's warm in the winter. You'll have plenty of privacy, no worries. Yes, establishing identities may be challenging at first, but there are plenty of reasonable explanations as to who we are. We could be Eva's cousins from Waco here house-sitting while they take a little trip to Hot Springs."

I giggled in spite of my stressed-out-ness. "That a pretty random combination of locations, but still, it has potential. You may be developing a creative bone after all."

"As for the outhouse situation, we'll check it in a minute. If there are any holes or breaks in the boards, I'll fix them in the morning."

"What if the snakes can crawl up through the toilet seat?" I half-sobbed out of reptile fear.

Level-headed as ever, Mick attempted to reason with his semi-hysterical girl whose fingernails were digging painfully into his shoulder. "Honey, do you really think any snake would want to be crawling around down there in all that . . . well, shit?"

I could still process plausible concepts and conceded, "Well no, probably not. But what about the corncob bin?"

Mick paused. This could be a problem for him. "I forgot about the corncob necessity."

"Yeah, 'cuz you chafe on Charmin Ultra. I don't know how you're going to stand ultra-abrasive."

"We might need to spring for the luxury of whatever passes as actual toilet paper these days. A trip to the local supermarket will also be on tomorrow's to-do list."

"I think nowadays they're just 'markets.' 'Super' versions haven't been invented yet," I reminded him. "You have a great plan. You're the Lord of the Great Plans, but what are we going to wear for this exciting goods-purchasing trek into town? You're a good two inches taller than Timothy, and Eva is at least one size smaller than I am."

"Maybe this unplanned excursion is at least well-timed. You really should be laying off the candy anyway," Mick teased, squishing a fat layer around my midsection.

"Stop that!" I ordered, slapping his hand away with my own. "My candy habit is your fault, thank you very much."

"And speaking of which, that needs to go on our shopping list."

"May I remind you: they won't have all your favorite chocolate candies."

Mick patted me on the back then stood up and stretched. "I really will survive. Now," he began, taking me by the hand and pulling me up, "let's light a couple of candles and inspect the outhouse. Then we can figure out our clothing ensembles before bedtime."

Upon standing, I dusted myself off and prepared to make the best of the situation. After all, who knew what poor Eva and Timothy were going to do with our lives? "Lead on, you masculine pioneer man, you. Hey, you do realize that people around here will force you to keep your hair cut. You know that, right?"

He ignored me. I needed to learn that technique.

The outhouse was in impeccable condition as outhouses go. The dirt floor had been swept until it was smooth and free of debris. There really was a corncob bin, much to my amusement, but there was no way any snake vermin were getting into it. Timothy must be an expert carpenter because each of his buildings were flawlessly put together and maintained from the main house to this outhouse to his tool shed several yards away. Mick was secretly relieved that there was a second bin next to the toilet seat which contained a package of something called 'Medicated Paper.' We felt a piece just to see what our backsides would soon be experiencing. It was better than a corncob but nothing like the fluffy softness available in our time. I told Mick he may not be wiping his butt on a cloud, but at least he wouldn't be wiping it on sandpaper either. He suggested adding moisturizing lotions to our list. He probably had the right idea there.

My outhouse fears allayed for the time being, we looked forward to sleep with understandable anticipation. Traversing time and space took a lot out of a person. I had already located a soft and snuggly nightgown and was tucked cozily beneath Eva's beautifully-detailed, handmade quilt. Mick had gone outside one more time to draw a bucket of fresh water from the little well beside the back door. I heard the door swing open then bang closed. He must have latched it somehow because there was a fumbling of metal against metal that I didn't quite recognize.

"Would you bring me a glass of water, please?" I yelled into the vicinity of the kitchen.

"As soon as I locate a glass, your wish is my command," he replied from the short distance.

"I thought your wish was my command?" I yelled back with inherent fliratatiousness.

Thankfully electricity had made it this far out into the boonies, so Mick was able to click the kitchen light bulb off. I'd always liked that sound. He arrived in the bedroom with two full glasses of the clearest water I'd ever seen. "Wow, that looks so good!" I exclaimed, suddenly realizing just how thirsty I was. After gulping half the glass, I realized it was the best-tasting water I'd ever had too. "This is the best water I've ever tasted. I mean, seriously!"

Mick was eyeing the super-starched nightshirt I'd jokingly laid out on a chair for him. "Water doesn't have a taste."

"I know, but in this case the lack of taste counts as a taste. There must be a spring down there."

"And limestone too, remember...sort of acts like a strainer for the water," Mick informed me, still staring at the stiff article of clothing. "Am I really supposed to wear this?"

"Well, you don't have to wear anything, but what would the locals say should word get around that you sleep in the nude?"

"I could tell them I'm French?"

I burst into giggling as Mick finally made his decision. He took off his t-shirt and made a first attempt at getting himself into what rural America considered proper sleeping attire at the time. The medicated outhouse paper was more pliable. "It might be easiest if I just set it upside down on the floor and dive into it. Or . . . help me, please. Maybe hold it over my head then lower it onto me?"

Still laughing, I crawled from beneath the covers and stood atop the mattress. Taking the garment from him, I slowly lowered it onto his upstretched arms then over his head. As I did, he eyed my own sleeping ensemble. "Sexy nighty, Grandma Mabel. Gets me hot."

"Gets me hot too. It's flannel," I replied, still concentrating on getting Mick into the shirt. Once in place, he vigorously moved his arms around in an effort to make it more comfortably bendable. The crunching sound produced vibrations that would've registered on the

April Arnold

Richter scale, had it been developed yet. "Any progress?"

He frowned. "A little, I guess. How can he sleep this way?"

"I guess he lies on his back and never moves the entire night. No wonder Eva prefers the couch, poor woman."

Mick's eyes darkened into bedroom mode as he nipped the tip of my earlobe. "Think you'll prefer the couch too? I might not mind so much if you cause a few wrinkles."

"Oh, I intend to!" I said and flicked off the bedside lamp.

After an hour or so of romantic fun and frolic, the need for sleep finally o'ertook us. Time and location displacement aside, we both slept better than we had in months The next morning found me still clad in my cotton flannel and standing barefoot in a barely-modernized country kitchen. The pressing task for the moment? I needed to figure out how to make breakfast for me and my man with the less-than-modern conveniences at hand. It was the rural thing to do. But where was I supposed to get the pertinent ingredients for such a thing? There was no recognizable refrigerator, so where would one get eggs? And bacon. Who was supposed to bring home the bacon, and where the crap did they put it?

I bumbled my way around the kitchen digging through the same cabinets we'd inspected the night before. Aha, there was flour. Now what about cooking oil? A big tub of something white reached my gaze. Wow, it was Crisco! My own grandmother used this stuff when I was a kid. We'd have to get our cholesterol checked immediately upon returning to 21st century life. I explored further and found a frying pan which I dutifully set on the stovetop. Mick had gone out back in search of wood for burning in the aforementioned stove while I assessed the general culinary situation.

The screen door opened and slammed. "I found some! Timothy has it flawlessly stacked behind the tool shed," Mick announced proudly. I suddenly imagined him measuring and documenting the precise angles of each wood chunk. He must be going crazy without the ability to document each precious number. As I opened what I assumed was the stove door, Mick deposited the fire wood therein. Out of habit, he turned toward the sink and tried to turn on a faucet. "Oh yeah. Is there any water left in the bucket?"

"A little," I said as I lit a match and tossed it in with the wood.

"I'll get more then. What's the word on breakfast? 'Hungry' doesn't even begin to describe the state of my rumbling stomach."

"Well, I'm pretty sure I can make biscuits with what's available. I can't seem to find any eggs or breakfast meat anywhere though."

"There's a chicken coop behind the outhouse," Mick responded. "It doesn't get any fresher than that."

Dear lord. Chicken coop. Live chickens sitting on top of their unborn, shell-encased young. An arrogant, vindictive rooster patrolling his chicken harem. I immediately turned paler than I already was. "Umm . . . do you think you could grab a couple for me since you'll be outside anyway?"

Mick was already halfway out the kitchen door. "Really, Katie? Are you still traumatized by your childhood 'when roosters attack' episode?"

I managed a pitiful, "Yes!"

He felt sorry for me and agreed to retrieve our eggs from the Chicken Coop O' Death while I mixed up something resembling biscuits. Locating a pan, I set it on the now-warm stovetop and melted some Crisco in it just like my Grandma used to do when making cornbread. Once melted, I plopped wads of dough into it and spaced each plop appropriately. Very carefully I opened the front door of the stove and slid the pan onto the grate situated safely above the now-mellowed flames. "I hope I don't burn them," I worried aloud. Thoughts of marauding chickens in cahoots with the rattlesnakes were impairing my ability to focus.

Biscuit placement accomplished, I continued my search for the elusive meat. Didn't average people living in this time have iceboxes of some sort? Nothing in the room looked much like an icebox, but then I was a spoiled gal from the too-pampered future. "Maybe it's on the porch with the bath tub," I theorized, immediately heading in that direction. Bingo! The wooden cabinet thingy with sawdust and water trickling from the back had to be it. Encouraged by my unexpectedly quick progress, I yanked the door open. Never in my life had I been so ecstatic to see a slab of bacon.

"I rock," I declared to myself and the termites that probably lurked in the wood beams then returned to the kitchen. The skillet now hot, I sliced a few slabs of what looked like quality, farm-raised bacon and confidently laid them down to fry. From the very first crackle of fat, I felt like a professional pioneer. "Round up the kids, Pa, and circle them wagons!"

"Is there an imminent Indian attack I wasn't warned about?"

Mick asked, laying several fresh—and poop-encrusted—eggs into the sink.

"It was the first pioneer-ish thing that came to mind," I replied, carefully turning the bacon over and dodging hot fat-splatters. They were like miniature heat-seeking missiles popping out of the pan in search of my bare skin.

"We're not exactly the Donner Party, you know. This is 1920, not 1820. There are automobiles, not covered wagons," Mick reminded me, sitting himself down into an old kitchen chair after depositing a brimming bucket of cold spring water onto the countertop.

"Yes, and we don't eat each other either. Now, where are those eggs?"

"In the sink."

I wiped my bacon-spattered hands onto the makeshift apron in the form of an old dishtowel that was tied around my waist. Upon seeing the filthy chicken embryos, I wasn't very hungry anymore. "You mean they really come out like that?"

Mick was thoroughly amused. "And human babies come out all clean and sterile?"

"But we don't poop on our young!"

"Actually, I think that can happen during child . . ."

"We don't poop on our young on purpose! This is disgusting," I said, still staring at the poor crusty chicken babies awaiting their cleansing.

Mick stood up with resignation, still smiling. "I'll wash. You finish the bacon and figure out where that burning smell is coming from."

"The biscuits!" I screamed and, yanking the dishtowel from around my waist, used it to open the stove door in order to remove the charred mounds of flour and lard from their place of execution. "I take it back. I'm a lousy pioneer. We all would've starved to death or resorted to cannibalism before even reaching the Oregon Trail. I'd have killed us off on the Iowa trail."

Mick laid a consoling hand on my shoulder and made strange strangling sounds which I took to mean he was trying not to laugh his smarty-pants butt off at the predicament. "It's okay, Ma Katie. There's still bacon and eggs which are now shiny clean. That will be plenty."

I sighed and tossed the unintendedly blackened biscuits into what I assumed was a trash bin. It was actually an old wooden box containing coffee grounds. To me, that conveyed "trash."

Determined to persevere so Mick wouldn't starve, I cracked the poop-free eggs into the bacon-greased skillet and scrambled them within an inch of their existence. "I suppose it will have to be enough until we get to the market. There's not much else in the way of food except half a loaf of bread, half a slab of bacon, and a few sausage links in the icebox. Which reminds me: what are we going to do for money? Something tells me that Bank of America has yet to place an ATM anywhere in the vicinity."

"Huh. Yeah, we will have to figure that out, won't we? Maybe the market owner will let us put it on an account of some sort. They allowed credit in *Little House on the Prairie* anyway."

"They probably would if we were Eva or Timothy, but since we're only supposed to be their phantom cousins no one in town has ever met or even heard of before . . . "

Mick's brow wrinkled in thought. "That's a good point. Well, I guess first we'll look around the house and see if there's any sort of money stash. People living in the country this long ago often kept emergency funds at home, especially the ones who didn't trust banks."

"And it's a good thing too since The Crash is less than nine years away. Okay, I'm going to find some manner of clothing I can squeeze into, and while I'm at it, I'll look around the bedroom for whatever cash may be here."

"And I'll wash the dishes when I'm finished eating. Aren't you hungry?"

I was already halfway to the bedroom. "No, I can never think of eating when there's a clothing crisis."

I could hear Mick rolling his eyes at me.

CHAPTER NINE

"I can't bloody breathe!" I panted to Mick as we walked down the dirt road that passed for one of the major streets. Pulling impotently at the dress that simply had nothing left to give, I had to keep reminding myself that, while we were somewhere in the middle of future Austin, we were in what amounted to a suburb in 1920 Austin.

Mick had easily found clothing that would work for him, although the pants were indeed a couple of inches too short. I'd have to locate a needle and thread somewhere. "It can't be that bad. You look fine," he remarked in his annoying sensible way.

"We're going to have to spring for a couple of dresses or something because my hips are wreaking havoc with what's already available. I'm determined that poor Eva will have intact dresses to come home to."

"So why can't you breathe if it's the hips that are too tight?"

I didn't know. There wasn't an adequate phrase expressing clothing discomfort that applied to the hip section. "I can't poop? Is that better?"

Mick grasped my hand with an acceptable amount of sympathy. "Well, look at it this way: Eva is stuck trying to figure out leather corsets and stiletto boots. Constipation is the least of your worries."

I laughed. "And something tells me she's going to love it! Timothy may have a heart attack, however. I wonder what they're going to do for jobs and such? Life is much more expensive and complicated and confusing in the 21st of all the centuries."

Mick began massaging my knuckles absently as we walked. "Which once again brings up the question of what we're going to do as well. I don't know much about farming, but I suppose I could learn. I'm a physicist who just figured out that some ghosts are actually time-warping people. Surely I can handle a plow and plant some seeds."

A sudden positive attitude rushed through my body. "Of course you can. And I can learn how to cook and use the outhouse in the middle of the night without falling into the so-called seat and put on make-up without a proper make-up mirror . . . this just might work!"

As we neared the market, Mick presented one more frightening yet necessary thought for consideration: "We also need to accept the possibility that we might be trapped here forever. It's unlikely that Timothy and Eva could repair the cylinders enough for even basic functionality. And if nothing else, it would take them some time to network with anyone who could."

I'd already been considering this every five seconds since being stranded here and returned his encouraging hand-squeeze. "It's okay. We'll make do somehow, and so will they. They're the resilient types, I know it. It's hardly scientific of me, but I have a strong feeling we'll get warped back into our rightful places eventually."

Mick nodded as he led me up the wooden steps and into the market. "No, it's not scientific at all, but that's what I love most about you."

We were being given "the eye." Several "eyes," actually. There were a few housewives and a couple of farmer husbands conducting various market-related business transactions around us, but none of that business was interesting enough to distract them from the strangers in town. One of the women—we quickly learned she was the store proprietor's wife—apparently had no inborn "stranger fear" and approached us almost the moment we walked through the doorway. "Good morning, good morning! You two new in town? Where are you from? My husband and me are from here, always lived here, and so did our parents and grandparents. My great-grandparents came over on the boat. No, not the Mayflower, one of the boats that landed in Galveston. Where are you staying? With family? You'd be welcome to stay with us, but we've already got all the family we can handle! The mother-in-law is in town," she added with a knowing wink.

Mick took the opportunity to answer a question or two while the nice but talkative woman paused to laugh at her apparently funny joke. "We're actually keeping an eye on Eva and Timothy's place while they go back East for awhile. I'm Eva's cousin, you know, and my Mama—Eva's aunt—is feeling poorly."

I chuckled to myself. "Feeling poorly?" He really had watched *Little House on the Prairie!*

"And who's this lovely lady with you? Your wife, I expect? My, but you're a pretty thing. Misplaced your wedding ring though, did you? I misplaced mine once. My wedding ring, that is. Turned out it fell into the milk pail during the morning milking. Did you maybe lose it in the chicken coop?"

My brain was dizzied by her rapid-fire questions. Not knowing how to respond, I stared dumbly at my naked ring finger. Hmm. This could be an unforeseen difficulty for early 20th century country society. Decent women didn't shack up with their men of non-husbandly designation.

Luckily Mick came to my immediate rescue. "Aw, she's always losing it somewhere. Last week she accidentally stuffed it into a sausage link. Yesterday morning I bit into it during breakfast . . . nearly chipped a tooth. But that's my Katie," he said and winked at me.

My face flushed with adoration and admiration and a strong desire to French kiss the boy right there in the canned goods aisle. I didn't figure that would go over well either, though, even amongst the properly married. "We have yet to be officially introduced, however," I began in an attempt to escape an awkward subject. "My name is Katie Burg . . . McClaren, and this is . . . "

"Burg-McClaren? Is that one of them modern, hyphenated last names?" the lady asked with a frown.

"Yes it is but only on paper. All our friends know me as just plain Katie McClaren. This is my, er, husband Mick." The term "husband" sounded foreign but groovily so.

We all three formally shook hands and sealed the new acquaintanceship as the lady finally gave us a name to go with the mouth. "And I'm Clara Simmons. My husband Carl owns this store and," here Mrs. Simmons paused to look around then whisper only to us, "and he runs a little side business out back around midnight." She winked and pointed at a corked jug half-hidden behind the counter. Moonshine. That so totally figured.

"We might have to arrange a late-night purchase one of these days, but for now there's a few more practical things we're needing," Mick said, trying to steer the conversation back into a productive direction.

Clara Simmons was having none of it. "So your Ma's not doing well, is she? What's wrong with her? None of us even knew Eva had family outside Texas. We thought they all came from around here. Guess you never really know everything about someone, even after a lifetime."

Mick paused as Clara took a breath. He fully expected her to continue soliloquizing, but to his and Katie's amazement, she hushed and waited for a response to her inquisition. "I think she'll be fine. She has bad rheumatism during summer, and this year it hurt so much she just couldn't take care of herself and needed a little help."

"Aw, God bless Eva. She has such a good heart. So does her husband Timothy. I suppose you've met her husband Timothy? He helped her get rid of a rattlesnake den in the old well beside Eva's place. Her place is the one next to Timothy's that got blown up when Eva threw lit moonshine into it."

"Lit moonshine?" Katie asked in amazement.

"Yes. She'd been hitting a bottle of her granddaddy's secret stash at the time. I don't think the poor girl was thinking too clearly."

"Now, Mrs. Simmons, about the things we need," Mick prodded.

"Oh yes, of course! I'm so sorry, I could prattle on all day if people would let me," she laughed.

No kidding, Katie and Mick both thought simultaneously. While Mick took care of their basic needs, Katie wandered around the variety store with wonder. These were the things people wanted and/or needed almost one hundred years ago. The concept was staggering to her, even though she'd dealt with the concept and resigned herself to being stuck out of time for awhile. What was this? A container of tapeworms? And it's being sold as—Katie flipped the jar around to read the instructions pasted to the back—a weight loss aid? Good mother mercy, people ate these things on purpose just to get thinner? And I thought 21st century women were loopy when it came to weight loss methods. I couldn't resist. "Hey Mick, look at this!"

Trying to make a decision between buying either two pounds of bacon or a pound of honey-cured ham that both cost the same amount, Mick was slightly annoyed at the distraction. Annoyance dissipated when he read the "medication" label. Hilarity ensued as he exclaimed, "Geez, and I thought you would do anything to lose weight! This is insane!"

"I know, right? Like ingesting a parasite is good for you no matter how 'sterile' they're proclaimed to be."

"Well, they used to bleed people for every medical reason under the sun. A headache, stomach ache, fever, broken toenail, all of these things would lose you a pint or more of blood."

While Mick and I continued our crackpot product-bashing, Clara glared at us in a much offended manner. "I don't see what's so funny. My sister-in-law has lost ten pounds since using this product once she got past the diarrhea . . . well, almost past. She still goes to the outhouse three or four times a day, but that's a lot better than it used to be! You should be careful about criticizing a treatment you've never tried yourself."

Mick's jaw froze mid-laugh as he mentally smacked himself. Suddenly feeling like her weight had been insulted, Katie resisted issuing a witty comeback to the poor woman who hadn't benefitted from ninety or so more years of medical advancement. "Of course, you're right," Katie replied. "It may be a wonderful treatment. It just seems peculiar that someone would eat a tapeworm—or any worm, for that matter—on purpose. We apologize."

Not one to hold grudges, Clara was all smiles once again. "Oh, it's quite alright. I suppose it does sound strange, now that I think about it. Now, Mr. McClaren, have you decided if it will be bacon or ham?"

Meat and tapeworms. Perfect. I continued down another aisle and let Mick finish gathering and paying for our purchases. I saw many another amusing products but decided to keep the details to myself for now. Since there was no television, we'd have to find something to entertain ourselves with in the evening. And speaking of evening activities, tonight was definitely going to include a hot bath. Mick was headed my way with two item-stuffed bags, so I opened the door for him. "How long do you think it will take to heat enough water for a bath?"

Squinting as his eyeballs encountered the midday summer sun, he didn't reply immediately. Eyes adjusted, he said, "Probably not too long. Back in the pioneer days an entire family took a bath in the same water."

"Ewww. No wonder people in this time have no trouble implanting tapeworms in their intestines. What if their little kids peed in the water? You know they did. All little kids pee in the bath water."

Mick nodded and grinned. "The lye soap probably killed any bacteria dead on contact. We'll see how long it takes to heat the water then decide."

They walked several steps in unexpectedly comfortable silence before Katie spoke again. "You know, it's weird. I don't feel all that uncomfortable here."

"Even without full make-up access?"

She elbowed him playfully. "I'm not that bad. Besides, I can do okay with what's available now. There won't be any runway model impersonations or anything, but . . . "

"Thank goodness!" was Mick's response to that. "I miss the sunglasses availability though. We're being bombarded with harmful UV rays."

"Maybe the ozone layer is still thick enough to protect us better in this time. Come to think of it, even if it is thicker, I still need to find their version of sunscreen. If I'm going to be working out in the fields and yard and such, I'll either have to wear long sleeves or sunscreen . . . and I don't fancy the idea of wearing long sleeves in 100-degree heat."

"I can't remember the exact year, but I don't think that stuff was invented until closer to World War II. I remember reading something about the soldiers first using it on the various battlefronts."

"Oh terrific," I muttered as we reached our house. "And I have the happy skin cancer gene running rampant through my chromosomes."

Mick opened the back door for me and kissed the top of my ear. "Don't worry, Katie-mine. I'll protect you from the skin cancer."

For some reason, I had a blast sorting through Mick's grocery selection and figuring out how best—and frugally!—to combine them. We'd found $25 stuck under their mattress which should go a long way if we were careful. Still, some manner of gainful employment must be procured. I wondered if Mrs. Simmons would consider letting me help out in the store. I could introduce a make-over counter!

While sorting the meat from the canned goods, I heard an odd scraping sound of metal on wood. "What are you doing?" I yelled.

"Moving the tub," came Mick's muffled reply.

"You can't put it in here yet. I still have to cook."

"I know. I was just going to have it ready by the door." Finished with that phase of the relocation, Mick wandered into the kitchen and watched my sorting and preparing. "Need any eggs?"

"Probably," I said. "I think I've decided to do meatloaf. That should be a foolproof meal for the wood stove-challenged, but then again, the biscuits should've been too."

"Whatever you make will be perfect. I'm starving again."

"Just wait until we start working in the field. I may not be able to keep up with your appetite!"

Mick winked. "Which one?" He smacked my bottom once again and headed for the chicken coop. Upon returning, he was carrying an armload of fresh veggies instead of eggs. We had a garden! The chickens could go to hades, for all I cared.

"Wow!" I cried happily. "We get to have salad! I'm so excited, you have no idea!"

Mick was pleased with his advantageous find and immediately began washing away the dirt. "Of course I have an idea. I'm the one that bought you the salad bar frequent flyer card at the pizza place downtown. Oh, but there weren't any eggs today."

"That's okay. I think there are a couple left from breakfast." I grabbed the decided-upon ground meat and trotted to the icebox. Opening the door, I grabbed the remaining two eggs. "I do not like green eggs and ham, Son of Sam . . . or something like that. And voila!" I said, brandishing my successfully retrieved ingredients as I returned to the kitchen. Instead of seeing Mick dutifully scrubbing vegetables at the sink, he was kneeling on one knee in the middle of the kitchen floor. I really needed to figure out where the mop was. Otherwise there was not a single thought in my shocked head.

"I know this is kind of sudden."

My heart was pounding but in the good way. "Maybe so, but I'm sort of used to it after all that's happened." I glanced around the room as I spoke.

"Mrs. Simmons raised an important point: you need to be wearing a wedding band, and instead of constantly inventing new ways for you to lose one, I figured why not buy you the real thing?"

Now I was confused and quickly careening toward depression. Amazing how emotions can do about-faces like that. "So this is just for show? I mean, this is only so people will think we're properly married and not shacking up?"

He knew exactly where my mind had gone. "Yes, but I also thought it was high time I made an honest woman of you instead of letting you continue playing the dirty little hooker you've been recently."

I laughed with relief but also because of his uncanny ability to know my mind's idiosyncrasies. "But I had the perfect outfit!"

"Yeah, but it's stuck ninety-something years in the future, thank the leather gods. What do you say? Would you be willing to spend the rest of your life married to a math nerd who may constantly be questioning your clothing choices?"

I knelt to the floor, flung my arms around his neck, and gave him the kiss of his life. "I wouldn't have it any other way."

He grinned, blushing all the while. "Good. Then let's see if this fits. I'm sorry it couldn't have been fancier, but the local supply of fine jewelry is seriously lacking . . . as is my future bank account."

"I don't care, Mick. It's beautiful! Plus it's actually silver which is perfect because . . ."

"Because you hate gold. I know. When we get back, we can pick out something nicer for your actual wedding band."

It, of course, fit perfectly. Knowing Mick he'd probably measured the circumference of my finger while I slept. I was beaming even more brightly than the perfectly polished silver. A tiny diamond was nestled in the center of the smooth-surfaced ring, its facets glinting happily anytime light brushed it. "You did good. Now what if I really do lose it?"

Mick rose to his feet then pulled me up too. "If you lose it, you'll just have to wrap tin foil around your finger. I'm too broke to support a ring-losing habit."

"I'll be so careful." Then, with newly-energized mischievousness in my eyes, I said, "Now since the water must be shared anyway, how about a bath of newly-engaged togetherness?"

Dinner waited a while.

CHAPTER TEN

The next morning I awoke to the glorious surreality of being engaged. While I never thought it possible this would ever happen, I had still fervently hoped. On paper, Mick and I were the unlikeliest of contradictory pairs, but anyone who knew us in real life would understand otherwise. Best of friends since childhood, all of our other friends were probably expecting such things.

As I wandered outside with empty water bucket in hand, I couldn't help but wonder what our children would be like. "Thoroughly confused" was a good possibility if their brains were half math and half English nerd. Can two such opposing forces exist within the same skull? I reached the well and began the semi-tedious process of refilling my bucket. Mick had gone back to the market to speak with Mr. Simmons. Somehow, he'd told me, he had to learn how to farm in as unobvious a way as possible so we wouldn't arouse suspicion with our citified ignorance. I, on the other hand, intended to devote my day to cooking under these more antiquated circumstances. I simply had to stop charring everything, or poor Mick wouldn't have a normal bowel movement for months.

Since our delayed dinner the night before had made the quickness of salad preparation necessary, today I would finally tackle the meatloaf project which meant gathering more eggs. During our post-engagement romp on the kitchen floor, I'd inadvertently smashed the two shell-encased embryos already gathered. Therefore, the knowledge that I had to brave the inside of a chicken coop made the straining buttons on my borrowed dress strain even further. I heaved in deep, rapid breaths of nervousness. Maybe one of the buttons would pop off and fly at the rooster's squawking, belligerent head thereby killing him like David killed Goliath. It could happen, right?

So now it's probably time to explain why I so illogically freak out upon sight of live poultry. Dead poultry is cool, of course. I'd eaten lots and lots of it. My live chicken fear began years ago around the age of seven. My parents kept a chicken coop fully-stocked with a dozen or so chickens and one rooster so we'd have a continuous supply of fresh eggs. As one of my chores, I was expected to a) take the evil beasts a giant bucket of water and feed, and b) collect the eggs. This sounded simple enough, so on my first trip solo to the chicken coop, I was relatively unfazed by the whole idea. All of that changed the moment I entered the coop. White feathered fiends swarmed around me as I tried to pour water into the troughs. When it was time to dump the feed into the feeders, two of the devil birds flapped upward and perched on the rim of my feed bucket within breathing distance of my face, although I'm still not convinced that chickens actually breathe. Don't their beaks have gills? Needless to say, I dropped the bucket and entertained no thought but that of escape; but as I turned around, there blocking my path was The Rooster. Hell's fire burned in his beady little eyeballs as he flew at me. Convinced he wanted to peck my face into bloody strips of flesh, I turned and ran around and around the coop in a crazed attempt to find the door that was in the same place it had always been, Beelzebub's favorite assassin flapping only inches behind. Finally, at the peak of the chickens squawking and rooster crowing at me in Hell-ese, I managed to open the door, slam it shut, and run wildly back into the house.

My younger brother was assigned chicken duty after that. Dad said the chickens were so traumatized by my mindless behavior that they didn't lay any eggs again for a week. He didn't use big words though. The smaller ones yelled in my general direction were effective enough.

So one may now comprehend my dilemma with regard to picking up even the single egg necessary to make lunch. As a soon-to-be wife, however, I figured it was my duty to overcome irrational fear and pass serenely through this company of poultry to retrieve my final meatloaf ingredient. After depositing the now-full water bucket on the kitchen cabinet, I grabbed a pair of thick work gloves and slid them onto my hands. I wanted as much protection as possible from any pecking beaks or slashing toenails. Raptor talons were more like it, I thought, as I clung to the idea of my would-be leather hand-gauntlets. Once I was out the back door and as far from safety as the outhouse, I began to shake. My steps slowed as my heart rate increased to about three hundred beats per minute. Keep walking, girl, just keep walking, I encouraged myself. As the coop came into full view, my earth began to shake, and my moon turned to blood. It was in there. Honestly, I could probably handle the chickens, but not It. Stephen King really should've used a giant rooster instead of a spider. I wouldn't have slept for a month if he had!

Miraculously I got my legs moving again. Step by wretched step, I approached my fate with about as much serenity as a blender set on "liquefy." Just as I'd worked up enough courage to touch the door handle, I finally saw It. It had somehow escaped the chicken coop prison and was strutting out from behind a tree to my right . . . and It saw me. It was déjà vu all over again as the creature launched into a furious assault upon my person, chasing me around and around the small building. I took off both gloves and threw them in his general direction, and they—of course—missed him entirely. When I finally managed to escape into the coop, It flew at the door several times trying to peck my knees. Two buttons actually popped off the bodice of Eva's dress as I huffed and puffed for dear life, but neither of them struck my nemesis. To make matters worse, after his vicious failed onslaught, It took up sentry duty in front of the door. He obviously wasn't letting his quarry go anywhere.

Responsible soon-to-be wife or not, I burst into tears.

"Hope the meatloaf is ready because we're going to need our strength. I picked up lots of tips this morning, but large amounts of energy will be required . . . like 'big bang' amounts. Katie? Are you in here?" Mick wandered through the house but found no sign of me. He heard a muffled yell coming from somewhere behind the house and decided to follow it. Once he swung open the back screen door, he thought he could make out the sound of his name. That was my "distressed" voice, if his ears didn't deceive him, and as he neared the chicken coop, he fully understood why I was using it. He couldn't quite figure out why I was half-naked, though.

"Mick! It is so about time! Kill this thing. Now!"

Mick knew he'd regret it later but couldn't help grinning at the sight of his fiancée—her upper half clad only in a bra—gripping the chicken wire until her knuckles were snow-whiter than normal. "Is this your way of telling me you'd like to role-play tonight?"

"Mick, you insensitive idiot, this isn't funny! If you ever want to have bedroom fun-time at any time in the future, you will wring that thing's neck this instant!"

"So I guess this means the meatloaf isn't ready yet?"

I was livid. Speech ceased to form as my eyes went cold and bore into his. This was my "fear me" face, and Mick had (supposedly) learned years ago precisely what it meant. When we were teenagers, he had inadvertently locked me in one of those portable outbuildings with an angry and terrified mockingbird. It hadn't been pretty. Ghosts and time/space travelers I can cope with, but avian entities? Forget about it.

Mick stupidly attempted the application of logic to our scenario. "But Katie, it's not our rooster to kill. I don't think Timothy and Eva would appreciate coming home to a rooster-less chicken coop."

"Tell them it ran away. Tell them it died of the plague. Tell them whatever, but I don't want to see It alive another second!" I glared murderously at the rooster still patrolling in front of the door. It, of course, had no issue with Mick's presence which led my mind to the only believable conclusion: It wanted me dead too. Ultimately, I guessed that was fair.

Mick sighed and tried one final alternative suggestion. "Okay, what if I chase it away? No doubt it will come back eventually, but you could at least make a good run for it."

Maybe that would work. Calming somewhat, I loosened my grip on the wire. Great, now I had wire lines imprinted in my hands. Reluctantly I said, "Fine. You chase the thing away, grab what eggs you can carry, and I'll go inside to start dinner."

"But you're already in there. Can't you get the eggs?"

"You're on your own with the eggs," I stated firmly.

Satisfied with the compromise as long as it would get me out of the chicken coop and back inside the house, Mick proceeded to yell like a wild fiend and chase the rooster in the direction of the tool shed. It was rather hilarious, actually, watching this reserved personality flailing his arms while running after the now-terrified rooster. I hazarded a giggle and rushed madly for the house. Safely inside and once again watching the Mick action, I laughed 'til my stomach cramped as roles suddenly reversed. Mick had become the pursuee. Within moments he found himself eyeing It from behind the wire, except his eyes blazed with exasperation rather than fear. He unwaveringly turned to retrieve the eggs then exited the coop, kicking the psychotic rooster across the lawn.

So yeah, It wound up dead anyway.

*****

The meatloaf was stupendous! Not that there's anything challenging about making decent meatloaf, though I've known a few people whose culinary attempts made me consider believing otherwise. Maybe it was the absence of a blackened top layer that brought out the flavor of such simple ingredients, but Mick and I both gorged our empty tummies on the savory tastiness.

"You did good, babycakes. This stuff is awesome!"

I won't lie: I was beaming with domestic pride "Thanks to you getting the eggs. And thanks to the existence of ketchup in 1920! Meatloaf just won't work without lots and lots of it."

"I thought the extra onions made it better myself. Most people seem to be stingy with their onion usage," he replied, pushing his plate away and leaning back in his creaky wooden chair. He patted his bulging stomach and smiled lazily.

There was something brilliant about this life of relative simplicity, I paused to acknowledge, although I could tell Mick was starting to miss his genius-grade calculator. Part of me almost hated the thought of returning to our rightful time, but other parts of me remembered learning about The Great Depression and Vietnam and the nuclear bombs parked in Cuba that aimed directly for Florida. Those experiences I could pretty much do without. "Tomorrow I need to weed the garden. I was able to get a good lay of the vegetable land while stuck in the chicken coop, and it's shockingly weed-infested."

Mick rose to clear dirty dishes from the table and set them in the sink for washing. "I can do that," I said, gently restraining his arm.

"No worries, I got this. You cooked, I'll clean. Besides, you've had a traumatic day and probably need some extra relaxation time."

What a sweetheart! "That does sound good. Wish we had a bottle of wine to help with that relaxation."

Mick grinned a sly grin as he scrubbed a ketchuppy plate. "Why don't you take a look in the cabinet there?"

"You didn't!" I exclaimed, rushing to the cabinet he indicated. Inside was a two-year-old bottle of California merlot. This man was the discovery of the century! Time warping was nothing by comparison. "How did you get away with this?"

Still smiling, Mick explained. "Mr. Simmons really does have a, shall we say, 'questionable' side business going on in the back room of his store. It's pricier than it would be if the stuff was legal but still worth it under the circumstances."

"You brought wine, and you're doing the dishes. I want you. Now."

Mick turned away from the sink and took a step in my direction, soap suds dripping all over the floor. "But I'm all wet."

"So am I. Come on."

An hour or so later, we both lounged on the front porch and brazenly sipped the alcoholic contraband. I pondered its lovely shade of deep burgundy and asked, "Have you noticed how every situation is leading to sex these days?"

"Yeah, we should've tried this engagement and marriage thing years ago."

"Not too many years ago. That would've been gross."

Mick emptied his glass and poured himself another. "Want some more?"

"Yes, please!" I eagerly responded, relishing the happy fuzziness buzzing through my body. Of course that buzzing wasn't only the wine. Mick had been having that effect on me for a while now. "Do you know if the sewing machine in the living room works?"

Feeling groovy himself, Mick was less guarded toward what could be a potentially disastrous question. "I would think so. Women used them more often these days. Why?"

"Because I want to try my hand at sewing stuff."

Having heard the actual words spoken, Mick snapped a bit more to attention. "Katie, you do remember what happened in home economics class, right?"

Damn, he remembered too. "Yeah, but that was a long time ago."

"It was six months ago."

"Was it? It feels like longer ago than that."

"Technically it's longer in the future than that, but the fact still remains that you don't know what the hell you're doing with those machines."

"If it's in the future, then it hasn't happened yet; therefore my sewing record is clean," I declared triumphantly.

"You sewed the would-be potholder you were making onto the teacher's Prada jacket."

"And? What kind of idiot wears a Prada jacket to teach school anyway? She deserved it."

"Is there anything I can say or do to convince you that this is a bad idea?"

"Nope. I'm determined. See my 'determined' face?"

Mick sighed and downed the remainder of his full-bodied merlot. "Do as you will then, my dear. But if I come home from the field tomorrow and find you fingerless and/or bleeding to death, I'm removing all sewing privileges."

"It's a deal," I agreed and kissed his cheek. "I'm only going to start with basic repair work anyway . . . like letting out side seams and the hems of your—er, Timothy's—pants."

"Yeah, those dresses have a habit of bursting open at inopportune times, don't they?" he commented with much glee.

"Laugh now, bubba, but what will you say when my boobs are suddenly exposed in the middle of a church social or something?"

"I'd probably say, 'Praise the Lord!' "

I had to laugh at that one. "You're such a guy."

Waxing flirtatious once more, partially due to the wine, he asked, "I thought that's what you liked best about me."

I climbed into his lap. "It helps."

"Seriously? Again? The back porch might be better for this kind of thing," he said, happily amazed at my sudden flooziness.

"It's already dark. Besides, every town needs a good scandal once in a while."

*****

Thankfully there was no scandal, at least not yet. People here retreated indoors at sunset and stayed there until morning except on rare occasions like the Fourth of July. You had to have a picnic with fireworks on the Fourth. Such practices made sense when ninety percent of a population earned their living by farming and ranching, but we were still adjusting to the slower-moving, earlier-to-bed lifestyle. That was likely to change starting today, however. Mick and I were both up at the pre-crack of dawn preparing for his day of hard manual labor. I scrambled eggs, fried bacon, and baked flawless biscuits like a veteran short order cook while he analyzed the many tools in the tool shed, trying to figure out each one's purpose. He returned to the kitchen just as I was putting everything on the table. "Any luck?" I asked.

He sat down hungrily, mesmerized by the scent of bacon. I poured a sizeable cup of coffee and set it next to his rapidly-filling plate. "Lots of luck if I knew what the tools were used for. It's times like this when I really miss my calculator."

"These tools should be easier to figure out than that mathematical nightmare."

"For you, Lady Shakespeare, yes they would be."

"I hate Shakespeare."

"Anyway, I did find several cotton harvest sack things. Mr. Simmons said the cotton is ready to be picked. Actually, he said it in a reprimanding sort of way like I should've known it was time weeks before it really was."

"Just remind him that we're Yankees."

"I did," Mick replied. "He apologized and dropped the subject."

I chomped down on a biscuit slathered with butter and honey. If I kept up these eating habits, I'd have to forget letting out seams and resort to buying muumuus. "Do you need any help hauling stuff out to the field?"

Mick swiped one last biscuit himself and honeyed it up. "I don't think so. The field is only fifty or so yards from the back door. More than likely I can handle carrying the sack at least that far."

"Well, lunch will be ready precisely at noon."

"I don't have a watch . . . or a cell phone."

I pointed straight up at the sky. "When the sun is right there, come eat."

"What if it's cloudy?"

I playfully slapped his cheek as he stood up and grabbed an old hat he'd found amongst Timothy's sparse clothing supply. "We'll have fresh veggies today, I think. There should be enough to make some sort of salad again."

He was safely on his way outside when he replied, "Good, because your fat rolls are reproducing!"

If the door hadn't hit him on his way out, I would have. The dishes were quickly washed, dried, and put away which left me plenty of cool-ish morning to spend in the garden. I didn't envy Mick's indentured servitude to the sweltering Texas heat all day. I'd have to see about making a gallon or five of iced tea for when he took breaks. Tea now brewing on the stovetop, I searched the cabinets for something like a colander. What I found was an actual colander which was even better.

Armed with my holey bowl and a hoe I'd found leaning against the tool shed, I walked purposefully to the garden. The hoe would be useful for old-fashioned weed whacking as well as snake murdering. Upon arrival at my wondrous patch of roughage-filled joy, I immediately noticed something amiss. The weeds were still there, of course, but scattered around the garden in multiple places were little depressions in the ground where plants used to be. Potatoes in particular seem to have been targeted by a phantom subterranean veggie stealer. What potatoes there still there I pulled up quickly, de-dirting them before placing them into the colander. By the time I got to the carrots, whatever it was beneath the ground was just getting started on them. Frozen to the spot where I knelt with thoughts of that movie *Tremors* tunneling through my brain, I watched a carrot top sink inch . . . by inch . . . by inch into the ground until it disappeared. "Friggin' gopher. There's a friggin' gopher in my garden!" I announced to the uncaring world.

Incensed at the violation of my vegetation, I brandished my hoe and started hacking it into the ground. When it came up all red and gooshy, I knew I'd hit my mark. "Look, dude, I'm really sorry I had to do that, but it's my garden, you know? I'm a veggie person. They make my taste buds dance and my bowels flow freely. You don't mess with a girl's bowels." And then I felt guilty for hacking a furry member of the animal kingdom to death. I soothed my conscience by reminding it that there were probably lots more down there anyway.

"Yeah, the little babies of the mother gopher you just sliced into pieces!" my conscience replied.

I was a bad person.

With a sigh, I chopped away at all the infringing weeds then laid down the hoe and began pulling what vegetables were ready to be harvested. All in all, we still had plenty: summer and zucchini squash, cucumbers, several potatoes despite the depredation, onions, a couple of decent-sized carrots, a head of cabbage, green beans, and two tomatoes that technically shouldn't have been yanked just yet, but I couldn't resist in case the gopher's ghost decided to haunt . . . and an actual head of pretty, fluttery, leafy lettuce! My colander literally overfloweth-ed.

Gopher death fading from my thoughts, I trekked happily away from the garden and back toward the house. While passing the tool shed, I noticed there were several tall, bushy dill plants dispersing their wonderful scent into my nostrils. Surely the colander could handle a few sprigs of the herb, so I pulled and crammed as many as I could in between the vegetables. Hypnotized by the aroma, I failed to notice another memorable aroma creeping in with the dill . . . until I heard the weird hissing sound. Nearly dropping my load, I felt fur swish quickly across my leg then looked down just in time to see the retreating backside of a skunk. "Oh, bloody hell!" I yelled and turned to flee from what emanated from that backside.

I didn't make it. The black and white beastie had sprayed me full on, head to toe, veggies and all. What was it with the animals around here? How did they find me, and why did they wish to destroy me? Tears of frustration mixed with chemical irritation flooded down my cheeks as I dejectedly retreated to the back porch. I stank. Badly. This dress would have to be tossed, and I very much feared that the veggies would too. Immediately upon entering, I grabbed the water bucket and filled it over and over with water, dumping each bucketful into the bath tub. I didn't give a rip if it was heated or not. It was already mid-morning and nearing 90 degrees. I didn't care if a visitor suddenly arrived and witnessed my full-blown nakedness. Well, that wasn't likely to happen. Skunk smell would create an anti-interfering neighbor barrier around the property for hours.

There was a box of Borax soap under the kitchen sink, so I decided to carefully utilize its ultra-cleaning power. It would hurt like hades, but this smell had to go. Mick would be back in a couple of hours for lunch, and now I had no idea if anything was even going to be edible. Clothing removed, I eased myself into the cold spring water, wincing every inch of the descent. Once my skin stopped screaming at me to stop, I reached for the soap and scrubbed away with the granular cleanser. Oh, I was so going to regret this! After five minutes of rubbing the crustiness into my skin, I sniffed a spot and thought some progress had been made. Of course, two or three layers of skin had likely been removed along with the stench, but at least Mick wouldn't pass out if I hugged him. My hair was going to be more difficult, so I shampooed it several times hoping it would be enough. For conditioner, I cracked a few eggs and rubbed the contents all over my "clean" hair. It would have to do for now.

After donning a light cotton robe, I slid into some house shoes I'd found shoved into the back of Eva's closet space then shuffled into the kitchen. I'd set the colander full of what used to be a bunch of edible happy thoughts into the sink. Slowly I leaned over to sniff them. Oh dear. This gave an entirely too literal meaning to the term "skunk cabbage." Determined to salvage what could be of my lunch plans, I began scrubbing away at each piece. Maybe if I scrubbed everything thoroughly and scraped off the tainted outer layers, they'd still be okay.

Two hours later when the big hand, little hand, and the sun were on the "twelve," I heard the backdoor open then slam shut. Mick stumbled into the kitchen and slumped down in his chair. "If ever there was a time for Guinness, it's now," he whimpered.

No matter how trying my morning had been—and it had been trying!—it was nothing compared to the hard work Mick had accomplished. And he had a full afternoon of still more sweat-inducing travail. "Want some tea?"

"Only if it's laced with many ice cubes."

"Is there any other way to drink it?" I handed him a big glass of near-to-overflowing sweet tea which he proceeded to gulp down in seconds. I refilled it then kissed his ear.

He smiled a tired smile. "This and death may be the only situations that don't end with sex."

I laughed. "Speaking of death, I killed a gopher in the garden today. It had eaten nearly all of the potatoes and was just getting started on the carrots."

"I'll have to call the ASPCA on you now."

"It doesn't exist yet."

"Oh, well in that case, kill as many as you can find, especially if they start in on the potatoes again."

Thankfully, washing and peeling off a layer of each veggie had removed all remnants of eau de skunk from our lunch items. As a nod to his masculinity, I fried the potatoes instead of boiling them then made a huge salad with the rest of the produce. "I hope you like fries with your salad," I said, handing him the ketchup.

"Always," was his muffled response. He was already chomping away with impressive speed. Poor baby, I hoped he wasn't overdoing it out there, but what choice did we have? Money had to be earned.

Mick paused between bites to indulge in a momentary frown of confusion. "What's that smell?"

I sighed, sat down, and dragged the entire bowl of remaining salad in front of me. "A skunk sprayed me."

"Animals don't seem to like you much."

"Tell me about it," I said, crunching my teeth into the first bite of fresh greens. All the animal animosity in the world was totally worth it as long as there was produce! And Mick. He came in a close second. Watching how impressively he was adapting to life here, all hardship aside, made me practically worship the hard-packed dirt ground he now walked upon. I was so elated I could have even hugged the rooster, but he was dead along with the gopher.

Mick pushed his empty plate forward and poured a fourth glass of tea. "That's quality tea . . . not from concentrate."

"Glad you like it. I'll bring another glass out to you in a couple of hours, but for now," I said, handing him an aluminum lunch pail-type thing full of water, "take this."

"The 1920s version of a thermos, huh? Pretty cool!" Then he kissed me and retreated toward the back door. "I'm holding you to that iced tea break too!"

CHAPTER ELEVEN

After tidying up the kitchen and once again pondering why I thought living so (comparatively) primitively was so fabulous, I invaded Eva's side of the closet once more. There had to be a way I could successfully let out the seams on a few of these dresses without stabbing through finger capillaries. I grabbed three of the most promising body-covering prospects and carried them to the living room. Being the mechanical wonder that he was, and because he had taken home economics in high school to get out of gym class, Mick had managed to show me the basics of using this particular machine. It was so much easier to navigate than my Mom's modern electronic thing that clogged up my every mental pathway.

Confidence growing, I slowly ran the thread through the needle then through the other thingies it needed to be threaded through. I checked the bobbin located in the "thread pit" beneath the needle and sewing surface, and the circular piece appeared to be intact. Difficult tasks accomplished, I began ripping out the side seams of a dress bodice. There seemed to be half an inch or so available for letting out, so I lined the adjusted seam edges up with the needle and let 'er whir away. There was something soothing about moving my foot up and down on the "power" pedal. With the pleasant monotony of that mechanical noise inspiring me, the first seam was finished quickly . . . and bloodlessly! "I am the sewing goddess!" I declared and started on the second side seam. That accomplished, I stood up, yanked off my robe, and tried the dress on right there. Yes indeed, this should do nicely!

"My awesomeness availeth much!" I yelled to the stray cat gazing curiously at me through a window screen then felt even more encouraged because the cat wasn't trying to eat me or mine. Sitting back down at the machine, I prepared to start altering the next dress. As I glanced downward to make sure my foot was properly placed on the pumpy pedal mechanism, I noticed several scraps of newspaper lying next to it, for whatever early-20th-century reason. Resting my cheek on the machine's surface as I leaned down to gather up the paper shreds, my foot suddenly pumped reflexively. Oh, the pain. "Holy mother of . . . !" I screamed as the needle romped viciously across my earlobe.

A knock at the screen door. "Katie? Katie, dear, are you alright?" a well-meaning but interloping voice asked. Apparently the wind had dispersed the skunk barrier more quickly than I'd expected.

"Mrs. Simmons?" I cried pitifully and not without a little embarrassment. "No, I'm not alright! Do you think you could come inside and get this needle out of my ear?"

Had she known me better and been Catholic, Mrs. Simmons would've been crossing herself, I thought in between waves of burning agony. I could see her from her knees downward as she anxiously made her way toward the sound of my death throes. A weak "help!" was all I could manage.

"Oh child, however did you manage this?"

"How I manage everything, apparently: by being alive."

"Now, now, we'll get you out of this. I'll have to back the needle up though. Do you think you can stand a little more of the pain? Aside from cutting part of your ear off, I really don't think . . ."

"I can stand it! Do whatever you must, Mrs. Simmons, I won't hold it against you."

Despite the throbbing stabs now penetrating into other areas of my skull, I felt truly sorry for the poor woman. No matter how obnoxious her conversational skills were, I'd be forever grateful and in her debt. "Now just hold still for me, dear."

Like I was going anywhere. "Don't suppose you brought any of that Midnight Special your husband sells."

"I certainly would have if I'd known!" she replied, quite seriously.

The whole process was over in a matter of seconds, but so was my brilliant career as a seamstress. One look at this bloody, swollen mess, and Mick would be locking the sewing machine in the tool shed. Honestly, I couldn't blame him. What man wants an earlobe-less wife? Well, maybe Van Gogh. I rose slowly from my seated-and-crouched position, sweat pouring from my body as semi-shock set in. "Thank you so much for coming along when you did, Mrs. Simmons. Your timing is beyond perfect," I said as she helped a very shaky me to the couch.

"Always happy to help. I actually stopped by to ask you a question, but you probably aren't in a chatty mood about now."

"No, not really, but if you walked all this way in the heat, you may ask anything you wish," I said with the best smile I could manage under the circumstances. "Please sit down if you'd like."

She did like and placed herself comfortably into Eva's chair. "I won't stay long, but I wanted to ask if you'd be interested in helping me out at the store for a few hours every day. Mornings are always so busy, and Carl and I aren't as young as we used to be. Time was we were there from sun-up to well after sundown without a single ache or pain. Although I hate to admit it, I really could use some help from about 8:00 until noon, if that would suit you and your husband."

In the midst of drenching one of Eva's dresses with ear blood, I replied, "That is a generous offer, Mrs. Simmons, and to be honest, we could really use the extra income. When would you like me to start?"

Mrs. Simmons grinned and stood, obviously not wanting to impose on my invalidity any longer. "As soon as that ear heals up. We wouldn't want you scaring off the customers!"

We both laughed, or at least I tried to. "May I see you to the door?" I asked and slowly walked her in that direction. "Thanks for coming to my rescue."

"My pleasure, dear! Let's see, today is Wednesday? How about you start work first thing Monday morning, as long as Mick is agreeable?"

"Oh, he will be," I assured her. "It's time for me to take him a giant glass of iced tea about now anyway, so I can ask him."

Mrs. Simmons was already ambling her way down the sidewalk. "Be sure to wear a bonnet! The sun, you know . . . murder on the skin, and it's not good for the baby either!"

As if ruining what used to be a darn good dress that wasn't mine and having to break the news of my sudden multiple ear piercings to Mick, Mrs. Simmons had raised an important and potentially terrifying point: it was entirely possible that I could be pregnant. What with all the excitement of the last few days, I'd forgotten to be worried about it.

Making my way into the kitchen and the half-full bucket of water, I dipped an un-bloody section of cloth into it. After placing the still-cold water to my injury, bleeding ceased quickly. But that wasn't the only part of my body that had seemingly ceased bleeding either. I was scheduled to start a week ago and hadn't. During my pre-birth control years, that wouldn't have meant a thing since good old Flo came and went as she pleased, but since being on such regulating drugs, my period struck like clockwork. Until now.

"Well, genius, what did you expect when your birth control pack ran out nearly two weeks ago, and you're now stuck in a birth control-less world? That whole spiel about having to be off it for several weeks before you can get pregnant is obviously bull-kaka!" At least Mick wouldn't totally freak out . . . at least I didn't think he would. Besides, how could I really know for sure if there was a little math-and-English swirl growing in my nether regions? "Wish that RXS Pharmacy was here right now."

I found some semblance of a rudimentary first aid kit, taped a bandage onto my ear, and dropped the finishing touches into Mick's tea glass in the form of ice. Donning an ugly bonnet as instructed because Mick understandably took the only hat, I slowly made my way out into the field. Mick was halfway finished with a return trip down the cotton row when he spotted his sweet tea salvation. He dropped the long canvas bag that was slung over his shoulder and practically ran toward me. His hat fluttered haphazardly away in the process revealing a tan line on his forehead. He was officially a redneck . . . or brownface?

Reaching me, he grabbed the glass and gulped. "Maybe breathe in there somewhere," I said with a grin.

Having emptied the glass, he panted for several seconds before saying, "Thanks, Katie, that was unbelievable!"

"I accomplish the unbelievable in multiple rooms now, it seems," I remarked with a wink.

He winked back then finally noticed my ear. With a frown of reproof, he announced, "It's going into the tool shed."

"I know," I replied with some dejection. "But I have good news too."

"You have more ice and tea?"

From behind my back I revealed another full glass. "You're amazing!" he paused to say before taking another big sip. "Now, what's the good news?"

"Mrs. Simmons dropped by for a few minutes. After she finished releasing my ear from the bloodthirsty needle's thrall, she asked if I'd like to help her out at the market in the mornings."

"For money?"

"No, for moonshine. Yes, of course for money."

"You had me at 'moonshine,'" he said.

"Anyway, I start on Monday."

"That's good because your ear looks like it was mauled by Rottweilers. There's no way anyone could stomach looking at it right now. Anyway, guess our financial worries are over, at least."

I paused and shuffled my feet in the dirt.

Mick watched curiously. "I think the dirt clod is dead. You should really stop mangling the corpse."

"Well . . . ," I began cautiously. "There's a second potential bit of news I need to tell you about."

"Potential news? When will we know if this news has reached full potential?"

"In about nine months."

My words didn't register with his brain immediately. After multiple seconds of staring blankly at me, the goofiest grin I'd ever seen on his face began to appear. "Are you serious? Katie, are you serious?"

"So you're okay with it? I mean, you're not upset or whatever at having to raise a child in such a displaced and technology-deficient fashion?"

He grabbed me and hugged me tightly. "Why should I be? Yeah, it's unexpected and it will be a lot more challenging without the use of our usual technology . . . "

"Just imagine not being able to introduce him or her to the joys of a logarithmic calculator."

He ignored that. "But the unexpected is exactly what I'd expect from you! Is it for sure? Do you know for a fact that you're pregnant?"

I suddenly found myself dizzy with warm, fuzzy relief as he took my hand and led me on a walk down the cotton row to retrieve his hat and that cotton receptacle bag whatever-it's-called. "There's probably a doctor somewhere around here who could confirm it, or we could just wait and see. Once we have more money saved, I would like to have regular check-ups, but then again, there's not much a doctor could do during this time period except 'just wait and see.' "

Concern creased his half-brown/half-white forehead. "Geez, I didn't think about that. There really can be some danger when it comes to that whole 'technology-less' thing. Will be you okay having the baby here? Is it safe?"

"People were safely born all the time in the 1920s. My grandparents told me so," I replied with mock seriousness.

He laid a protective arm around my shoulders. "I know, but this time it's happening to you and my little astrophysicist in there."

"I prefer to think of him or her as the next award-winning novelist."

"Whichever, as long as you both survive the ordeal."

"It's a pregnancy, not open-heart surgery. Okay, so maybe it's open-*leg* surgery, but . . . " I kissed him wholeheartedly for his husbandly/fatherly devotion. " . . . we'll be just dandy. And who knows? We could easily be back in the very antiseptic, very epidural-ful 21st century nine months from now anyway."

"That would make me very happy," he said then proceeded to kiss me for about five minutes without ceasing.

*****

Through expertly deceptive means, Mick and I managed to borrow the community-accessible "Simmons car," as it was known in the immediate vicinity, and drive to a neighboring town to get truly and properly married. He was as forward-thinking as any human being could be when it came to the scientific applications of life, but when it came to family, Mick was as old-fashioned as they came. I approved in this instance, however, my own mind wanting the assurance that our child would be "bona fide." On the trip back, we stopped at a roadside stand to buy some potatoes from a farmer selling his fresh and fragrant goods. Obviously he had yet to become embroiled in the War of the Gophers.

And I'd also wound up on the losing end of breakfast that morning. This baby was already wreaking havoc with my innards. "You feeling better now?" Mick asked.

"Oh yes, much improved. In fact, I'm so hungry I could bite into this raw potato here and now," I assured him, brandishing one of the earthy-smelling spuds. The smell of freshly-dug-up dirt was one of my favorite smells in the world. Heck, there were still dirt particles hiding happily in each little potato indention. Modern-day supermarkets really should rethink their sanitary dirt removal processes. It killed the vegetable ambience.

"Hold off on that, we're almost home. You don't know where that thing has been."

"Yes I do. It was in the ground in Mr. What's-His-Name's field."

"Okay, you don't know where the ground has been . . . or Mr. What's-His-Name."

"True. But if it's okay with you, I think I'll bake these instead of frying them today. I'm still regurgitating grease from this morning's ham-fest."

"You seemed to enjoy it at the time," Mick observed.

"Oh, I did! But afterward there was all the pink vomit to clean up. Really, I don't think the preacher's wife appreciated my presence in her living room much."

Mick laughed. "Fair enough. Baked potatoes it is then with lots and lots of cheese and butter and crumbly bacon."

"I also threw up the bacon."

"What? When?"

"After enjoying it for a midnight snack last night. Well, it was enjoyable going down, at least."

"Yeah, bile-flavored bacon isn't the best. Hmm. Now I don't want the bacon either."

We dropped the car off at the Simmons' house and, after many interrogation attempts on the part of Mrs. Simmons as well as many admonitions on proper maternity maintenance, escaped homeward to enjoy what was left of our nuptials day. If we ever got back to our proper time, we'd be world record- holders for number of wedding anniversaries.

"I never thought I could be satisfied by a sight like that," Mick mused. "I never thought about how meaningful work could be without logging a lot of laboratory time."

"What sight?" I asked as we lazily sat on our back porch watching the sun retreat behind a distant hill. Purple, orange, red, and pink clouds crisscrossed paths with the lovely burning ball of gas. Both mentally and verbally, I referred to this place as "ours" on a consistent basis now, even though subconsciously I knew and contentedly accepted the truth. Eva and Timothy rocked, and I'd joyously return their home to them upon their impending arrival. At least I assumed it was an "impending" arrival.

"The sight of stacks of full cotton sacks. Before now, I'd never even seen one of those sack-things, and now I'm stuffing them full of Timothy's cotton. Tomorrow I'm borrowing the truck from Mr. Mason down the road and hauling it all to the gin. Want to come along?"

"Farmer Mick, who'd have thought? But you're right. There is something extremely satisfying and meaningful about this life, morning/afternoon/evening sickness aside. Yes, I think I will tag along if you can wait until I'm finished helping Mrs. Simmons with her market-ly duties . . . and getting some baking necessities. I'm in desperate need of wedding cake."

"That's right, I forgot you start work tomorrow, O modern woman o' mine," he said, kissing me atop my head. "And we really should have cake. It seems like the commemorative and celebratory thing to do. I need to get an early start on the work to be done, unfortunately, but should be home by lunch."

"I should be back to my old frying self by then. I was thinking of experimenting with hush puppies . . . or corn fritters, I haven't quite decided."

Mick suddenly pulled away from me with much excitement. "I almost forgot! Speaking of puppies, how would you like to have one?"

"Well, I'm more of a cat person, but all the families around here do seem to have a dog. And if nothing else, it could keep away any unwanted roosters. What kind of canine is it?"

"A border collie. Mr. Mason's dog just had a litter of pups, and he offered me one in exchange for fixing his radio."

"I think I'll name him Buckbeak. You know, bring a bit of neo-modern fantasy into our world!"

"Buckbeak the Dog?"

"Yes. I'm suffering from Harry Potter deprivation. And besides, what could be more awesome than a dog named after a gryphon-eagle thingy that can fly?"

"You're strange."

"And you love it."

"That I do. I'll bring Buckbeak by after the cotton business has been taken care of."

"Yay!" I said, clapping my hands excitedly. Dogs could be annoying, but puppies were joyful, joyful. "And I'll make a bed for him in the kitchen, at least until he gets bigger."

An empty tin cup unpredictably flew off the ice box and crashed into my head. My eyes widened as a wave of chills washed over my skin. "That's not natural," I mumbled, my vocabulary momentarily stunted by shock.

April Arnold

Mick saw the whole thing and felt my scalp: a lump was already beginning to form. "What in the bloody hell . . . ?"

CHAPTER TWELVE

"You are going to pay for any damages to this property, aren't you? If not, I'll sue, and you'll be out even more cash!" the angry pharmacist declared.

Timothy stared wordlessly at the man, his mouth managing a stutter or two. Since they were obviously not under physical attack, Eva felt it safe to step forward and forcefully reply, "The only damage, sir, has been to our own equipment. As you can clearly see, the building is just fine. Now, we will remove our machines as quickly as possible, but in the meantime, I would appreciate it if you would back the hell off!"

Now Timothy was staring wordlessly at Eva as the pharmacist testily conceded, "Fine. Just see that you do, and if I do discover damages, I'll be tracking you down!"

As irate store manager man stormed off, Timothy managed to say, "I've never heard you curse."

"Time travel makes me cranky, evidently," she said, placing her hands on her hips and assessing their overall situation for the first time. "Well, this is a grand mess if ever there was one."

"Where do we start?"

"Well, I suppose we should find someplace to take all this junk. I hate to throw it away since it's probably the only way we'll be able to get back home. And it's probably expensive."

Timothy nodded his head in agreement then noticed the broken-down house next door to the pharmacy lot. "Hey Eva . . . isn't that . . . that's your old place!"

Eva followed his gaze until her own eyes rested on the house she'd only recently blown up. Well, relatively recently. "Oh my, it is! It looks terrible. I wonder why nobody ever tore it down?"

"Don't know, but we could carry all this over there. It looks like the living room might be in good enough shape to protect it."

"It's haunted, you know," said an unknown voice.

Eva and Timothy turned around to see yet another employee—a calmer one, this time—emptying garbage into a big green metal container bin. "Haunted, you say? How do you know?" Timothy asked.

The boy on trash detail was excited to be as helpful as possible.

"Well, I don't know personally, but a couple of friends of mine went ghost-hunting a few nights ago and caught an EVP on tape!"

They "caught an EVP?" Was this some sort of dangerous animal? If so, it must be very tiny if it can be caught with tape. Or maybe it was a disease. Oh joy, the first experience with interpreting futuristic terminology. Eva inhaled a deep breath and forged ahead as best she could. "And what did they do with the EVP on tape?"

"Uhhh . . . listened to it? See, Katie had her tape recorder going when Mick dropped a candy wrapper on the floor. He never goes ghost-hunting without candy. Anyway, after they left the house, they played the tape back and heard a voice say, 'Pick that up!'"

Eva felt the blood draining from her face and emptying into her stomach thereby making it all jumpy. "And why would a voice say that?"

"That's the coolest part!" employee-dude said giddily. "Katie had just told Mick to pick up the candy wrapper!"

"Interesting," Timothy said, just to make sure no one had forgotten that he was standing there too.

"So yeah, if you did want to keep all this stuff in the house, it would be mostly safe, at least from people. Everybody is scared to go near the property now."

"From people? Do ghosts often vandalize personal property?"

Pharmacy worker-peon laughed at Eva's quick wit. Most people did. "You obviously haven't seen *Poltergeist*!"

No, and she wasn't sure she ever wanted to see whatever the crap he was talking about. Regardless, the decision was made. Eva thanked the boy whose name happened to be Andy and got something called a "cell number" from him in case they had more questions about the house. Apparently Andy deemed himself a sort of historical documentarian on the exploits of Katie and Mick. "You can call or text me anytime," Andy assured them. "I'm in class during the day, but I work here at night and on weekends."

Eva had been afraid he lived in a prison after all the "cell number" talk. That's all they needed: to team up with an escaped convict.

"You're in secondary school then?" Timothy ventured since the kid was obviously well past primary school age.

Andy paused to consider the unusual way of referencing "high school," then decided to move ahead with the conversation anyway.

"College . . . or university, rather. Mick and I are both teachers' assistants in a couple of the advanced physics classes, so we hang out after class a lot."

Hang out. Hang out what, the laundry? Some fellow random escaped convict? Male bonding activities were quite different in the future. "Physics? As in quantum physics?" Eva asked.

Becoming as animated as Mick had anytime his favorite subject was mentioned, Andy verified, "Yes, that's one of the classes. I just started the advanced stuff and haven't quite gotten the hang of it yet, but it's so interesting."

There he went with the "hanging" again. "We've heard that maybe this quantum physics thing might prove ghosts are actually living people from . . . another time, I believe?"

"Hey, do you two actually know Katie and Mick? That's what they're trying to prove."

Oh no, she'd said too much. It was Timothy who came to her rescue. "Nah, Eva thinks too much for her own good and came up with the idea on her own."

Ever so grateful, Eva filled in the remaining blanks in their story as best she could. "And yes, we have met them. We're actually here to look after their house since they'll be away doing more research on ghost-hunting and advanced physics and . . . yeah."

Timothy was really getting into the act now. He could be a slow starter sometimes, but once he did start, he was totally committed to the venture. "But their directions weren't too clear," he began. "Could you draw us a map to the house, maybe?"

"Do you need Mick's place or Katie's? I'm not sure how to get to Katie's, but it would be a lot cleaner than Mick's, that's for sure. If you don't mind doing some serious housekeeping, this is how you'd get to his apartment. It's not far from here either."

Andy proceeded to draw out a tremendously detailed map, including little trees and grass tufts, a flower or two, and an accurate depiction of road kill. "It's Texas," he explained with a knowing grin.

Hiding their extreme feelings of "overwhelmed" and "bewildered," Eva and Timothy thanked Andy once again then promised to get in contact with him if they needed anything, assuming they could figure out how to operate all these new-fangled gadgets and not become roadkill themselves before finding Mick's residence.

Their brains dizzy with far too much information, the displaced couple emerged from behind the pharmacy and began moving Mick's time-warping equipment into Eva's haunted house. "This is exactly what I saw the first time they appeared in my living room!" she said, pointing to a particular spot on the charred living room floor. "It makes perfect sense now."

Equipment-moving accomplished successfully and without dropping anything important, they embarked upon their trek into the extreme unknown. The automobiles that whizzed by them were difficult enough to fathom. There were so many colors and shapes and sizes, all of them moving at unbelievable speeds. Andy's sketch wasn't an exaggeration! And then there were the buildings. Every inch of ground was covered with a building or road made of a strange substance. Their cotton fields were nowhere to be found, having been replaced by "city" as far as their senses could see, hear, and smell. Each step seemed to bring on new and frightening revelations of just how quickly the world had changed in less than a hundred years. "Can you believe all this, Eva?" Timothy whispered as he grasped her hand. "Only a couple of months ago, we were walking on this very spot going to the dance and blowing up snakes and chopping the cotton fields and getting married right there at . . . Lulu's Quickie-Mart."

For once, she was the speechless one. Eva managed a hand squeeze in return followed by another deep breath to hopefully clear her head which it didn't. All it did was clog her nasal passages with the smell of asphalt baking in the stupidly hot summer sun.

Timothy smiled at his typically-talkative, take-charge wife. "We'll figure it out, Eva. It will take time, but we'll figure it out."

He always knew when to step up, Eva thought. She smiled back at him, his words reanimating her vocal cords. "Yes, we will. It will likely be the hardest thing we've ever done, but we'll do it. We got rid of the snakes, after all."

"You got rid of them along with half the town . . . and you were drunk to boot," he half-smirked.

"But we achieved our goal. I didn't see any reptile vermin creeping around my property. Oh, I think we're here. Check the map and see if this building looks right."

Timothy compared the drawing to the renovated plantation house-turned-apartment building looming unimposingly before them.

"I think so. It says here Mick's room is number seven. Guess we can just go inside then?"

"It's the best plan I can come up with," Eva replied as they pushed open the front door. "Isn't this the old Mason place?"

Timothy stopped mid-step. "You know, I think it is! Sure looks different now, doesn't it?"

"What doesn't?" Eva replied with not a small amount of sarcasm as she began looking at numbers painted onto doors. "Here it is: number seven."

Timothy turned the knob and quickly discovered that it was locked. "And we seem to have a problem."

"Just another one for our ever-lengthening list. It's locked, isn't it?"

"Yeah. If Mick was going out of town, and we were supposed to keep an eye on his place . . . "

" . . . then logically he'd have given us the key before leaving. Damn."

Timothy grinned at her second curse word of the day. "You're becoming a foul-mouthed hussy, you know that?"

Eva couldn't help but grin in return. "Yes, I really mustn't make a habit of such things."

"I don't know. I kinda like it," Timothy replied with a wink.

"And you're becoming a . . . "

"A what?"

"A typical man! Now let's think: maybe there's an extra key hidden somewhere. My mother always thought there should be a way to hide a house key in a rock then put the rock in the flower bed or under porch steps where it would look like part of the scenery."

"Your mother always was peculiar."

"It was a good idea! But there's no flower bed or steps or a hollow rock to put anything in, so that idea is out the window. Hey, I wonder if we could get in through a window . . . "

"How about we look under this funny piece of carpet that says 'welcome to the math zone' on it?" Timothy asked, kneeling to pick up the door mat. "Well, what do you know?"

"Great! What a creative idea, hiding it there. Now let's see what this place looks like."

Timothy unlocked the door and pushed it open. The rooms were small but adequate, or would have been had there not been dishes, various articles of clothing, wadded up paper, and containers of half-rancid food scattered across every available inch of floor space. "Andy sure was telling the truth, wasn't he?" Timothy said.

Eva picked up a food-stained t-shirt and stared at it with much disdain. "Alright. I'll get to work washing clothes. You pick up all the dishes you can find and stick them in the kitchen."

Timothy walked into the small kitchen where every bit of countertop was already spoken for. "Stick them where in the kitchen?"

She groaned. "Just do the best you can, I guess." As Timothy got to work, Eva steeled her nerves for a complete exploration of what would be their living space for now, at least. Massive messes aside, she was thrilled to find an indoor "outhouse" with running water and fully-functional toilet. Eewww, it would all need to be thoroughly scrubbed, however. "Hey Timothy, we won't need to find any corncobs!"

Thump, thump, thump came the sounds of Timothy's approaching footsteps. "My, my. This is really something." He turned one of the bath tub knobs and wondered as water flowed forth. He was enthralled by all things mechanical. "So now I'm thinking this might not be so bad after all!"

"How's the kitchen coming along?" Eva asked as she opened cabinets and inspected their contents: a couple of raggedy towels, an empty package of something called "toilet paper," some soap remains, and a mouse corpse still stuck in a trap. Yeesh.

"It's going alright. I got all the dirty dishes off the floors anyway . . . at least I think I did. Is there another room besides these?"

Eva slammed the cabinet door shut in disgust. She'd deal with rodent death later. "Maybe one more room. I saw a closed door next to the front door when we came in," Eva said, making a beeline for that aforementioned door. Upon opening it, they found two very large, white, box-shaped machines with funny dials and punchable buttons. One had a lid on top that opened, and the other had a door that opened from the front. "Huh. I wonder what these things are?"

Fascinated as per usual by newer, more improved machinery, Timothy opened the lid on the first big white box. "There's wet clothes in this one. And they smell. See?" He yanked out a mildewy t-shirt and practically shoved it up Eva's nose.

Eva sniffed and, sure enough, this was a case of neglected wet laundry moldering in an enclosed space. Surely this wasn't some sort of automatic clothes washing machine? "Do you think this could be what it looks like?" she asked excitedly.

"Like a machine that washes your clothes just by pushing a button? Could be."

Eva quickly pointed out precisely that button. "Look! It says 'start!' And what's this other machine? I'll bet it dries clothes!" She opened the front door of the miraculous drier and saw a perfectly dried load of mostly-fresh-smelling towels. "We didn't go forward in time. We died and went to heaven!"

A thought suddenly occurring to him, Timothy returned to the kitchen and started opening more appliance doors. Eva followed and asked, "What are you looking for?"

"If there's a machine that washes and dries clothes, maybe there's one that washes and dries dishes too. And here it is!"

Eva gawked in amazement as her husband lowered the dishwasher door to reveal a load of food-and-spot-free dishes. "I . . . I . . ."

Timothy watched with much amusement as Eva was rendered speechless for the second time in a two-hour period. "We'll have so much free time on our hands, we won't know what to do with ourselves."

"A machine that washes dishes . . ." were the only words that came to mind. She could just cry out of sheer jubilance. Really, she could!

"So maybe we should get this place cleaned up and then find something to eat." Timothy opened another appliance door and shivered at the blast of cold air. "It's freezing in there!"

Eva was on the verge of passing out from the astounding sights that kept jumping out at her. "It's an ice box. Look. There's ice." A couple of cubes dropped out of the ice maker and into the massively overflowing bucket. "And it makes its own little chunks."

Timothy closed that door and opened the one beneath it. "It's cold but not freezing cold. This must be for storing things you don't want to freeze like cheese or bacon or even milk. Imagine how much longer food would last if you kept it cold like this, even in the summertime."

"There's not much in here though," Eva pointed out as she pushed aside a bottle of ketchup and can of beer in order to reveal a single package of deli-sliced turkey that appeared to be turning green. The dead mouse looked fresher. "You're right, we need to find a market nearby once we've cleaned things up."

"We still have to figure out how to use all these machines too, or they won't do us much good," Timothy said practically. "I'll see what I can do with the dish washing machine, and you see about the washing and drying ones."

*****

Two hours and two headaches later, they had managed to figure out the dishwasher but were having trouble with the clothes washer. The hot, warm, and cold options were self-explanatory, but what the heck was a "permanent press?" Did this thing iron everything too? "I think we need a break," Eva declared. "Besides, it will be dark in a few hours, and we need to locate the nearest place to buy food."

Timothy had just discovered the owner's manual for the washing machine and was starting to skim through it when a realization struck: "How are we going to buy food without any money?"

"Oh dear," Eva sighed. "Maybe Mick keeps some under his mattress too? I'll go check." She walked quickly to the bedroom and dug around beneath various spots of the mattress. Nothing. In the midst of her exploration, she suddenly heard the sound of running water coming from the washing/drying machine room. That man could figure out any mechanism ever designed, she thought with a proud smile. Eva stopped at a desk and opened several drawers. There were numerous calculators in various stages of functionality, a variety of multi-colored pencils, countless pieces of paper covered in complicated equations, and a half-eaten bag of chocolate candies. Just as she was about to give up and go give her man a much-deserved pat of congratulations on the back, she noticed a plain white envelope tucked away in the very back of the top desk drawer. Upon pulling it out, she read the words: new computer fund. Inside she found almost $500 in bills of varying amounts. With a huge mountain of guilt, she took the money and mentally promised herself that they'd somehow find a way to earn money and replace whatever they spent.

"Eva, it's working!" Timothy called, walking down the hall toward her location.

She met him halfway and brandished the envelope. "I found $500. He's been saving to buy a new computer, whatever that is, but we can make it up to him. Surely he'd understand that we need money to live on. And of course we'll find jobs of some kind, won't we? Heavens, what in the world could we possibly do in this time?"

Leading her into a semi-clutter-free space on the living room couch, Timothy did his best to reassure her. "So far we can wash dishes and clothes and probably ourselves."

She permitted herself a tiny grin.

"Really, I'm not sure what we'll do, but certain jobs can't be that different from jobs in our time. You helped Mrs. Simmons out at the market that one summer, remember? Well, there are markets around here too."

"But all these mechanical contraptions everyone uses these days! Each one is so different from another."

"You're smart, Eva. You'll learn how to use them and be just fine. Maybe we can ask Andy if he has any ideas."

"Let's try to find something on our own first. I don't want to arouse too much suspicion, and since he actually knows Katie and Mick, he could easily become suspicious."

Timothy took her hand and pulled her into a standing position. "Well, we got dishes washed and stinky clothes washing. Let's see if we can find our way to the market. I'm getting pretty hungry about now."

Eva surveyed her still-surreal surroundings for the fiftieth time that hour trying to mentally absorb just one piece more. "I had no idea that candy wrappers could cause such problems."

Timothy took a couple of twenty-dollar bills out of the envelope and folded them carefully into his pocketbook. "They rank right up there with boll weevils. Come on, let's see what else we can get into."

"Plenty of trouble, no doubt," Eva muttered as she re-retrieved the envelope from the desktop. Who knew what things would cost in the here and now?

CHAPTER THIRTEEN

It didn't take long for the couple to locate an adequate grocery-buying location. After only fifteen minutes of walking and a nudge in the correct direction by a helpful yuppie jogging down the sidewalk with her yorkie, Eva and Timothy found themselves staring wide-eyed at their friendly neighborhood superstore. Future people had to be kidding! "Can you believe this?" Timothy asked.

"You could fit our house fifty times over into that building! What are they selling in there, whole herds of cows?"

"After ninety or so years, I'd be surprised if you can't buy a whole cotton crop-in-a-box already harvested."

"I don't know if this is going to be another adventure or another headache."

Timothy shook his head and visually panned the length of the store front one more time before grabbing Eva determinedly by the hand and pulling her toward the sliding entrance doors. "My money is on the headache . . . or Mick's money, that is."

They were sensorily overloaded five minutes after walking through those doors. Aisles and aisles of food lay to their right, all manner of clothing covered square footage directly in front of them, and to their left . . . who could say? "Did we make a list?" Timothy asked feebly.

"I didn't think we'd need one. Usually we just walk up and down the few aisles, see what we need as we go, then pay for everything. But this . . . we'll need to modify our strategy here."

"It could take hours."

"If we even survive. Dear heaven, what is that woman wearing?"

Timothy tried to stare as respectfully as possible from behind an issue of the Enquirer he'd just grabbed from a magazine stand. "I don't…I don't think that's a woman."

"Well of course it's a woman. She's wearing a dress and heels, isn't she?"

"She seems to have some spare, er . . . parts underneath the skirt then."

Eva swiped the magazine from her blushing husband and made her best attempt at respectful staring too. He was right. Goodness me. "We have more to learn than I thought we might," she said, returning the magazine to its rightful place.

"Should've known that would be the case after seeing the dishwasher and ice-spitting machine and big metal boxes that wash and dry clothes."

Eva made the mistake of actually reading an Enquirer headline: "Man Gives Birth to Boa Constrictor, Wife Less Than Pleased." She paused to skim the remainder of the would-be "news" magazine cover before slamming it back into the rack. "Infidelity has gotten more complex too. You know, progress isn't necessarily as wonderful as advertised."

"Hey, this is nice," Timothy said in his "excited" voice. That simply meant it was varying from the monotone for a moment. "A metal cart on wheels. This sure will come in handy."

"We had carts on wheels in our own time, if you'll recall."

"I know, but they weren't so . . . shiny." Timothy glanced around the monstrosity of a store one last time before adding, "Maybe we should split up and meet back here. You can take care of whatever groceries we need, and I'll look around everywhere else just in case there's something we haven't thought of."

Eva well-knew her man. He just wanted an excuse to scope out all of the more modern inventions. Ah well, how often does one get the opportunity to do such things? "Alright, we'll meet in an hour and pay for everything. Don't get carried away now."

"When have I ever gotten carried away?" he asked with a grin.

He had a point. This was the sensible man who had her starch his socks because he didn't want Eva to waste water washing a separate, extra load of clothes. She couldn't help but smile as she watched him carefully maneuvering his shiny metal cart with wheels off into the glorious retail sunset. Then she turned and tackled the produce section. It must be admitted that grabbing a plastic-packaged bag of clean lettuce sure beat fighting off the gophers for one or two half-eaten plants from her garden. As she leaned in to inspect each lettuce head, she was surprised when it suddenly started raining on her. Eva jumped back and looked upward. Nope, the ceiling was intact. Apparently this store felt the need to recreate rainshowers for the benefit of its vegetables. They even had fake thunder rumbling in the background. "What, are there no more thunderstorms in the future?" she mumbled. "No doubt they've invented a machine to control those too."

After gathering together various veggie basics and laying them neatly into her cart, the meat section came into view. Now this, she had to confess, was the best discovery yet. There was nothing more unpleasant than cow slaughter . . . or sheep slaughter or chicken slaughter or—ugh!—pig slaughter. And look! Fish slaughter! Eva suddenly realized that personal giddiness had ensued as she practically waltzed over to the fresh seafood section. Little did she know that the term "fresh" was often used too loosely in the realm of bargain-priced food.

"Good afternoon, ma'am, may I help you?" a friendly seafood counter lady asked.

Eva was dazed by the relative variety of dead sea-dwellers. Half of this stuff she'd never even seen in a store before. "How much would a pound of shrimp cost?"

"Farm-raised or coastal?"

"Umm . . . coastal?"

Apparently unaware of her seafood-purchasing inexperience, Eva watched as the seafood counter lady double-checked the price. "That would be $18.95, ma'am."

Eva had been leaning over the glass top of the fish display case in order to see all it contained. Her chin slammed into said glass when she heard the price, speechless from normal speechlessness and the blazing pain working its way through her jaw.

"I know! Shrimp is on sale this week. It's a steal, isn't it?"

A steal? Only if the fishing boat and all hands on deck come with it, Eva thought. "So what can I get for $5?" she asked. Even that amount she considered an extravagance.

The fish lady looked at her kind of funny but only for a second. "Well, we have salmon on sale this week too. I can probably get you enough of that to feed two people for $5."

"Why is the salmon so inexpensive?" Eva very wisely wondered aloud.

"Overstocked," the lady replied, already cutting and weighing the fish.

Now, to the average 21st-century fish-buyer perusing bargain store fish selections, "overstocked" would've set off clanging warning gongs. To poor, unsuspecting Eva, it simply made thrifty shopping sense. "Thank you so much. My husband and I are visiting from . . . far away, and we wanted to have something special for dinner tonight. What would you recommend serving with this?"

After getting several great menu ideas, Eva happily tripped up and down aisles collecting the necessary side-dish ingredients as well as some fresh dill and lemons in which to cook the salmon. That's what the seafood counter lady said: bake the fish on a cedar plank with fresh dill and lemon. Unfortunately she hadn't been told where she could chop down the necessary cedar tree. Eva added asparagus to her existing produce supply—stupidly expensive at $3.00 per bunch—and a bag of frozen dinner rolls. For some odd reason, she felt like she was cheating on something precious as she removed the bag from the giant freezing cabinet and did her best to make sure no one was looking. Her mother would have been mortified to learn that her only daughter was purchasing and not baking her own bread . . . and purchasing it frozen, no less. Eva felt an inexplicable sense of loss as she continued down the frozen food aisle.

She wandered up and down each and every row of packaged foods she encountered, purchasing a few more cooking and baking supplies as well as ingredients, then tackling whatever cleaning and bathroom supplies they might need. She stood in the toilet paper aisle a good five minutes just taking in the 2-ply, ultra-absorbent glory. A twenty-four-pack of Charmin Ultra very quickly and guiltlessly found its way into her cart. "Some things are worth it," she muttered, then rounded the final corner into the non-alcoholic and adult beverage aisle. Maybe a teensy bit more splurging for special occasion purposes. Having no clue what any of the beers or wines tasted like, she made her best guess and grabbed a sampling of both: light beer and a pink-colored fizzy drink that promised to be fruity. If "light" and "fruity" were in the descriptions, they had to be among the best, right?

Eva was humming a random tune of comparable happiness while keeping an eye out for Timothy. The salmon needed to get home as soon as possible if it was to maintain edibility integrity, so she was pleasantly surprised to see her husband leaning casually on the handlebar of his beloved wheeled cart. To her equal surprise, it contained very little. To her even more equal surprise, he'd bought a few clothing items. Thinking ahead was generally not his forte.

"We'd best hurry. I got us something special for dinner and don't want it to spoil. What did you find?"

"Oh, several things. I got a pair of denims for myself and a few shirts. It's a good thing you brought the rest of the money. Imagine paying $10 apiece for a shirt!"

"It's a good thing you didn't see the price of fish then. We could've been proud owners of a bend in the Colorado River for what a pound of shrimp cost."

"Never had shrimp but always wanted to try it."

"Well, when you're prepared to swap a kidney for it, you can try it. Now what's this?" Eva asked as she sorted through a layer of socks and unmentionables to discover a bright green shirt with "Girls Rock" written across the chest. She gave Timothy one of "her looks."

"It was on something called a 'clearance' for $2. It must be a local landmark that wasn't discovered in 1920, this 'Girls Rock.' We should ask around and go exploring."

"Maybe," Eva commented. "But first we need to find out where Katie lives. I'd rather just borrow her clothes than spend still more money on new ones, especially as high as grocery prices are. And what about other bills? My guess is you can't get lighting and water for free these days since they come out of faucets and bulb things instead of underground wells and candles."

"No, but it wasn't free where we come from either . . . and if you'll remember, we also had light bulbs," Timothy agreed as they pushed their carts into one of the check-out lines, or as Eva described them, "one of the most obnoxiously long lines of rude people wasting time waiting to pay for their useless junk."

Arriving at Mick's apartment once more, Eva carefully unpacked the helpfully reusable plastic bags and set each aside for later consignment to a specified drawer space. The items lately liberated from sack-dom she carefully arranged into cabinets, a small but useful pantry, and what she had just learned was called a "refrigerator." Once conveniently arranged, Eva turned her attention to preparing the food she'd just purchased. They'd never found any choppable cedar trees, so she'd have to make do with a regular baking dish. She found one made of thick glass in a drawer beneath the oven and nodded approval. While sorting groceries, she'd also found a cookbook specifically for preparing seafood. Yay!

While Timothy fumbled with the large rectangular screen mounted onto a living room wall, Eva turned a knob on this amazing oven to the "preheat" setting. She then adjusted the temperature knob to the appropriate level indicated by Mick's cookbook that he obviously never used. "Cookbooks are supposed to have stains," Eva muttered to herself. Hers were sprinkled with dots of floury egg mixture and shortening with a dusting of sugar crusted together by vanilla flavoring . . . just for good measure, you know.

"Hey Eva, what do you suppose this thing does?" Timothy asked through the open window space that divided kitchen from living room. He walked into the kitchen while frowning with great concentration at Mick's universal remote.

Eva patiently took it from him, somewhat miffed at being pulled away from the entertaining task of flouring and deflowering Mick's virgin cookbook. She tapped the rectangular black plastic plank thingy with buttons on it against the countertop. "Well, I can't quite say. Have you tried pushing any of the buttons?"

Timothy just stared at her.

"Of course you have, you're a man. Keep pushing them, and I'm sure you'll eventually discover the answer." As she spoke, she randomly hit the "power" button while aiming it at the cable box. Colorful-but-silent scenes were suddenly being enacted in lively fashion on the wall-mounted screen.

"You did it! Are we supposed to be hearing something too?"

"Your guess is as good as mine," Eva said, handing the remote back to him. "You figure that out while I get dinner going. Oh, and here ya go." She handed him a can of now-cold beer.

Timothy was confounded once more as he tried to figure out how to open a can of what he assumed would be a wonderfully refreshing beverage. "It's tough when what you want is right in front of you, but you still can't get to it." Remote in one hand and incorrigible beer can in the other, Timothy returned to the living room for further product analysis, frown of concentration still carved into place.

Eva returned to her task of dinner preparations and picked up one utensil she actually did know how to use: a kitchen knife. Unable to find a proper cutting board, she'd retrieved a plate from a cabinet and proceeded to chop the fresh dill into the finest of pieces. That done, she removed the salmon from the re-fri-ger-a-tor (she still had to think the word slowly to get it right) and placed it carefully into the glass dish. It smelled weird, but what did she know about how salmon was supposed to smell? The only fish they typically ate back home was catfish that grew up in the muddy creek bottoms, and they smelled abominable . . . like muddy creek bottom mixed with rotting death. The lemon juice would probably fix all that in this instance anyway, and besides, salmon were fancy fish that swam about in freshwater streams instead of stagnant creek sludge.

The little red-orange light on the stove turned off with a sudden pop that made Eva jump and sling her knife into the air where it promptly stuck point-first into the ceiling. Grand. Now it would fall on her unsuspecting head like deadly, really hardened bird poo. Grabbing another knife from the wondrous wooden block o' knives on the counter before her, she sliced into the lemon and squished several squishes of the juice onto the salmon slices. She then sprinkled liberal amounts of the gloriously-smelling dill along with some salt and pepper atop the juice-soaked meat. Yes, the smell was disappearing beneath waves of citrusy herbalness. "Cover with foil and bake for 25 minutes," she read aloud from the cookbook. Carefully opening the oven door, anticipating the wave of heat that would suddenly escape, Eva slid the dish onto the topmost oven rack before her face was baked off the bone. "Wow. That beats a wood stove any day."

Now for a taste of that alcoholic fruit fizz, she thought excitedly. Bouncing happily to the fridge, Eva removed the bottle and unscrewed the top. Not even bothering with a glass, she took a massive swallow and smiled at the sweetness. In all her mind-numbing ignorance, she was actually enjoying it. "On to the asparagus!" she said with a bit more exuberance than was required. Wine coolers and empty stomachs don't generally mix.

Just as she finished rinsing the lovely green spears and prepared to start hacking off the tough ends, a shriek of voices exploded from the living room. Knife number two stuck into the ceiling. Timothy must've found the sound button, she thought. Eva leaned over the sink and peered through the open window space between kitchen and living room. Timothy was alternating between clamping his hands over his ears and madly pressing buttons on the magic sight and sound wand in an attempt to reduce decibel levels. "How do you turn this confounded thing off?" he uncharacteristically yelled.

With a sigh of amusement, the dutiful wife shoved wads of another miraculous invention called "paper towels" into her ears and proceeded into the living room to assist her helpless husband. She took the remote from him, analyzed the buttons for a moment, then punched one of the down arrows. After several more punches, the deafening screams were transformed into a pleasant choir of fun and funky nuns. "Catchy tune," Eva said as she turned over the remote once more. "You might want to write down each button discovery made so there won't be a repeat of this evening's disturbance of the peace."

To emphasize Eva's suggestion, a loud pounding resounded from the ceiling above their heads. A muted, "Hey! Keep it down! Where do you think we are, Madison Square Gardens?"

"Yes!" she yelled back and returned to the kitchen.

"What's Madison Square Gardens?" Timothy asked, still rubbing his ears.

"I don't know, but I couldn't let him have the last word."

"No, That's not like you at all," Timothy said with inherent sarcasm.

Eva laughed. "I think the salmon is done if you'd like to set the table. The asparagus won't take but a few minutes, and apparently the rolls can cook in the micro . . . wave . . . for one minute. I guess that's the other box with a door on it hanging above the oven."

Timothy gathered up plates, knives, and forks along with a couple of those ingenious paper towels and exited to set the table. Eva opened the microwave door and placed the entire bag of rolls inside. Punching in one minute and hitting start, she stirred the asparagus sautéing in a chunk of butter. After an unexpected "ding" from above her head, Eva deduced that the rolls must be done. She opened the door, carefully touched the bag, and discovered that they still felt cold. "Maybe one more minute," she said and punched in the additional minute. Asparagus fully cooked, she removed the vegetables from the heat and dumped them onto a plate. The microwave dinged. She opened the door and discovered a melted mass of blue plastic and half-cooked dough. Oops.

"Timothy, we won't be having rolls tonight!"

*****

After what turned out to be a respectable first dinner prepared utilizing unknown 21st-century techniques, Timothy and Eva sat excitedly on Mick's couch and channel-surfed for a couple of hours without stopping. Each new channel and show revealed an overwhelming discovery of things yet to be, discoveries made even more exciting after a few more beers and the entire bottle of pink beverage. Timothy's personal favorite was The History Channel, a revelation that finally ended the "surfing" portion of their television-watching evening. They were airing specials on ancient Roman warfare, presentations to which Timothy was absolutely riveted. Although she too found it interesting, Eva opted to head bedroomward and scope out the sleeping situation. She ignored the initial gurgling disturbing her usually placid stomach.

She reached the bed itself and inspected the condition of the sheets. They smelled a bit stale but were otherwise clean and sleepable. An hour or so of airing out would help. She left the bedspread, blanket, and sheet pulled back and fluffed the pillow. *wonderfully* fluffy pillows! She suspected that Katie might have had something to do with those. She was correct. Left to his own devices, Mick was perfectly happy to sleep on a rolled-up bathroom towel.

The bed arranged, Eva wandered into the walk-in closet. She reached for the typical string that would turn on the light but found none. Instead, she fumbled around and discovered a plastic flippy button on the wall that moved up and down. She flipped it up, and the light appeared. "This is terrific," the whispered, feeling awed into respecting the rising flood of technology. Rifling through the poorly-hung articles of male clothing, Eva happened upon a decidedly odd clothing addition toward the back. At least she had to assume that it was clothing since they were hanging in a clothing closet.

Eva removed a strange corset made of what appeared to be black leather. It had an equally strange metal something in the back that slid up and down. Aha, this must be the new-fangled replacement for lace-up strings. Draped over the lower portion of the corset's hanger was a pair of pants made of what appeared to be black leather. Why would anyone wear this underneath a dress? Eva turned to leave and tripped on a big chunk of something: the matching black leather stiletto boots. "What in the world . . . ?" She picked them up and marveled at the oddity as a wild, crazy, and relatively characteristic idea struck her: what if she tried it all on? Suddenly giggly and giddy, Eva ditched her 1920s get-up and figured out how to unzip the corset. She managed to get it into place before attempting her first round of squeezing into the leather jeans. There was no way. Bending over was impossible from within the confines of her black leather chest-prison. So she removed the corset THEN shoved herself into the pants THEN put the corset back on. She zipped her feet into the boots, attempted to take a step or two, and landed on the bed in a twisting, stumbling crash of awkwardness. "People walk in these? Really?" Eva finally managed to make a few successful steps without teetering then looked at her reflection in the full-length mirror hung on Mick's closet door. She was shocked at her brazen hussy-ness. "At home I'd be arrested . . . and everyone thought the fringe was tawdry!"

Timothy was engrossed in a virtual mapping of Julius Caesar's famous victory at Alesia when he heard a peculiar rhythmic stomping moving down the hall and toward his position. For a split second he wondered if he should run. Once Eva appeared, he was sure of it. "I see . . . so an entire cow had to die for that?"

Eva blushed intensely as she attempted flirtation. "So what do you think? That Cosmopolitan magazine said this was a sure way to impress your man."

"I'm thinking we should probably avoid that store section in the future. What are those things on your feet? Do they help you reach top shelves easier?"

In a way she couldn't quite explain, Eva was suddenly depressed. "So you don't like it?"

Timothy didn't say anything immediately, afraid that whatever he said would be the wrong thing.

"Ah well. Katie said Mick didn't like it either. I'll just go risk life and limb and re-clothe myself in 1920s finest."

Timothy smiled, relieved at not being forced into confessing his true feelings about Eva's insane clothing experiment. It was amusing, however, to watch her cling to the wall as she cautiously made her way back to the bedroom.

"Well, Eva, if he wasn't ready for two-inch heels and a starchless lifestyle, what makes you think he would be thrilled with a twenty-first-century whore outfit?" She sat slowly down onto the bed, unbroken-in leather groaning with each movement. As she propped a foot on her knee and began unzipping one of the boots, she felt something intestinal give way. This would not be good.

"Wicked overstocked salmon!" she muttered as she tore the boots from her feet and tried to unzip the pants. The damnable notlaces thing was stuck. Her heart pounding in concert with her rumbling innards, Eva hobbled down the hall to enlist the help of her husband. "I can't get this metal doohickey down! It's stuck, and I need to use the toilet thing! And why aren't you sick yet?"

"I don't know," he replied, moving quickly in his distressed wife's direction. Unable to think of anything else beyond processing the sudden onslaught of diarrhea and Eva's inability to fight back, he offered. "Let me see what I can do."

Eva was alternating between jumping up and down and whimpering while stomping each foot, none of which was helpful to Timothy conquering the zipper. "Hold still, honey, I can't get a grip on it."

"I . . . can't . . . hold . . . still! That salmon's swimming downstream and fast!"

Timothy couldn't help but chuckle. Big mistake.

"Not funny! Not at all funny!" she yelled, red-faced and in gut-curdling agony.

He finally got a firm grip on the zipper and jerked it downward. Nothing happened.

"My intestines are going to explode right here. Do you want to be responsible for cleaning up my exploded intestines?"

I'm not the one who told you to put those pants on, he very silently thought to himself. He rushed to Mick's junk drawer and dug around amidst the clutter. Aha, pliers! Returning to his wife—who was now writhing about on the carpet and clutching her abdomen—he grasped the zipper with the pliers and yanked as hard as he could. The entire seam ripped to pieces, zipper flying in one direction, bits of leather in another. Eva leapt up off the floor and flew into the bathroom, slamming the door behind her. A sudden exhalation of, "Aaaaahhhhhhhh . . . " emerged from behind the door as Timothy approached it. "You gonna make it?" he asked.

"Oh dear lord . . . " was all she managed.

"How about we have meatloaf tomorrow night?"

CHAPTER FOURTEEN

It was just like Timothy to be recalcitrant to the point of avoiding sickness. While Eva was making countless trips back and forth to the helpfully efficient toilet, Timothy was snoring blissfully away for the entire night. The man had no compassion. It was with a huff of disgusted derision that Eva glanced at the red-lit clock situated on a night stand next to her husband's sound-asleep head: 6:15. Might as well get up and make breakfast.

Her gastrointestinal tract finally calm—probably because it had been completely emptied in the last eight hours—Eva headed toward the kitchen to figure out the modern way of preparing bacon, eggs, and toast for her man. Eating aside, there was much to be accomplished today, particularly where finding lucrative employment was concerned. What *were* they going to do? Maybe she could get a job working with the seafood counter lady so she—Eva—could warn unsuspecting customers about the Satanic salmon. It would make sense that Timothy should be able to find work as some sort of mechanic. There were machines and automobiles aplenty, that was certain, but how complicated were they to repair?

"After breakfast we should probably figure out how to take baths," Timothy remarked as he shuffled nonchalantly into the living room looking well-rested, his hand immediately grasping the glorious remote control. In a matter of seconds he had expertly turned on the TV, cable box, and sound system.

"Well, that took him no time to master," Eva mumbled to herself as she separated the pre-sliced bacon and laid each carefully into a frying pan. "Don't get too attached to these future entertainments, now. You do still have a wife that needs your attention."

Timothy smiled as he changed channels. "Why do you think I suggested a bath?"

Eva was momentarily speechless. "Why husband o' mine, I do believe you're in danger of becoming a romantic!"

"Becoming a romantic? I thought I already was one," he replied with what passed as a sultry grin, at least for him.

Eva blushed over her scrambling eggs. This place might just be good for them after all. After a carefully eaten breakfast, Eva cleared away the dishes and deftly loaded them into the dishwasher that was rapidly becoming her very best friend in the whole wide world. If they ever got back to their correct time, she was really going to miss the glorious automatic detergent dispenser and rinse cycle and auto-dry and spin cycle and permanent press . . . no wait, that was her other best friend, the clothes-washing machine. At any rate, the twenty-first century had its good points.

Her stomach and intestines properly digesting their eggs and bacon, Eva headed to the bedroom closet to see if there were any practical clothes in which she could go job hunting. She could hear Timothy showering behind the closed bathroom door, his tone-deaf voice singing away at "Spread a Little Sunshine." So much for romance. She grinned despite their as-yet-unrealized watery rendezvous then began the clothes-sorting process. There was always the really bright and conspicuous "Girls Rock" shirt thing Timothy had frugally purchased, but somehow it simply didn't elicit a sense of professionalism. Eva laid it aside and critically inspected the leather-free shirts, dresses, and jeans Katie had hanging in Mick's closet for emergencies. If they were married, why did they need two different homes? Must be a futuristic thing.

Timothy exited the now-steamy bathroom garbed in one of Mick's much-too-large bathrobes. "You ever seen anything like this, Eva? It's like a big towel with sleeves. Only problem is now it's soaking wet which kind of defeats the purpose, don't you think?"

Eva had just buttoned herself into a plaid, belted tunic that had potential. She glanced amusedly at her husband now dripping water all over the carpet. "Did you use the towel I laid out for you to dry off first?"

"Huh," Timothy said as revelation struck. "I thought this towel coat would take care of that."

"Only if you want to dry off and mop floors at the same time. Now what do you think of this shirt/dress thing? Would you hire me?"

"Hire you for what?"

"I don't know, maybe a store clerk? I thought we could go back to our grocery store and see if they need help somewhere. Personally, I feel that they could use a new fish counter person, but that's just my opinion."

Timothy looked her over carefully and finally nodded approval. "It's a bit shorter than what you'd normally wear, but at least it isn't made of something that ever moo-ed."

"Hardy, har, har!" Eva replied, smacking him with the clunky shoe she was about to slide onto her foot. "And what about you, sir? Any ideas on where you'll be looking for gainful employment?"

"I thought we could go back to that RXS place and talk to Andy. Since I don't know what a 'cell number' is, I thought I'd better just talk to him in person."

"Or talk to his parole officer."

"What?"

"Nothing." Eva took a deep breath and took in her surroundings yet again. "It all moves a lot faster here, doesn't it? It will take me months to process everything."

"Years, even."

"Yeah . . . well, we'd best get you out of that sponge with arm holes and into something presentable. I've looked through Mick's wardrobe and found a few things that were least likely to fall off of you."

"Does he have any belts?"

"I believe so."

"Then I'll be fine."

"Fine" turned out to be a very relative term in this instance. Timothy couldn't understand why his newly-purchased denims and long-sleeved cotton shirts (he didn't know they were called t-shirts) weren't up to par, but Eva thought he needed something nicer. Denim and leather had the same connotations in her mind: inappropriate for job searching. As they exited Mick's apartment building and walked into the rapidly-warming morning sun, the entire block was treated to the sight of Timothy dressed in entirely-too-long lemon yellow plaid walking shorts that would've looked like ghetto pants if they hadn't been held up above the butt-line by six-too-many inches of leather belt. Eva had discovered a lemon yellow polo shirt that perfectly matched the shorts as well as a pair of worn brown leather man-sandals with—you guessed it—matching lemon yellow socks.

Timothy was understandably uncomfortable. "Am I really supposed to wear socks with . . . these?"

"Aren't you supposed to wear some sort of socks or stockings with any shoe?"

"The Romans didn't."

Eva stifled a giggle. He really did look rather ludicrous, but what other option did they have? The clothing he'd purchased the day before was far too casual for their present undertaking, although come to think of it, she had no real concept of what would be appropriate in this time period. Jeans bearing the name of "Wrangler" simply didn't sound correct. "At least there's minimal leather involved."

"Is that going to be our reasoning for every stupid outfit we end up wearing?"

She laughed outright and took her husband by the hand. "It's as good a validation as any. Besides, we'll get used to it in time. A month from now our old clothes might seem ridiculous."

It was Timothy's turn to sigh. "Do you think we'll be here that long?"

"I don't know, honey. I honestly don't. But I think we need to be as prepared as possible to be here for the long haul."

"I've never been on a haul that long, even during cotton harvest. Well, I mean to speak with Andy about all this . . . see if he can help us figure how to fix Mick's magic time travel machine. Andy said he was in school with Mick, so he probably understands this quantum physical subject. Who knows? Maybe I can give him a hand with putting it back together."

"That won't earn us any money, but then again, maybe the reassembly process should be your top priority. Maybe in that whole process you could learn how to apply quantum physics to farming," Eva said with a wink and gentle elbow-jab into Timothy's unsuspecting side.

His face cracked a smile. "I was thinking the same thing. Imagine how much time and money could be saved if we could time warp the boll weevils right out of the field?"

"I knew you'd have this all thought out."

"You'd be surprised."

"So, my forward-thinking darling, I shall bring home the bacon, as it were, and you can help Andy figure out how to get situations correctly reversed. It's a good plan."

"I'm a good planner," Timothy said, returning the playful elbow-jab.

"There was never a doubt."

"But, Eva?"

"Yes, dear?"

"Just don't bring home the salmon."

"I'm way ahead of you there!"

Their first stop of the morning was that notorious superstore, place of capitalist joy and groundbreaking fashion faux pas. Lemon-flavored Timothy would actually fit in great here. But in all seriousness, if he was going to be whiling away his hours at scientific and technological advancement, Eva really was going to have a find a way of making decent money. "Who do I talk to, I wonder?"

Timothy was recovering from another round of sensory overload and took several seconds to comprehend what she'd just asked. "Well now . . . maybe a manager of something?"

"Let's go talk to Seafood Lady!" Eva said with inspiration.

She grasped the semi-bewildered Timothy by the hand and dragged him toward the Land of the Fish's Revenge.

Upon arrival at their departmental destination, Eva quickly discovered that today it was Seafood Man on duty . . . or Seafood Child, rather. Seriously, just how long had this kid been out of diapers? Not that diapers wouldn't come in handy where that colon-dissolving salmon was concerned. "Hello, excuse me? We were wondering if we could speak to your manager?"

The boy had a slightly terrified look in his eye as he replied, "Look, if it's about the salmon, then . . . "

"No, no," Eva began, exchanging a meaningful glance with her citrus-colored husband. "I was just wondering if there were any jobs available. I really need work right now and thought this might be a good place to start looking."

Seafood Child had just been deveining a new shipment of shrimp and unwittingly wiped their intestinal contents across his cheek when he struck his "I'm thinking" pose. "As a matter of fact, we do have an opening. There were a few 'incidents' yesterday because of some outdated fish that was sold."

"You don't say," Eva remarked.

"The girl who sold the fish was fired, and I'm just temping until we find a full-time replacement."

Timothy couldn't stand it anymore. "Son, um, you have fish guts all over your face."

Seafood Child suddenly remembered what he'd just been doing and turned an appropriate shade of green upon the realization of what sort of substance Timothy must mean. "Oh great. Alright, you two just wait here, and I'll go get my manager . . . as soon as I disinfect my face!"

"That sounds promising," Eva said.

"Which part? Getting the job or that kid washing his face?"

"It's a tie," she said as the manager approached them.

"So I hear you're looking for a job?" the friendly manager man asked, first focusing on Timothy.

"Yes, I am," Eva promptly responded. "I can start right away too, if you like."

Manager Man extended his very clean hand out to her, and Eva shook it firmly. "That sounds wonderful, but do you have any experience working with seafood or any other type of meat? Can you weight and package it properly, for instance?"

Eva looked at Timothy who small-smiled encouragement. "Well sir, I've helped my family butcher chickens and hogs since I was a little girl, and we had to weigh portions properly before taking them to market." Manager Man was nodding his approval, so she must not have said anything too outdated.

"So you have experience with organic techniques and regulations. That's excellent. What about seafood?"

Here Eva paused again. She used to help her Dad catch and clean mudcat, or at least as clean as they could get. Would that be classified under the same heading as "seafood?" "I've worked with salmon (technically true) and have experience with cleaning and filleting catfish."

"What about shrimp deveining?"

"Oh yes, no problem."

Timothy elbowed her again.

"Well then, I think we should give you a try! It pays $10 an hour, but I'm afraid I can't offer you health benefits."

Wow, ten dollars an hour? She'd be rich in a month! Plus she didn't know what health benefits were anyway, so why should the absence of such a thing matter? "That will be just fine. When would you like me to start?"

"Would tomorrow at 8:00 a.m. be too soon?"

"No sir, that would be perfect! I'll be here."

"Very good! Josh over there will train you on all the equipment necessary to do the job."

Josh of the Now-Clean Face waved a friendly lobster in their direction. Eva waved back. "See you in the morning then!"

As they were exiting the store, Timothy voiced an afterthought. "Hey, Eva? Now that we have an income and can stop using Mick's computer money, can we go look at some men's clothes? I've got to get out of this."

"Sounds good. I need to get a few items myself since my new workplace probably wouldn't approve of the black corset either."

So seventy dollars and twenty minutes later, Eva had several workable clothing options while Timothy was happily sporting his budget couture in khaki pants, a plain navy blue button-up shirt that was on clearance, and brown loafers . . . complimented by plain white socks, starch-free though they were. Timothy wasn't one for impulsive action, but he felt quite sure that once they got home, these yellow monstrosities would be going directly into the garbage . . . or perhaps a large bonfire.

"I'm hungry," Eva said, rubbing her rumbling tummy. Fully recovered from the night before and having carefully sampled only a small amount of breakfast, she was more ravenous than ever. "Let's see if we can find a place to eat. Surely there's something like that on every street corner these days."

Now that he was acceptably attired, Timothy was far more amenable to extra stops being added to their day's routine. "I could eat. What's this place up here, and why does everybody like yellow so much?"

Eva looked in the direction indicated by Timothy's finger and read "fast food." Sure, why not? "Yeah, that will work. What do you think they serve?"

"I don't know, but it's probably good enough. And fast too, or so they claim."

"Guess we're about to find out."

After arguing with the order-taking teenager over the concept of extra-large portion sizes and nearly fist-fighting with an angry five-year-old that didn't get the appropriate number of ketchup bag-things in her kiddie meal, Eva and Timothy stumbled to an empty and sticky table with their trays of pseudo food. "On what part of a chicken does one find the 'nugget?' " Eva asked, slowly opening her corrugated box of pre-formed poultry parts.

Timothy was just as slowly opening his box that clearly stated the name of his particular burger . . . as if he didn't remember what he ordered. What he discovered was a partially-flattened beef patty of sorts with a weirdly-colored liquid substance oozing out the sides. "I don't know, but I'm already starting to regret this orange whatever-it-is."

"Looks like some sort of sauce . . . not mustard, I don't think," Eva said, attempting to make an educated guess. She'd taken her first bit of the mysterious chicken part and was okay with it. The barbecue sauce in the tiny cup helped.

He took his first bite and made a very unhappy face. "This ranks up there with Mrs. Simmons's lemonade."

"Mine's actually okay. Try the fries. They're really good."

Timothy discovered that he could, at least, enjoy the crispy sticks of grease-flavored cholesterol especially after he finally got his ketchup bag open. "You want this thing they call a hamburger? If I eat it, tonight will be a repeat of the last."

"Here, you can have my nuggets," Eva offered, swapping entrees with her husband. Thankfully, her taste buds were tolerating the Thousand Island dressing masquerading as a unique kind of sandwich condiment. Hopefully her insides wouldn't have a problem with it either. "We forgot to get something to drink."

Timothy nodded as he mopped up the last of his ketchup with the last of his fries. "Let's get a drink somewhere else. I can't take any more of this extra-large value talk right now."

"But I thought you loved a bargain," Eva said with a knowing smile.

"This lunch just cured me of that."

"Miracles do happen," Eva remarked as she gathered up their trash and deposited it into a conveniently-labeled receptacle labeled "trash." No, really? Is that why is smelled like rancid puss with a hint of last year's compost? "I may be out of time, but I can, at least, still find the garbage can."

CHAPTER FIFTEEN

Who'd have thought special sauce could produce such a "special" reaction in her poor Timothy? In the midst of their trek to see Andy at the pharmacy, Timothy was suddenly o'ertaken by a fierce need to find a toilet, so there upon Mick's porcelain throne he remained for the entire night. Eva could only imagine what would've happened if Timothy had eaten the entire sandwich or whatever it was. "Plague in a box" was a far more accurate description. Eva, however, was forced to remain sleepless for the second night in a row due to the tortured moaning frequently emanating from behind the bathroom door. Men were babies in any century. At precisely 6:15 the following morning, Eva was in the kitchen preparing their usual repast. She heard Timothy stumbling down the hall and plopping onto the living room couch. "Three, two, one . . . " she counted down, the TV, cable box, and sound system springing to life right on cue. Apparently he'd been mostly delivered from gastrointestinal evil because he'd begun his now-morning ritual of channel surfing.

"Would you like a piece of dry toast?" Eva asked in a patient, wifely manner.

"Oh, I could probably choke down some of it," he half-whimpered, already absorbed into the latest History Channel special.

Eva brought him a plate with a perfectly-toasted slice of bread on top. "Coffee?"

"No, it would only make things worse," he replied and nibbled at the toast.

"Do you think you'll feel up to a chat with Andy in a while?"

There was a long pause as General Custer battled with an indigenous warrior. "What was that? Oh, yes, maybe this afternoon."

"Well, I have to get to work, you remember. Come to think of it, I'm not sure when I'll be finished and back here."

"Mmmm."

Eva shook her head and retreated to the bedroom. Showered and properly clothed, Eva surveyed her outdated hairstyle in the foggy mirror. "I should probably do something about this" she muttered, adjusting one of the hairpins determined to plummet floor-ward. Deciding that this was as good as it was going to get for the immediate moment, she returned to the living room to give Timothy a good-bye kiss on the cheek. "I'll be home as soon as I can."

A bewildered Timothy looked up at her. "Where are you going?"

"To work? Remember? I have to make money so you can help Andy figure out how to get us back into our farmhouse."

"Oh! Right!" he said, jumping up from the couch. He teetered just a bit, still weak from lack of food and sleep. "This is worse than that bushel of green apples I ate last year."

"No, honey, nothing could be worse than that."

"Maybe not. Well, I'll get cleaned up and go see Andy then. I think I can find my way back to the place."

"Be careful," she told him then gave him the previously planned kiss on the cheek.

"You too. Don't eat the merchandise."

"Am thinking we should give up food for a few days."

"I don't disagree with you. See you tonight."

With not a little nervousness, Eva left Mick's apartment and walked determinedly in the direction of her new job. What in the world was she getting herself into? Sure, they had to have an income, but what did she really know about any of this? Well, she knew what bad fish smelled like now. That was something. But what did good fish smell like? Ugh. Her mind twisted and turned in and around such thought progressions during her entire walk to work. As she entered the store, she was surprised to see so many people shopping madly this early in the day. How many worthless odds and ends did a person need in this time period, and why were they so desperate to get their hands on it at 7:30 in the morning? She inhaled a "do or die" breath and proceeded to the seafood counter. Josh was already there slinging dead fish tails into a bucket. "Good morning," Eva said, extending her hand.

"Hi," Josh replied, doing his best to wipe goo and scales off his hands. "It will be great to finally have someone around who knows what they're doing."

Yes it would, Eva thought. What she actually said was an evasive, "I'm happy to be here. I suppose we should just jump right in then, yes?"

"Absolutely! We just got a shipment of fresh shrimp in that needs deveining. You know how to do that?"

"Oh sure," Eva responded, her heart rate suddenly ramping up to supersonic speeds. She attempted to exude a nonchalant confidence as Josh handed her what she assumed was some sort of deveining tool. Ah well, ultimately a knife was a knife.

"You can put the shrimp into this container after you've finished with them. Put the sea poo into this container here," he directed, pointing to both containers respectively.

"You bet," she said, trying desperately to still her shaking hands.

"I'll show you how to work all the equipment you'll be using once we've finished with this morning's shipments. They need to be done ASAP for freshness reasons."

ASAP. She guessed that meant "work fast," so Eva proceeded to do so. The first few shrimp were pretty much mangled beyond recognition by the time she'd gotten their intestinal tract removed . . . this was certainly an apt first task for her after the past two nights spent in what they'd learned was called a "bathroom." After the outhouse back home, she preferred to term it "ecstasy." No snakes, no spiders, no corncobs, and gloriously thick and soft "toilet paper." She wondered how Katie and Mick were coping with their various "technologies" right now.

"Good job," Josh remarked, pausing to assess Eva's progress. "You're a natural."

"Thanks," she replied, tossing one of the last shrimps into the appropriate container. At least I'm learning a trade, she thought. This might actually come in handy if they got back to 1922. She could open a seafood store! Of course, they didn't live near the coast, but maybe there could be a way to use ice blocks for transporting fish up from the coast in one of those new Fords. Their icebox at the house kept food edible quite well, and that refrigerator in Mick's apartment seemed to function under the same theory.

"So where are you from?"

The question took Eva off-guard, and she nearly deveined a finger. "Oh, well, you know, we come from . . . Waco. Yes."

"No kidding! That's where I'm going to college in the fall."

"How nice," she said. That response seemed safe enough.

"Yeah, I got a full football scholarship, and there are worse places to be."

There was no point in even attempting a lucid response. Thankfully Josh was too reabsorbed in his task of de-tailing fish to notice. She had no idea that friendly small talk could be so stressful then wondered how Timothy was handling his own task at hand.

*****

"I don't like shoes," Timothy mused as he approached the pharmacy building. His next challenge would be to find a store that sells cowboy boots. You simply can't pick cotton in these low-cut, floppy things. Dirt would get into them and turn into sweat-mud within minutes. "But there isn't any cotton, Timothy," he verbally reminded himself then lost his train of thought over the wonderment of automatically-opening, sliding glass doors. "How about that," he mused, moving in and out of the doorway, watching the slab of glass slide open and closed, and looking intently for the motor that allowed for such smooth, rapid movement.

"Excuse me?" a voice said. "I'm sorry, sir, but could you move away from the door? It's hot, and all the cold air is getting out."

Blushing with embarrassment, Timothy mumbled an apologetic, "I'm sorry, I was looking at this door here . . . never seen anything like this."

The voice which also included an entire face gave him a strange look until he suddenly realized who this newcomer was. "Timothy, right? I'm Andy!"

Andy's hand was extended and shaking his own before Timothy could recover speaking abilities. "Yes, um, Timothy. Yes, I'm Timothy. Nice to see you again."

"Good to see you too! Hey, have you heard anything from Mick or Katie? I've been trying to call, but they never answer and never return my voicemails. I'm kind of starting to worry about them."

How he wished Eva was here! She could've come up with a plausible explanation in seconds and maybe even been able to figure out what a voicemail was. Instead Timothy had to rely on his own deft thinking and sleight of tongue. "No, we haven't heard from them." Genius, right?

"Okay. Well, if you do, would you give me a call? You still have my cell number, yes?"

Timothy finally comprehended Eva's earlier "parole officer" reference and found himself desperately drowning in his own confusion. "I think Eva has it."

"Great. So what can we do for you today?"

Timothy wanted to run hide in that giant bin labeled "beach balls." He was so out of his depth . . . or maybe out of his shallow, considering how little he knew of this world. "I . . . I was just wondering if I could talk to you for a minute . . . if you're not busy, I don't want to interrupt."

"Sure, I have a few minutes. What's on your mind?"

Way too much, Timothy thought. "You know about that quantum physics invention Mick built? The one we moved to the old house across the way?"

"Mostly I just know *of* it. Mick and I talked about it a few times, but I was never involved with the practical hands-on development."

"Oh," was Timothy's downtrodden response. "Well, but you understand how it all works?"

"I understand the theory behind it, or at least I sort of do. Quantum physics applied practically gets pretty out there."

"Out where?"

"Out . . . never mind. I only meant that it can get extremely complicated."

"I see," Timothy replied, rapidly losing what confidence he had at the realization that he didn't in any way "see" much of anything these days.

"What do you need to know about how it works?" Andy prodded. He had a feeling this was going to be a very interesting conversation.

Might as well just lay it all on the table, Timothy thought. "Alright. This is going to sound, well, 'pretty out there,' but I need you to show me how to fix Mick's machine. Eva and I are from 1922, and when Mick and Katie did whatever they did with that machine, they got stuck in 1922, and we got stuck here."

Andy's reaction was nothing like he'd expected it to be. "So it worked? Wow! I always knew he was good, but honestly, I didn't think anybody could be that good. Geez, I have so many questions! What are you doing for money? How are you both adapting to twenty-first century technology? The sheer speed at which everything moves now must be scary as crap!"

"Crap?" Timothy asked, mostly just relieved that Andy both accepted and comprehended this futuristic lunacy.

"Oh, sorry. 'Crap' is another word for sh . . . " Here Andy paused, suddenly realizing that such a commonly-used swear word nowadays might offend a 1922 resident.

"You mean shit. I get it," Timothy nodded with both

comprehension and a hint of newfound camaraderie. "To answer your question, we're both still feeling kind of lost. Eva got a job at the huge grocery place down the street working in the meat department."

"She's worked as a butcher before then?"

"She helped me slaughter and cut up a pig to eat last winter."

"Oh," Andy said with mild shock. "Yeah, I guess that counts as experience then. How does she like it?"

"Don't know. It's her first day. To tell you the truth, neither of us understands how she even got the job. But then again, Eva is very good at getting folks to do what she wants."

Andy grinned. "A charmer! Well, that will get both of you through most sticky situations no matter what time and space you're occupying."

"Are meat sections sticky?" Timothy asked, mystification taking over yet again.

Here Andy paused. "Come to think of it, they tend to be. At any rate, you have an income. That's awesome. And you're staying at Mick's place, so you should have computer and internet access too."

"Inter-what access?"

Noticing that their conversation was drawing some strange glances from the local RXS Pharmacy shoppers, Andy motioned for Timothy to follow him into a back office where they could hammer out the details of inter-dimensional time travel more privately. "I think we're going to have to start from square one."

"How many squares are there?"

"Lots! First of all, do you know how to use a telephone?"

Timothy inhaled a deep breath of relief. Finally, something he recognized! "Of course. Eva and I have had a phone for a few years now. We always have to wait for old Mr. Flanagan to hang up before we can use it though . . . his kids live all the way in Birmingham, and he doesn't get to see them much. So they can talk for an hour at a time some days."

Now it was Andy's turn to be lost. "Okay. You all have your own phones but have to share the same line?"

"Sure. Don't they have party lines anymore?"

"Only outside the dance clubs. Okay, the first thing we have to do is get you a cell phone. Here, look at mine." At which point Andy pulled a new smartphone from his back pocket and swiped it to life.

"Basically this is just a hand-held computer that also lets you talk to people long-distance just like a regular telephone. It lets you do tons of other things too, but we can get to that later."

"You mentioned a computer earlier too. What's that?"

Andy stared at the poor displaced man, not impatiently, but with plenty of pity. "Tell you what: my shift ends in about half an hour. Why don't you wait here, and then we'll go back to Mick's place so I can fully educate you on everything . . . well, most of what you need to know."

"Will any of it have to do with orange-colored sauce?" Timothy asked with trepidation.

*****

With a swipe of his finger and a few touches on the screen, Andy's phone sprang to 4G life. He was physically shaking, he was so excited at this new development. "There's no way I could've gotten any friggin' luckier! Finally I get my chance at the top," he mumbled as he entered the men's room for even more privacy. He locked the door behind him as a voice answered his call.

"This better be good. I'm about to go into a meeting with the dean and our client, and it's not going to be a pleasant encounter unless you have something substantial for me."

"I do!" Andy assured the voice in a hushed-but-frenzied whisper. "He did it. His machine allowed him to travel through time and back again, and even better, I know where the machine is being stored!"

There were several seconds of silence before the voice replied, "And does he know that you know where the machine is? It's doubtful that Mick would leave it haphazardly lying around unguarded."

Andy giggled. He always giggled when he was pleased with himself. It was annoying. "That's the best part, sir! Mick and his girlfriend are stuck in a different time! They got trapped there, and their two contacts got trapped here. I'm with one of the contacts right now . . . about to go back with him to their apartment to teach him how to use our technology."

"For once you're not wasting my time. You actually did something helpful . . . shocking. There may be hope for your thesis yet. By all means, accompany this contact, but don't leave the apartment until you hear from me. The next move must be discussed with our client before we take any, shall we say, more decisive measures."

"Yes sir. I'm on it," Andy replied then clicked the phone off. Gross condescension and non-stop insults notwithstanding, he was very pleased with the just-concluded conversation. It was about time the professor demonstrated a healthy respect for his dedication to the project.

As Andy exited the restroom, Timothy was rapidly advancing toward it. "I beg your pardon," Timothy began. "Were you finished?"

"Oh yeah, for sure," Andy replied with an even bigger grin than before. "I'll meet you out front, and we can head to Mick's place."

*****

"I don't know when this particular scallop arrived in our store. I don't make a habit of stalking our seafood!" Eva snapped. She knew that she was behaving in an unforgivably unprofessional manner but, quite frankly, didn't give a fig anymore. The woman standing in front of her would try the patience of . . . well, someone with a lot of patience.

This particular rude customer was determined to have her way too. "Don't take that tone with me, lady! Where's your manager? I want to talk to your manager!"

Josh reluctantly appeared from behind the corner where he'd been hiding for the last fifteen minutes. "So . . . what can I do for you, ma'am?"

The woman sized him up within seconds and firmly decided he wasn't good enough to address her complaint either. "What, do they hire right out of junior high now? Getting a head start on the vocational training before those selfish college recruiters can nab them?"

Josh's entire demeanor shifted into attack mode at such a crack. He'd been getting teased for his baby-faced features all his life and wasn't about to take it from this . . . not nice person. "Excuse me, ma'am, but neither I nor Eva here deserve to be treated so disrespectfully. Now what can we help you with?"

Eva grinned covertly, trying not to laugh at the puffed-up, offended expression on the overly-dressed woman's face. Seriously, who wears a three-piece suit to buy low-priced fish? Eva had only just arrived in this time, but she was still well-aware of when an outfit was ostentatiously out of place!

The overly-dressed woman took a deep breath to calm herself.

She would not stoop to the level of mere meat-chopping peasants. She was the wife of an important government figure, after all. "I merely asked Eva when these scallops arrived. They must be completely fresh before I'll purchase them."

The verbal smirk at the speaking of her name made Eva cringe. "And I merely told Mrs. Government Official that I wasn't in the habit of following out seafood deliveries around from birth to ingestion."

Josh paused then nodded, assessing the situation. He'd heard plenty of reports from his co-workers around the store about this particular customer. Her "government official" husband was head garbage truck driver, but she acted like he was George W. Bush himself. "I think I can solve this issue to everyone's satisfaction. Now, ma'am, if you would like to smell each scallop before purchasing them, I would be happy to let you do so."

The woman frowned. "Why would that help me? I don't know what a good or bad scallop smells like."

Eva inwardly admitted to having some empathy toward her there.

Josh's sickly sweet smile indicated to Eva that he was about to go in for the very-rewarding kill. "Oh, well then allow me to educate you: a bad scallop smells very much like your government-official husband's mobile office space."

"Ah!" was all the suited woman could muster as her face turned as red as the lobsters on display.

"And I must add that if you'd like to be assured of unparalleled freshness, this is probably not the wisest place to be shopping for seafood."

Eva raised a hand and added, "I can vouch for that."

"My husband will hear about this!" the woman retorted, pushing her shopping cart away in an indignant huff.

"Will she tell him, do you think?" Eva asked, slightly nervous. She just got this job and didn't want to lose it over scallops.

"She'll tell him, alright, and then he and I will have a laugh over it on garbage day," Josh replied with a smile. "We've known each other for years."

"But she doesn't know that."

"Obviously not," Josh said, finally letting the laughter escape.

Eva joined in the levity, so relieved and amused that she even considered buying some of the scallops to take home for dinner.

They really had just arrived that morning. She simply hadn't liked that woman's attitude and thoroughly enjoyed messing with her.

CHAPTER SIXTEEN

Eva knocked on the door for the fifth time, her grocery bags getting heavier with each passing second that Timothy ignored her. "Hey!" she yelled then stuck her ear to the door. These scallops weren't going to cook themselves.

The lock clicked, and the door opened. "Hi there!" Andy said with an overly-developed smile. "Timothy just started the last level of *Call of Duty*. He's really good at this!"

Eva stumbled through the door and into the kitchen with her slowly-ripping plastic bags, the obnoxious sounds of stuff blowing up and guns firing providing the soundtrack for cooking dinner. Great, yet another technological time-waster into which Timothy could absorb himself. By the time they got back to their appropriate decade, he wouldn't even remember how to plant a cotton seed or murder a rattlesnake . . . unless he could do it using a remote control or that hand-held thingy Andy kept referring to as a "mouse." It would be ironic though . . . a mouse killing a rattlesnake. Speaking of which, that dead mouse was still in the bathroom cabinet.

"I got scallops for us tonight. Andy, would you like to stay for dinner?" Eva called into the living room. Andy was deeply engrossed in the game playing out before him, fascinated by Timothy's ability to master twenty-first century electronics in such a short amount of time. Neither man uttered a word in response. "Josh said cheddar mashed potatoes and sweet corn relish would go well with them. What do you think?"

Crash, boom, blood-curdling screams of mind-boggling death.

"I got some more of your favorite beer, and I thought I'd go wild with some champagne. This sparkling wine was on sale and sounded very classy."

"You need to steal that Panzer so you can blow up the bunker."

"I just cut off my finger and am bleeding profusely as I speak."

"No, no, use the M-16 instead. Moisin-Nagants only work for covert sniper missions."

Eva nodded her defeat then went back to putting away the groceries. The precious green bottle of $3 "champagne" she placed into the freezer. A stiff drink was needed more quickly this evening. She then pored over the scallop recipe she'd gotten from an obliging co-worker to make sure she had the technique down correctly. The things would be ready in no time, so she decided to start by hacking up potatoes for oven-roasting. She grated cheese, smashed and grated sticky garlic cloves, and finely-chopped green onion. "Bacon would be really good with this too," she muttered then grabbed a few slices for quick frying. "Maybe I'll open up a seafood shop AND restaurant when we get back. For now, it's champagne time!"

After a quick glance at the potatoes happily roasting away in the 450-degree heat, Eva pranced to the freezer—assuming one could "prance" the five or so feet from oven to freezer—and retrieved her prize. Perfectly-chilled or not, she needed to start sipping. Timothy's apparent indifference to her existence and her earlier encounter with the Wicked Witch of the Workplace had her primed for self-indulgence. The bottle was surprisingly well-chilled, so Eva decided to dispense with a glass and sip straight out of the bottle yet again. Screw class. She was from the country, after all.

"Tasty," she said, and took several swallows of the sweet, bubbly liquid. Her head was already getting slightly fuzzy as she removed the bacon from a burner, cut it up into small pieces, then returned it to the pan and burner along with garlic and onion. Several shakes of salt and pepper later, her concoction smelled wondrously delicious. Several more slugs of cheap champagne later, Eva was feeling wondrously delicious. "No beer today, no beer today. You can't buy beer on Sunday . . . " she sang to herself, removing the potatoes from the oven and dumping them into a big bowl. Shaky and goofy from her comparatively rapid alcohol intake on a still-empty stomach, she promptly dropped the glass baking dish onto the floor and watched with giggling amusement as it smashed into a dozen pieces. "Incoming! Incoming! All bunkers for themselves!" she cried, brandishing the half-full champagne bottle in the air. "Tell the colonel they've captured the Weiner schnitzel stand…bang, bang, bang!" Still holding the bottle in her left hand, Eva aimed her fully-automatic serving spoon in her right. After several more guzzles of sparkling sweetness, she plopped down onto the floor from sudden lack of an ability to stand.

By now, she had both Timothy's and Andy's attention. Andy's ever-present grin was pasted onto his face, but Timothy stared wide-eyed and open-mouthed at his wife. Eva saluted them both with her spoon hand and drank several more draughts from her bottle of perpetual happiness. "And now, if you'll excuse me, I must mash the scallops and sauté the potatoes. Please carry on with the killing of Nazis, whatever that is."

The smile disappeared from Andy's face as sudden realization struck. For them, World War II was a complete unknown. Maybe it was time for another type of computer education.

Timothy was already advancing to the kitchen to assist his inebriated spouse who was cross-legged on the kitchen floor trying to get her thumb unstuck from the champagne bottle. "I put the bottle to my ear and couldn't hear the ocean. Can you clean it out so I can hear the ocean? I think the scallops are homesick."

Timothy shook his head and grinned to himself. Eva never could hold her liquor especially after that incident with her grandpa's homemade moonshine. "Never mind the scallops. We're about to eat them anyway."

"Poor scallops!" Eva lamented with several sniffles of sympathy. "They just wanted to go home."

"Come with me, honey. Let's get you to bed, and I'll finish cooking dinner."

"Don't drink my French champagne," she admonished, the bottle still stuck to her thumb thanks to swelling caused by the trauma of trying to remove it.

"You already drank it all, sweetie," Timothy said, helping her into bed. The bottle would just have to stay where it was until her thumb returned to normal size. "You sleep now," he instructed gently. "I'll make sure the kitchen gets cleaned up. Will join you later," he said then kissed her forehead.

"The scallops say thank you," she whispered, drifting quickly off to sleep.

Returning to the kitchen, Timothy encountered a flustered Andy smashing away at the potatoes. Nervous about how much history he'd inadvertently revealed, he rambled along in quick sentences. "I was just about to add the cheese and bacon and whatever else is in the pan there. Maybe we need some milk too? Or butter? The scallops are a mystery to me though . . . never tackled seafood before. Should they cook on low heat or high heat? Oh, here's the recipe . . . no more than three minutes on high heat. Huh. I'm surprised."

"It's okay, Andy," Timothy assured him, grabbing the milk and requisite butter from the refrigerator. "I might not think on my feet as quickly as Eva does, but it didn't take long to figure out the game we were playing."

"I'm really sorry," Andy said with total sincerity.

"Well, at least we'll be prepared when the time comes to live through it. Truth be told, the fact that there will be another war doesn't surprise me. Eva and I have had a lot of conversations about whether or not something like that could or would happen again, especially so soon after the first war. You just confirmed what we already thought."

Andy was genuinely distraught by his own lack of discretion and just plain stupidity. In the absence of anything better to do, he placed a clean sauté pan onto a burner and began heating it. After a minute he added butter as per the recipe's instruction. "Well, if you have any questions about it, I'd be happy to answer them if possible. If not, you could find out anything you wanted to know on the internet."

"At least I know what you're talking about now," Timothy responded, popping the top on his first beer. Suddenly he felt like Eva had the right idea. "Now let's take a chance with those scallops."

Andy left Mick's apartment feeling much less confident in himself than he had upon arrival. Despite helping to cook a dinner that turned out awesomely, he was second-guessing himself left and right. What would the Professor say if he knew how nonsensically Andy had behaved tonight? "You've fallen victim to one of the classic blunders," Andy mumbled aloud. As if in accordance with the Fates who had already placed doom and a sizeable mountain of guilt on his imminent horizon, Andy's phone vibrated in his pocket. With a jump and increase in heart rate, he retrieved the device and slid a finger across the top. "Hello, sir. No, I can meet you. The device is in that broken-down building next to the pharmacy where I work. Oh, well no, why would you know where I work?"

Andy gave his Evil-Mastermind Professor directions and arranged to meet at Eva's old house as soon as possible. He was suddenly less sure about this course of action than he had been around three o'clock that afternoon. Somehow Eva and Timothy had awoken some spark of human . . . well, humanity in him, a surprising occurrence considering the fact that his entire dissertation grade rested upon delivery of Mick's invention to the Professor and his "client." But now it was too late. He'd revealed precisely where the equipment was and had no choice but to follow through with this present course of action. In the long run, wouldn't Eva and Timothy be better off here than the past anyway? Of course there was also Katie and Mick to consider. Damn.

Upon arrival at the old house, Andy discovered that an entire special ops team had been deployed for this particular recovery mission. A windowless armored truck was parked nearby waiting to be loaded down with damaged time-travelling equipment, and Professor was giving specific instructions on exactly how to load it. "Well, no mystery now who the client is," Andy said to himself. This was starting to get kind of scary. Maybe it was time to consider a college transfer!

The Professor glanced up from his notebook long enough to acknowledge Andy's presence. "There you are. I don't think we need anything else from you tonight if you'd like to go on home. We found all the parts and pieces, I believe. The Major assures me that everything can be loaded quickly then we'll be on our way as well. I'll see you in class tomorrow."

The hell you will, Andy thought. Knowing better than to argue but still miffed that he'd been dragged all the way here for no reason, Andy turned on his heel and retreated in the opposite direction. He had a good mind to go back to Mick's apartment and tell his new friends everything. Yes, he admitted to himself, he considered them friends. How could he not? They were innocent and, well, real people. That was tough to find nowadays . . . maybe any days. Andy unexpectedly found himself alternating between moving in the direction of his own place and that of Mick's. In a moment of momentous decision-making, he resigned himself to camping outside Mick's front door. He'd wait until morning if he had to, but he absolutely must enlist the help of his new BFFs.

Besides, he ultimately confided to himself, he—Andy Michael Everett III—was one of the good guys. Nobody with a name like that could ever believably pull off a black ten-gallon hat.

****

Eva's headache knew no bounds as she kissed Timothy good-bye and ambled miserably toward the door. The smell of fish deliveries was the very last thing her stomach needed this morning, but what choice did she have? Money had to be earned. Upon unlocking the door and turning the knob, she tried to push the door open. What the heck was blocking her forward mobility? She got it open just enough to peek down at the floor at which point she discovered a sleeping Andy curled up mostly peacefully. Timothy walked up behind Eva and peered over her shoulder. "He only had the one beer. Hey Andy, wake up!"

Eva kicked gently at the base of the door, hoping the vibrations would inspire the kid into wakefulness. Andy jumped, opened his eyes, looked up at two amused faces, then stretched for several seconds. "Is there any of that amazing potato concoction left? I'm starving."

"You slept outside our door just so you could get seconds?" Eva asked.

"Fourths, actually. Hey, those potatoes were the bomb! But no, I have something way more important to talk to you about. Eva, you should probably call in sick today."

Eva nodded in agreement, gagging involuntarily. "I should've done that anyway. Sparkling wine is the devil, and buckets of dead shrimp excrement is the last thing I can physically handle right now."

"I thought math equations were the devil," Timothy remarked.

"Sparkling wine is his illegitimate twin."

Three hours—one hour of which consisted of Andy apologizing uncontrollably—and a whole second batch of potatoes later, Timothy inhaled a deep breath of "this is a lot to process." Eva tapped her fingernails on the dining room table as her brain ran quickly through the larger-than-1920s-life information Andy had just revealed to them. If the government wanted Mick's invention, what could they possibly do to prevent it? They were talking about conspiring against a government that had helped win two World Wars and achieved multiple global military successes ever since. What could they possibly do to get that equipment back? "How much of Mick's research and experiments do you understand?" she finally asked Andy.

"On a general level, I understand most of it very well. But on a practical, I-can-make-this-stuff-work-again level . . . I just don't know. What I can do is shift into high-intensity research mode myself. If we could just get the equipment to a secure location where the components could be taken apart, I might be able to figure some important things out. I need to get my hands on that hardware."

"But you said the government people were hauling the

equipment away last night," Timothy reminded him.

Andy frowned for a moment as his terrified brain pondered the challenges before them. "I know, but my Professor doesn't have a clue that I've said anything to anyone about the proposed project. I'm supposed to be in one of his classes in a couple more hours. As much as I'm scared to death to show my face, it's possible that he'll accidentally let it slip where the equipment is being stored." Andy paused to take a deep, death-defying breath before irrevocably committing: "I have to be there. I will be there."

In a rare physical display of acknowledged friendship, Timothy patted Andy encouragingly on the back.

Eva's sensitivity was already offline thanks to the intensity of their collective, universal moment. "So we'll just steal it back then!" she declared, totally destroying the profound manly moment.

"It's a totally dumb and ridiculous idea on multiple levels that 100% depends on all three of us having the best luck of our lives, but it's also the only option we have," Andy admitted.

"Except the option of being stuck here forever. But how will we move all of it?" Timothy asked. "Even if we could find an automobile big enough to carry all the parts, you can bet Eva and me wouldn't know how to drive the thing without getting us all killed. There are bicycle riders here who move faster than our old Fords can go."

Eva wrinkled her forehead in deep thought. After several seconds of her own ponderations, a smile of satisfaction creased its way across her face. "So how do you two feel about garbage trucks?"

"Umm . . . they provide a valuable service to the community?" Andy attempted.

"That they do! And they're about to provide a valuable service to the whole universe, assuming you'd be willing to drive it. My boss is friends with the head of city sanitation, and tomorrow is trash day."

"Trash day . . . " Timothy considered.

"The day of the week when the garbage trucks stop in at all the businesses to pick up their trash and haul it off," Eva clarified. "If we could get Josh's friend to lend us a truck for a few hours . . . "

"But what explanation will we give? Hey, we need to borrow your truck so we can steal top-secret government equipment and save the world as we know it? This whole plan already sounds like the plot of a really bad made-for-cable movie," Andy said dubiously.

"Tell me about it," Timothy agreed, sagely nodding his head.

Eva paused to consider what the hell a made-for-cable movie was—and why Timothy was suddenly an expert about it!—as well as this aspect of her newborn strategy. "We could say . . . yeah! We could say that the store had extra trash to haul this week and could we do it after-hours so as not to invade city employee relaxation time."

"I don't know, Eva," Timothy began. "It sounds too easy."

" 'Easy? You call that 'easy?' " Andy said with amusement. Eva and Timothy both stared blankly at him. "Oh, sorry...y'all haven't seen *Star Wars* enough to quote it yet."

Eva recovered with a quick shake of her head. "In any case, the fact that it's so easy, so ludicrously simple is why it will work! Josh was just telling me that the city was having to cut down on overtime hours for their employees . . . something about an economy that's 'down,' whatever that means. He also said that the store has had to hang onto some of its trash because there wasn't enough time in the workday for all of it to be collected every week. We'd be doing the city and the store a service, not to mention my nostrils. Leftover seafood trash is not something you want to hang onto!"

Timothy nodded as he considered her explanation. "Well, if all of that's true, then it's a doable plan . . . that is, if Andy can find where the equipment is hidden and if we can break into the building where it's all hidden without getting caught and if we can load the equipment and escape without getting caught and if . . . "

"I didn't say it was a flawless plan," Eva admitted, "but what else have we got?"

"Agreed. It's the best—and only—option," Andy reiterated with finality. "Okay, I'm heading to class now and will be back here with news as soon as I can. It's probably smart if we don't use any sort of cellphone or internet communication for this. It's too traceable."

Timothy doubted that, based on the complicated nature of the equipment and procedures he'd only just begun learning, but took Andy's word for it anyway. "Then we'll wait here for you."

"Great," Andy replied, the shakiness in his voice betraying a lack of confidence. "Now hope like crazy that everything will go our way, and I do mean everything."

CHAPTER SEVENTEEN

"The cup can fly," I said numbly, still rubbing the sore spot on my head where the magical drinking utensil had smacked into it. That sudden, peculiar coldness in the air had gradually disappeared, and we were back in our sultry Texas summer evening once more.

Mick's logical, reasonable scientific mind was already assessing the unexpected occurrence. After several seconds of me staring questioningly at him, he shook his head. "Either those are a colony of Tinkerbells zipping around out there instead of fireflies, or something funky is going on here."

"Tinkerbells?"

"Fairy dust. Makes stuff fly."

"Oh. But cups can't think happy thoughts."

"I know. That's why I'm leaning toward something of the funky going on."

"I suppose it's time I came clean, sweetie. I have pregnancy-onset telekinetic powers and was waiting until this precise instant to demonstrate my skills."

For a brain that needed a solid explanation for every single thing that happened ever, the injection of humor into inexplicable situations had become a necessity for Mick over the years. "Well, demonstrate without bashing your head in, please. I kind of like it as it is."

I smiled and nodded having already accepted the only logical reason for what had just happened. "It seems obvious that this place is haunted, Mick."

Surprisingly, Mick nodded his instantaneous concession to the fact. "After all these years of watching your ghost shows, you'd know."

"And don't forget all those successful ghost hunts of our own," I reminded him, slowly returning to my sarcastic self.

He snickered. "And we're both living proof that strangeness may be applied scientifically to everyday life. It might actually be good to have someone keeping an eye on you while I'm out in the field doing that harvest thing . . . keep you from burning hair off or blowing up the kitchen."

"I don't think that whoever it is wants us to have a dog though.

The cup smashed into me as soon as we started discussing the impending puppy arrival."

The cup had been lying appropriately motionless where it had landed after assailing me. Suddenly it scooted across the floor, through a hole in the screen door screen, and onto the gravel path outside. Mick agreed. "I'll tell Mr. Mason that a dog is out of the question."

It was kind of weird how we both calmly acknowledged the fact that there was ghostliness living alongside us in our place of residence. In our own time, the concept would've sent us into a frenzy of vodka-and-Guinness-imbibing. But now? Now it felt like the most logical and "okay" idea in the world. Time-travelling could do that to you, I guessed. Hopefully Eva and Timothy wouldn't hate us forever for inflicting supernatural entities upon their home. Regardless of explanations, crazy or otherwise, we both woke up the following morning feeling terrific and ready to embrace whatever came our way. Even the little one living inside me decided not to induce vomiting this morning. The elation that came with keeping breakfast down was intoxicating!

"Are you sure you'll be alright getting to the store by yourself? If you can wait just a few minutes, I'll go get Mr. Mason's truck and drive you before getting back to the morning's cotton-picking," Mick offered protectively.

"No worries, my good man. Little Jane Austen McClaren is being a very good girl for mommy today," I replied, rubbing my gradually-expanding tummy lovingly.

Mick frowned. "Jane Austen? That's not on the baby name list."

"We don't have a list yet, so it could be!"

"Then we'll never have a list," Mick declared and kissed me on the nose.

"If it's a boy we can call him Stephen King McClaren!"

Mick laughed harder than he had in days. "Since you're obviously just fine this morning, I'll be on my way. Pick you up at noon then?"

"Sounds like a plan," I answered, grabbing his shirt front and pulling him down to my level for a quick-but-sloppy kiss.

"You really are feeling good today," he said with a grin.

"Yes, I am. And it's kinda nice to have a kiss that isn't vomit-flavored, huh?"

He laughed again, smacking my backside before walking out the back door and out into the fields. I'd come to love the sound of that old wooden screen door slamming shut. None of the back doors in our time had that sort of aural personality.

Mick had managed to let out a couple more of Eva's dresses since I couldn't do it without incurring extreme blood loss—he was really quite impressive with a sewing machine—while I mentally vowed to replace each and every one of them once Eva and Timothy returned. She was far too slender to believably wear my "fat pregnant woman" versions of her clothing.

Gathering up my things, which included a makeshift handbag containing a bit of money, I began exiting the house via the front door. From out of nowhere, I felt something smack me in the butt as I retreated. Turning around, I saw that hideous orange-and-puce-checked bonnet everyone insisted I wear lying suddenly motionless on the floor. Nothing and no one else was anywhere in sight. "Fine, fine, I'll wear the ugly thing!" I announced to thin air in my best frustrated voice before shoving the monstrosity onto my exposed head. "But I'll have you know it clashes horribly with this dress!"

Leave it to me to be a magnet for an opinionated and pushy ghost. In spite of this, I found myself semi-skipping down the road to the mercantile or grocery store or whatever the proper name for it was. I breathed in the gorgeous early-morning, summertime air. During summertime in Texas, there are approximately two waking hours' worth of pleasant outside time. After 9:00 a.m. or so, the combination of heat and humidity made being outdoors intolerably stifling. Additionally, the danger of death by sweat-induced drowning went up considerably. But it was precisely within the pleasant two-hour window of time that I found myself, enjoying the chirpy songbirds and sparkling dew still clinging desperately to liquid life on blades of green grass, the green grass still clinging desperately to the last remnants of chlorophyll that 100-degree temperatures allowed. There was no form-fitting leather and only minimal make-up involved, yet I was incredibly gratified with all things set before me.

"Good morning, Mrs. McClaren!" Mr. Simmons called from the front porch of the store as I approached the steps. He was sweeping away at the wooden boards just as I remembered Mr. Olsen doing in the *Little House* shows. Good thing Mick and I had both watched it so much! Mrs. Simmons had her faults, but I was thrilled to goodness that she in no way resembled Mr. Olsen's Harriett. Mr. Olsen—er, Simmons—extended his hand to me in a friendly good-morning greeting. "We're glad to have you here to help out! My wife is a hard worker, but neither of us are as young as we used to be, I'm afraid."

I heartily returned his handshake and replied, "Well, I'm just happy I can help. Your offer was well-timed for us as well," I smiled, laying a hand on the tiny bulge hinting at its existence beneath my dress skirt.

"Yes, my wife told me the wonderful news! Congratulations to you and Mick on the addition to your family," Mr. Simmons said with much sincerity. "Now we'd best get you out of this heat . . . not even 9:00, and it's already almost 90 degrees. Can't have you getting overheated on my watch!"

Mr. Simmons ushered me indoors with much ushering and led me to the back room where Mrs. Simmons was stirring a pitcher of pale yellow liquid. She looked up and grinned when she heard us enter. "Mornin' to you, Katie! I thought I'd make a special treat for your first day: my own special lemonade. There's even ice for the occasion," she declared proudly, handing me a glass brimming with the tangy refreshment.

With much gratitude, I took a huge swallow, anticipating the impending refreshment . . . and immediately wished that I hadn't. It was the sourest, most painfully torturous stuff that had ever attacked my taste buds! It took each and every muscle on my face to force my mouth from a grimace and into the expected smile. Fates above, why did you wish this horror upon me? The baby would absolutely be taking offense at this lemon-flavored travesty! But I had to say something . . . something complimentary. All I wanted to do was throw the glass and the entire pitcher out a window—open or closed—then run screaming toward a bottle of flavored vodka in an attempt to purify my tongue. But I had to be nice. "Oh, it's lovely, Mrs. Simmons. I don't think I've ever tasted anything quite like it." That part was honest, at least.

Mrs. Simmons never noticed any hesitation or revulsion whatsoever, thankfully, and beamed brightly as she continued, "Well, help yourself, dear. I made it all for you to enjoy."

Oh, the impending enjoyment!

"Now let's see about getting you started, shall we? Here's an apron to keep the dust off that pretty dress." I turned cooperatively around so Mrs. Simmons could tie the apron on securely. "Not too tight, is it, dear?"

I was still trying to force the taste of the profane beverage from my mouth and memory so was momentarily distracted from answering her question. As a result, she kept pulling the ties tighter and tighter. That combined with citrusy poison made my precious tummy-bundle rebel, and rebel vehemently. After a few happy hours of unusually calm stomach activity, I promptly emptied its contents all over the unsuspecting Mrs. Simmons's back room floor.

"Dear me, I believe that may have been too tight," Mrs. Simmons observed, quickly loosening the ties.

I wiped my mouth as quickly and politely as possible with the apron. "I'm so sorry, Mrs. Simmons. Let me clean up this mess for you."

She laid an understanding hand on my back and said, "No, no, Katie, I'll take care of this. You throw some cold water on your face and recover. I'll meet you out front in a few minutes. Heaven knows I had plenty moments like this myself! Well actually, both my sister and I did. We were expecting at the same time, you see, and it was the holiday season. We were at our grandmother's house, and it was Thanksgiving, and there was an episode with some rotten cranberries that . . . "

"Thank you, Mrs. Simmons," I very quickly interjected lest her description inspire more heaving innards. "I'll be back in a few minutes so we can get started," and I practically ran out the back door, making as mad a dash as possible for the well. As I did, I overheard my new boss lady muse aloud, "Grandmother refused to host a holiday after that."

After my embarrassing gastronomic explosion, the day improved rapidly. It was surreal in a good way getting to experience firsthand how regular people lived sixty or so years before my own life began. Listening to Mrs. Simmons explain the general workings of the store as well as some of her favorite products, I found myself fascinated to the point of being transfixed. Even her way-too-detailed examples of which anti-constipation meds worked best and why had an oddly inoffensive effect. I mentally thanked my little one for being so kind to my insides as Mrs. Simmons got to the part about the size, color, frequency, and even scent of her husband's bowel movements. "And that was the last time we used this particular brand. I told Mr.

Simmons we should stop carrying it, but he said Old Man Forsythe swore it was the best product around for getting rid of termites."

"What?" I asked with much disbelief.

Mrs. Simmons only shrugged. "That's what he told me. Whether it's true or not is another story, but we've kept the product on the shelf ever since."

"How many such products of questionable quality are there?" I hoped she wouldn't be upset by my question, but I needed to know which ones should be avoided at all costs . . . and which ones had practical applications other than those advertised.

To my relief, Mrs. Simmons smiled. "Not many. He lets me put my foot down from time to time . . . says it keeps me loving and lovable."

I laughed. "A wise man indeed!"

"Oh yes, over the years he learned to put a little more thought into which battles should be fought and which ones should be fled! But, of course, I do the same for him. Mr. Simmons really is a very good man."

From the contented, peaceful smile on her face, I could tell that she meant every word of it. I needed to start taking mental notes from this couple.

"And besides, he never complains if I have one too many nips of the—what did you call it?—Midnight Special?"

"I have great respect for him already! Those nips can be life-saving sometimes."

Mrs. Simmons giggled and winked. "That they can. Now let's see, where were we? Oh yes, products of questionable quality. Well, in my opinion, this entire section could go. Women around here don't have much use for any of it," she said, gesturing toward their version of a cosmetics counter.

Now we were going to have problems. Make-up was one of my bare necessities, much to Mick's chagrin, and I'd fight for their inclusion within store inventory with all my willful might. This was a battle that must not be avoided! As sweetly and calmly as possible, I replied, "Well, maybe they simply don't know how to use the products properly. I could help with that."

Mrs. Simmons nodded. "Yes, I noticed that you seem to enjoy them. You do look lovely . . . not like a painted barfly at all."

I mentally shrugged it off. I'd been compared with worse.

"That's because I've been practicing for many years and finally found what worked for me. If you'd like, we could have a special 'makeover day.' We could invite all the ladies in the area into the store for a demonstration on how to correctly apply make-up. I'd be happy to play teacher!"

"Hmmm, a makeover day. That just might be a good idea. It would get more people into the store, if nothing else."

"Yes, and maybe you could have specials on other products as well . . . like buy one pound of bacon, get half a pound free or 'two cans of corn for the price of one' . . . something like that. A few extra sales now and then on popular products will almost always increase business."

Mrs. Simmons's eyes lit up at the prospect of increasing cash flow. "Summer is usually the slowest time of year for business, but your ideas could help change that this time! Let me talk with Mr. Simmons this evening and see what he thinks. For now, let's get you started on learning the cash register."

The excitement of our upcoming girly-yet-potentially-moneymaking project provided a pleasant distraction from the fact that this particular cash register probably came over on the Niña, the Pinta, or the Santa Maria. In fact, I think the gargantuan chunk of iron just might have sunk one of them.

Just as I was experimenting with how to get the till open without it shooting across the room and crushing a customer's skull, an unknown female face walked through the front door. This unknown face was deeply etched with determination and focus. Glancing semi-frantically around for a Mrs. Simmons who was now nowhere to be seen, I pondered just how quickly I could inadvertently tick this person off with my extreme ignorance and inability to use the ill-advised cash register. Crap. I had to say something welcoming. I had to be helpful even if I was in no way helpful. Smile, Katie, for pete's sake! "Good morning, how may I help you?"

The resolute face, which was also connected to a body (in this story, that fact can't necessarily be assumed), strode up to the counter behind which I stood. Her hands smacked an as-yet-unknown object firmly down onto said counter while her unusually resonant (i.e. loud) lady voice demanded, "I want my money back on these beans."

I stared at an empty can of pinto beans. "And what seemed to be the problem with the product?"

"Don't get smart with me, missy!"

"I'm not trying to get smart with you, ma'am."

"I can't stand you painted-up, citified girls thinkin' you know everything about everything and us country folk are dumber than Christmas."

I couldn't resist. "How dumb is Christmas?"

"Why, I never! Where's Mrs. Simmons? I'll have a word with her about your sassy mouth, and you'll be out on your backside before dinner!"

I really needed to get a grip on my very poor and unprofessional attitude. "Mrs. Simmons had to run an errand, but I'd be more than happy to discuss this situation with you."

"Well . . . my 'situation' is that my husband took one bite of these beans and got sick. He was in the outhouse all night and can't work now because he's too tired, still layin' around in bed pesterin' me with all his whining. I want my money back and a free can of beans for my trouble!"

"You said your husband was sick after only one bite?" I probed.

"Yes, got stomach pains right away. It wasn't a full minute before he was moanin' and groanin' for dear life. Terrible frustration, that man . . . no gumption to speak of."

I frowned. "Mr. Mason isn't sick then?"

Mick frowned. "Well, if he is, he did a great job of hiding it while chopping up that tree stump he just dug out of the ground."

Mrs. Simmons nodded knowingly. "His wife tries that stunt once a month or so."

I contemplated the totally empty bean can for another few seconds, debating my response as well as just how much I should allow myself to enjoy it. "So who ate the rest of the beans?"

Anonymous woman stared blankly at me for a split second. "Well, I did. No sense letting 'em go to waste."

"But you're not sick."

"Well no, I'm, I'm . . . "

"I'm sorry, ma'am, but I'm afraid we can't refund money on a can of beans that was, apparently, perfectly safe to eat."

"No! He was sick, I tell you! Them beans were contanimated."

"Contaminated."

"What?"

"Wow."

Mrs. Simmons made her reappearance none too soon, I can tell you that! "Why Mrs. Mason, how are you today? Isn't it a lovely morning?"

Further angered by her present state of confusion and inability to coerce this stubborn and snippy-mouthed city girl to her will, Mrs. Mason was none to kind. "No it is not a lovely morning, not when I've got a sickly husband layin' around keepin' me from my work!"

Mrs. Simmons gave me a quick "oh, dear" look. "And I take it that these beans were the cause of it all?"

Mrs. Mason launched into an even more detailed, dramatic, and embellished account of Mr. Mason's fateful bite of beans. I lounged against the supportive cash register due to pregnancy-induced foot pain, all the while marveling at Mrs. Simmons's ability to not only endure, but soothe the ruffled lady's nerves. Mrs. Simmons placed a kindly hand on Mrs. Mason's back, walking her calmly to the front door where she handed her an item hidden from my view. Without further ado, the drama was over as abruptly as it had started.

"What did you give her?" I asked, eyes wide with disbelief mixed with admiration.

Mrs. Simmons turned a bit red and giggled. "A box of that termite laxative!"

We were both in the throes of paroxysmal laughter when Mick walked in, bemused at our jovial states. "What did I miss?"

"Hi, honey!" I called, running up to him and planting my lips onto his. "You missed nothing that can't be discussed later. How did the cotton-hauling go?"

"Great! Apparently I got an excellent price for what we've harvested so far. At least that's what Mr. Mason said."

I heard a peculiar muffled sound coming from somewhere behind Mick's back. "Whatcha got there, hmm?"

"A surprise just for you," he replied, carefully bringing his hand forward and revealing the sweetest little kitten I'd ever seen.

"Kitty!" I yelled and took the wriggling little gray darling from him.

"Hopefully there won't be any other-worldly objections to a cat. They're useful what with all the mice-killing and such. Besides, I know how you like cats better than dogs."

I was giggling and cooing over my new kitty, kissing its little nose and behaving in an all-around juvenile fashion. "Thank you so much, sweetie! But you get the honor of naming him. Ummm, is it a 'him?' "

"It's a 'him,' and I think we should call him Einstein. It seems appropriate." He was still grinning, apparently quite proud of the gesture as well as the choice of name.

"So can I name the baby Jane Austen?" I attempted.

"We'll discuss that later too," he said, planting another kiss on my nose. "I'm going out back to talk to Mr. Simmons about getting more cotton bag things."

"We should probably figure out the right name for those 'things,'" I suggested.

"We really should. So you'll be finished in, what, half an hour?"

"Gracious, is it almost noon already?" Mrs. Simmons exclaimed. "I've got to get lunch on the table. Yes, dears, we'll have things well in hand very shortly. Go on out back, Mick, and I'll have Katie here ready to go shortly. It's time you both got some food in your stomachs as well!"

"Whether it stays there or not is another story," I commented, returning to tinker with my cash register.

Half an hour and several large cotton-hauling bags (or simply cotton-hauling sacks, we finally discovered) later, we arrived home for an hour's worth of relaxation before Mick had to be back out in the field. It was a darn good thing Timothy only impregnated a couple of fields with the fluffy white commodity because this work was entirely too backbreaking. Mick was healthy and could take care of it just fine, but it still kind of worried me especially now that we were going to have a family. He should be carrying around specs for the next intergalactic space rocket, not dragging giant bags of cotton behind him for hours on end in the middle of surface-of-the-sun summer heat.

I set Einstein down on the kitchen floor to scamper about and explore his new abode then absent-mindedly began stirring sugar into the tea pitcher. Mick went to retrieve eggs from the chicken house into which I would never set foot again, dead rooster or not. The cramping of my fingers reminded me that I'd probably dissolved the sugar by now. Spoon set aside, I went for the bowl of seasoned potatoes I'd smashed earlier that morning in preparation for a quick noon meal. Since Mick liked them so much, I figured I'd fry up another batch of the potato pancakes. Dr. Adkins would be so ashamed, but then again he'd never had to work a cotton field or fight with Columbus's cash register . . . while pregnant and under the influence of that lemonade from the twentieth Circle of Hell! Seriously, it had to have earned its own special circle.

Einstein was happily gnawing on my big toe when Mick returned to the kitchen. "Seven eggs today, and look: potatoes from the one and only plant that survived The Great Gopher Feast of 1922!"

"Oooo!" I said, excitedly taking the few potatoes from him. "I think tomorrow I'll make potato salad in their honor."

"Is that how one shows honor to potatoes? By pulling them from the ground and eating them?"

"Better us than the gophers! Besides, do you know of a more appropriate way to honor food other than by eating it?"

"There might be some logic in there somewhere. Ah! Tea!" Mick cried as he laid the eggs in the sink, dodged a rampaging Einstein who was frolicking with a candy wrapper, and gulped down multiple glasses-full of this most excellent Southern beverage of choice.

As I placed the fried potatoes and a giant salad on the table, I happened to glance down at the floor where Einstein continued to toy furiously with . . . an empty bag of Skittles?

"Okay, so have you been experimenting with any interdimensional candy deliveries lately?" I asked, tapping my foot nervously on the floor at which point Einstein—finding my vibrating foot far more interesting than the candy wrapper—attacked it once more.

CHAPTER EIGHTEEN

Mick was too busy masticating his lunch for my question to immediately register inside his brain. "What was that?" he finally managed between bites.

I reached down, picked up the kitten-mauled Skittles package, and laid it emphatically onto his plate where he would be forced to acknowledge its existence. "Do you have something you'd like to tell me?"

Mick gaped at the object before him which wasn't a pleasant thing to watch considering the half-chewed lettuce and teeth-smashed potatoes threatening to dribble from his mouth. "I didn't do that," he said simply.

"So no midnight experiments with ion tubes or short-wave transponders or . . . or whatever?"

Mick stared at me as if pregnancy had suddenly shorted out my logic circuits. "Yes, since you bring it up, I've been having secret meetings with top-level scientists in the middle of the cotton patch every afternoon. The gophers are actually our private message couriers, so maybe you shouldn't hoe any more of them into the Great Rodent Beyond. Our projects are complicated."

Nodding my head and sighing, I plopped down in front of my plate and valiantly attempted to eat something. "Touché. I just thought that maybe . . . well, that maybe you'd discovered a way to bridge the time gap and weren't telling me because you didn't want me to be disappointed if you failed, and this wrapper package whatever was a step in your experimental procedures."

Mick smiled and took my hand that wasn't toying heartlessly with a tomato slice. "Honey, I'd tell you if any possibility of our escape came along. We're a team in more ways than one, you know."

"You mean other than baby-making?"

"Yeah, that."

"I know, and to this day I can't figure out how I've ever really helped you, what with that omniscient calculator of yours and the Man of Scientific Mystery brain you have manipulating said calculator. I think the baby is going to take after you, by the way. I swear he or she was kicking out calculus equations in Morse code while I was trying to sleep last night."

Mick laughed so hard that tea spewed from his nose. "If that's what happened, then this kid will put even me to shame! I think there is one thing we have to consider where the Skittles package is concerned, though: since that candy wasn't on the market until sometime in the early 80s . . . "

"Taste the rainbow!"

"Yes. As I was saying, it's likely that someone else has found a way to contact us."

My mind had moved beyond candy and was unexpectedly focused on not taking offense with my unborn child for possibly being a math nerd. It took me another second or two to fully realize what Mick had just announced. "What? You mean maybe Eva and Timothy found a way to fix your time-bendy machine? Or maybe it was our new ghost friend."

He shrugged and poured himself a fifth glass of tea. "The first thing you said. I can't think of any other explanation. They could've run into Andy somewhere along the way—he's always trying to hang out at my place, as you know—and he has a working knowledge of what I was trying to accomplish. If the machine components are still mostly intact, Andy certainly has the mental capacity to steer them in the right direction or maybe even repair the system himself."

"Huh," I remarked, patting my hand apologetically against my belly. "We should probably keep our eyes open for signs then, yes? I mean, they could be sending more objects through anytime. Hey, we should figure out a way to answer them! Any ideas?"

Chomping on the last precious ice cube remaining unmelted in his glass, Mick replied, "Give me the afternoon to ponder it. That's one thing about picking cotton: it gives a person plenty of quiet time to think."

"Yay!" I gleefully exclaimed, bouncing light-heartedly up from the table and inadvertently stepping on Einstein's tail. He screamed and ran away. "In that case, I'll see about making something special for dinner tonight! Maybe Mrs. Simmons has some fresh basil in stock."

"Yeah, I think she keeps it right next to the fresh sushi," Mick remarked. He kissed my cheek and burgeoning belly then headed out the back door, an empty cotton sack dragging behind him. That's my hard-working man, I thought contentedly as my shopping list mentally wrote itself.

Very shortly I was to discover how pointless it was to let my shopping list mentally write itself. Honestly, what culinary miracles was I truly expecting to find amidst the rows of salt-cured hams, toilet sandpaper, and termite-exterminating Ex-Lax? We were dealing with a rural general store, not Dean and DeLuca! After several moments of wishing Eva and Timothy would experimentally warp something tastier than candy wrappers our way, I settled half-heartedly on a handful of "special" food purchases: macaroni, a couple of cans of tomato sauce, some dried spices and herbs that sort of resembled something Italian-esque, and a couple of lovely looking steaks to make up for the absence of fresh basil. That was one good thing about Texas during pretty much any era: terrific fresh beef! I had grand plans of baking a loaf of bread too, so yeast had been added to my shopping basket as well.

"Baking some bread today, dear?" Mrs. Simmons asked as she watched me ringing up my own receipt. It was good cash register practice.

"Gonna try. I haven't attempted this in years, but anytime I ever did in the past, the bread never rose right."

"Oh, well, you need to put the dough in a very warm spot for half an hour before trying to bake it. It's sure to rise then. I remember when my mother was trying to teach me how to bake bread. It was so cold—the weather, not the bread—that we had a terrible time trying to find a spot in the house warm enough for the bread to rise. We ran out of wood for the stove and had a terrible time kneading with numb fingers—kneading the dough, not the wood—but finally managed to bake a decent loaf. My poor mother swore I'd never be able to bake anything respectable, but she comforted herself with the knowledge that I could at least make good lemonade!"

"Oh yes," I replied, hoping that the crinkling of my paper grocery bag would sufficiently stifle the sounds of choked back laughter threatening to erupt from my throat.

Upon arrival home, I "refrigerated" what needed to be and shoved the rest of the stuff into a cabinet for Einstein-proof protection. Sure, he was a kitten, but cats of any age or size tended to possess preternatural leaping abilities. Dinner safely put away, I grabbed my bucket and that repulsive bonnet and headed for the garden. A few fresh tomatoes and an onion should help transform canned tomato sauce into a marinara masterpiece, right?

Tip-toeing around the chicken coop, I cast furtive, sidelong glances in its direction. The rooster-demon was dead, but I still got chills every time I came within fifty feet of chicken wire. Just as I was about to safely exit the "fifty feet" zone, my sidelong glancing caught sight of . . . something. I froze mid-step, clutching the bucket handle so tightly that my fingers were turning purple. It wasn't. It couldn't be. But, holy mother mercy, it was! True to the freaky nature of this geographic location and my freak-of-nature husband's science experiments, there was the ghost of that blasted rooster strutting around like he never died in the first place. "But I can't kill it again!" I whined desperately to myself, rapidly scanning my surroundings for anything that might beat a ghost-rooster into submission. Ultimately I did what anybody would do in my situation: I screamed at the top of my heaving lungs and hid behind a tree trunk.

Mick must've broken an Olympic speed record sprinting from the field and to my aid. Cotton wads dangled from his work hat and clung to the five-o'clock shadow sprouting in a virile fashion. It looked like the hat was snowing on his face. "What? What's wrong, Katie? Are you in labor?"

I pointed in the direction of our poultry anomaly. "There! Do you see it? It wants me. It came back for my soul!"

Mick did look slightly taken aback by the sight but quickly recovered and erupted with mad merriment. I found this to be the inappropriate response. "Seriously, you're going to stand there and laugh at me when Satan has obviously sent his spawn to torture me into insanity?"

Breathing in huge amounts of air, Mick tried his best to cease sniggering. "Only you could speak Shakespearean under the influence of sheer terror."

"I hate Shakespeare!" I short-temperedly and somewhat irrationally reminded him.

He had calmed down sufficiently by then to lay a comforting hand on my shoulder. I had a good mind to shove that hand off and storm indignantly back into the house. "This is a good thing," he continued in a voice freed from the influence of hilarity.

"How is this a good thing? Ghost-roosters free to roam the Earth and do who knows what to unsuspecting little me and mine? How will you feel when your progeny in here is forever plagued by an avian specter bent on his or her demise?"

He stared at my face for several seconds just processing me. Then, "No, it's a good thing because it means that, for whatever reason, the electromagnetic fields are building in strength."

"Great! Too much EMF makes you sick, and I'm pregnant!" I reminded him. "I don't need any help with getting sick." I just wanted to pick my tomatoes and onions and get the hades back into my secure, feather-free kitchen.

"Yes, my martini-loving darling, but . . ."

"I could use a martini."

"The baby can discover alcohol without our help."

"Yeah, I know. Isn't that what I just said? And where did that term of endearment come from anyway?"

"Phrase of endearment."

"Whatever. So you were saying in a 'calm-down-Katie' fashion?"

"I was saying that an increased electromagnetic field means that Eva and Timothy getting through to us can happen much more easily. It may be that Andy has been able to repair the system after all."

I took his hand in my bucketless one and dragged him with me to the garden. My mind was trying to manage this information within the parameters of the emotion-tossed brain of a pregnant woman who had just seen a ghost-rooster. "Find me a couple of decent onions, will you?" I directed as politely as possible while under the influence. My own fingers were perusing tomato options.

"You okay?" Mick asked tentatively, testing the soil around each onion bulb lest his wild-eyed wife decide to gopher-slap him.

It took several seconds for me to answer. There was a worm crawling on my tomato that needed squashing. "Yes. Now I am okay to a respectable degree. Ghost-hunting shows aside, seeing the apparition of that horrible rooster unnerved me. I can handle apparitions of serial killers or even devil-gnomes, but . . . but that thing hit too close to home."

"Understandable," Mick said, clearly in "understanding mode."

"Plus I'm confused about where we are, where we're supposed to be, where I want to be. I kind of like it here. I've adjusted. But I know we don't belong, and I know I don't want to go through labor without an epidural!"

"And they don't make a shade of face powder that matches your complexion."

"I know, right? What's up with that?" I muttered in agreement, finally putting the offending worm to its eternal rest. I briefly wondered if it would come back to haunt me as well. Damn . . . and what about the gophers?

"How's this?" Mick asked, holding up a particularly lovely and aromatic onion.

"Ooo, that's perfect!" Visions of the marinara sauce I would soon be creating forced all animalistic spirits from my imagination. The dill plants looked beautiful today too, and since there was no skunk protector in the vicinity, I grabbed several sprigs of the fragrant green herb. I cared little whether they properly belonged in marinara or not. They were going to be used, by golly!

Mick put his arm around my shoulders and steered me toward the house. "I know what you mean about wanting to be wherever and belonging wherever that is. I've started enjoying myself out there in the cotton rows, even though I dehydrate in under half an hour. There's something to be said for manual labor, especially labor that produces something so useful."

"Your calculations produce usefulness too," I conceded. "But I get it. Simplicity can be fulfilling."

Mick nodded. "That's it exactly. But we do need to go back if we can manage it. Who knows how miserable Eva and Timothy might be living our lives? And yes, there's the epidural thing."

"On that we're firmly decided! Anyway, I'm good now. Come in and grab some iced tea before heading back out. I've got to start simmering the sauce."

"Molto bravo, bella mia!" he said, taking me in his arms and kissing me emphatically.

I spent the next several minutes trying to decide if it was his love for me or the iced tea that inspired such romantic gestures. Content with either conclusion, I ditched the bonnet and donned a much cuter light green-colored apron with frilly ruffles around the edges. I looked like a 1950s housewife minus the high heels and a calendar that said "1950"-something. What misogynistic creep decided high heels should be worn while cooking, vacuuming, or—heaven forbid!—cleaning the toilet? Thank goodness Halston and Bob Mackey and whoever had more common sense these days, whatever "these days" meant.

Setting myself to work, I tossed a chunk of butter into a pot so it could melt while I peeled and chopped up onion and tomato for sautéing. Immediately after the butter splatted onto the pot bottom, I remembered I first needed hot water for the yeast to rise. "No microwaves or hot water heaters in the vicinity for a few decades yet," I reminded myself, removing the butter from the pot and placing it on a plate far from Einstein's gaze. He had quickly discovered from whence his food came and was already plotting invasion and conquest.

The stove happily blazing, and the pot prepping to burst forth with bubbles at any moment, I proceeded with my peeling and hacking up of the fresh dill, tomato, and onion. I salted, peppered, and herbed the hades out of the garden ingredients then waited for the water to boil so far more interesting cooking could take place. Finally the yeast was happily warming into life, and butter was melting away in the pot. Veggies and seasonings dumped into it, I stirred and stirred until everything congealed into a sweet-smelling concoction. Adding the tomato sauce, I stirred then lidded the pot to let it simmer without my interference. Was I good or what? All this thinking and planning ahead was going to get me into trouble one day.

A claw sliced across my bare foot as Einstein mewed excitedly up at me. "Come to think of it, you didn't have lunch yet, did you? Hang on," I said to him and sliced a hunk of fat off one of the steaks. "Bon appetite, mon kitty!"

Einstein tackled the cow fat like he hadn't eaten in a week. Halfway through his noontime gnawing, he uncharacteristically paused to stare off into vacant, thin air. For several seconds the fat wasn't touched, but then it was vehemently batted aside, apparently due to the arrival of something far more interesting. I watched with some concern as Einstein batted away at what must have been...invisible string? He swiped at the empty space around him, bouncing into the air and swiping his paws at something only he could see. It finally occurred to me, of course, what must be going on. "I'm happy that you approve of cats, anyway," I said to whoever was playing with my kitten.

Then shrugging my shoulders, I let Einstein continue frolicking with his unseen playmate. This bread wasn't going to bake itself!

Several minutes and countless flour poofings onto my clothing later, I kneaded my dough into an acceptable mound. Placing it into a bowl and covering said bowl with a clean dish towel, I searched the house for a suitably warm place for "the rising." The back porch ultimately proved to be the premiere spot, so there the bowl was placed. "Half an hour in the sun should do you good," I said to the inanimate dough. "I, on the other hand, would burn like a dynamite fuse in that length of time." And mentally cursing my unfairly fair skin, I retreated back into the kitchen to check my sauce concoction's progress. A tiny taste let me know it was quite satisfactory . . . better than burned biscuits anyway.

"Knock, knock!" I heard someone call from the front door. "Katie, are you there? You're not bleeding, by any chance, are you?"

I grinned and realized who it must be. Grabbing another dish towel and wiping my hands as I walked to the door, the amused face of Mrs. Simmons greeted me. "No, no blood today . . . well, unless you count the steaks."

Mrs. Simmons was quick to get to her point. "I can't stay but a minute, dear, not with my own supper to get on the stove. I just wanted to bring you this sign I made earlier advertising our new services."

"Services?" I asked, taking the sheet of paper from her. Aha, she had made an advertisement for my new make-up counter! "This is wonderful! But might I make one suggestion?"

Mrs. Simmons answered sincerely. "Of course, Katie! This is our exciting new business venture, after all."

"Well, I think we should let everyone know that their first cosmetics consultation will be free. You know, when I look at facial contouring and skin tone and then use one or two of the products on them as a demonstration. Then if they're interested in learning more, we could charge a small fee for any, let's see, any follow-up consultations."

"I like it!" Mrs. Simmons exclaimed, her face lighting up as dollar signs ignited in her eyeballs. "Perhaps if enough of the ladies are interested, we could even put on some sort of demonstration for the rest of the community . . . you know, possibly arouse more interest in the . . . what did you call them? Oh yes, cosmetics."

"I think that's an excellent idea! Will you be mailing these flyers out or just hanging them up around town?"

"Oh, I thought I'd mail out a few to the surrounding communities. They aren't so far away that the ladies might not be willing to drive a bit further for, for . . ."

"For feminine education's sake," I added by way of finishing her thought.

"Exactly! Well, I'm glad we're thinking in the same way, dear. Now if you'll excuse me, I'd best get back to Mr. Simmons's chili and cornbread." Here she paused to ponder the distant horizon before continuing with, "I think we'll be seeing some changes in the weather overnight. The air feels heavier. Best bring the plants indoors!"

I crossed my arms and considered her words. "Now that you mention it, there is a peculiar feel to it, isn't there?"

"Well, I must be off! Be sure to keep the windows open in case another tornado comes," And with that bit of bizarre conversational injection, Mrs. Simmons skipped blithely back to her store/home, if a woman of her roundness could be said to "skip blithely." I was happy that she was so happy, and I was also happy that I was going to be working a job that was actually enjoyable. It never occurred to me what repercussions might come of said enjoyableness.

Breezing back to the stove, tornadic thoughts were pushed to the furthest recesses of my mind. It made sense that people would worry about such things around here in this time. Tornado Alley hadn't found itself a new alleyway yet.

I, however, was too busy being inspired once more by flights of foodie fancy to worry about such things! Any fascination with violent weather would have to wait as I fired up my own life-altering invention: a sort-of grill comprised of a cookie-cooling rack sitting atop the open stove-flame. Laying the steaks onto it, I checked the sauce. Perfect! It wasn't long before Mick came tramping through the screen door and into my kitchen, sniffing the air for any telltale signs of smoke or charring in progress. "Mmm. That smells great. Hey, I'm going to take a quick bath, okay? I can't tell where the sweat ends and I begin, and it feels like I'm leaving a puddle if I stand still for too long."

"Sure, babe. Take your time 'n enjoy the cooldown."

He slapped my rear end a bit less energetically than usual and ambled to the metal bath tub thingy. After several seconds of him sloshing into position, there was total silence. Then, "Uh, Katie?

What's this rock-like lump sitting in the bowl here?"

Fudge! The bread! "Oh for the love of . . . that's my homemade bread that needs baking!"

"Well, sweetie, I think the summer heat beat you to the baking part. It has a very well-defined crust."

I rushed to my precious pile of bread and discovered that the outside had indeed started baking itself into crispness, but upon further manual inspection, I soon discovered that the inside was just a doughey as it was over an hour ago. "It just isn't fair," I sighed.

Mick splashed several droplets of water at me and added sympathetically, "But I bet it will still make some respectable Italian biscuits with a little butter and garlic on top."

I nodded. "Good call. I'm on it."

And so it came to pass that our special Italian dinner turned out to be special after all. The marinara was pretty darn top notch considering the confines under which I was culinarily creating, and to make matters better, Mick had sneaked in a bottle of red wine out of Mr. Simmons's private stock. Hey, it was 1922. A glass of wine wouldn't hurt the baby as far as present-day medical science knew!

CHAPTER NINETEEN

We were awakened entirely too early the next morning by the banshee screamings of gale-force winds and giant trumpet blasts of thunder. Lightning sliced through the sky at regular and frequent intervals, and there was a distinct tinge of green contrasting with the black of roiling storm clouds. Rolling over, I reached for Mick and a few more minutes of lazing about in the blankets. Even noisy storms made me feel safe and cozy, and what better place to feel safe and cozy than beneath the covers of one's own bed with one's own hubby?

My hand felt blank space where my husband should've been. I opened one eye and focused it on Mick standing tensely at the window. He'd drawn the curtain aside and was staring at Mother Nature's mayhem happening outdoors. Before I could ask what was wrong, he announced without expression, "And that's the end of the harvest. Not a single boll will survive this storm."

Concerned by the concern in his voice, I dragged myself and my belly from bed and walked to his side. A hint of fear wandered in and out of his eyes as I recalled Mrs. Simmons's declarations from the previous evening's brief encounter. "You've already managed to harvest a good bit of it. There wasn't that much still left, was there?"

"Half a field or so. That's a big chunk of Timothy and Eva's money being washed or blown away, and it's my fault."

"Oh honey, your brain is capable of controlling and manipulating more than most mortals, but even you and that hand-held trigonometric wonder can't control the weather."

"Yeah, but it's my fault they're both stuck in another time. If they'd been here, they might have been able to read the weather signs or wind vectors or . . . "

"Barometric pressure?"

"Yeah, thanks. I don't know. I just can't help but feel responsible."

"But even if they had been here, and even if they could tell sooner than we could what might be coming, there's no way Timothy could've gotten an entire half a field harvested before the storm hit. It's not humanly possible. Besides, you were totally beat when you finally came in for dinner last night . . . or supper, rather." It was "supper" in the country, not "dinner."

"He could've gotten more of it though. He would've known not to stop working when I stopped last night. A few more hours, and who knows what could've been brought in from the wind and rain?"

I grasped his cheeks in my hands and directed his mouth to mine. "Sweetie, you're a certifiable genius, but you still haven't quite achieved 'God' status. And if you ever do, I don't think I'll like you very much anymore."

That got a smile out of him. "Of course you're right, although I'm not sure it's wise telling you so."

"At least not this early in the morning," I added. "Who knows how badly I'll blow it out of proportion by noon?"

That got an all-out laugh out of him as I continued contemplating the violent outdoors. "That's assuming we don't all blow away first. Wow, I haven't seen anything like this in years and years!"

We spent another precious couple of minutes indulging in some heavy petting smack in front of the window for all to see, assuming there was anyone rowing by our window to see. To our surprise, there was "anyone" out, a fact that was made known to us by a wild pounding on our back door.

"What the . . . ?" Mick gasped and rushed for the porch. I grabbed my summer robe and followed quickly after him. Upon reaching the screen door and fighting the wind to get it open, Mick pulled a soaked Mr. Simmons into the house. "Mr. Simmons! Are you alright? Is it Mrs. Simmons?"

Mr. Simmons was inhaling deep breaths of air now that he could do so without drowning. "Twister . . . twister comin'! Just got word from friends of ours down in Austin proper. It's headed this way and movin' fast!"

My brain oscillated back and forth between excitement and terror. I'd been in the vicinity of tornadoes several times in my life but had never seen one. They were always obscured by trees or rain or both. For years, one of my not-so-secret wishes was to see one live and in person, but now that the chance was about to present itself? I didn't think I liked it overly much. "Is there a cellar somewhere nearby?" I asked Mr. Simmons, clutching my stomach protectively. The baby apparently knew what was up too because little Jane or Stephen was kicking at my insides like a molested mule. So much for the continued stomach placidity of recent days.

"Under the tool shed!" he yelled over the roar that was just now coming into our range of hearing. It really did sound like the rumble of a distant train, although that train seemed to be chugging closer and closer by the second. Without losing a single iota of time, Mr. Simmons grabbed Mick—who had already grabbed me—and was shoving us out the door. As he did, an updraft of wind ripped the door from its hinges and sucked it up into the sky.

"Come on, Katie!" Mick shouted into my ear. Apparently I had frozen in the middle of a newly-formed raging river-let as soon as I saw the door fly upward. It took the controlled and emotionless urgency in Mick's voice to get me moving once more. "We're almost there, baby. Keep walking. Don't stop."

One muddy bare foot trudged in front of the other until all three of us were in the tool shed and sloshing our hands around on the ground feeling for the cellar door. Mr. Simmons finally grasped a handle and pulled. Water splashed all over and around us as a tremendously welcome hole in the ground was revealed. "We never even knew this was here," Mick mused, helping me down the few steps and into the cool subterranean expanse.

Mr. Simmons had already "landed" and was lighting a lantern. When the wooden door banged closed and was firmly secured by Mick, the deafening roar had become a dull, buzzing hum like that of a bee hive . . . an inestimably massive, Guinness-Book-of-World-Record-breaking bee hive. "Timothy's grandpa dug this cellar out sixty years ago, or thereabouts. It's come in handy more than a few times since, especially this year."

Mick watched Mr. Simmons walk around the tiny room, feeling the wood-covered earthen walls to make certain they were still sound. "How do they look?" Mick asked.

Mr. Simmons gave the room another once-over before nodding his satisfaction. "She'll do. But once this passes, we should probably shore it up in a couple places."

I was staring wide-eyed at every square foot of the wall foot-by-foot. A cold shiver wracked my body each time I saw a handful of dirt fall from between the cracks. "But we'll be okay for now?"

"Without a doubt," Mr. Simmons replied, smiling for the first time. "I left Mrs. Simmons in our cellar, and it's in about the same state. I wouldn't have left her if I hadn't known she'd be safe, but I had to make sure you two were alright, not being from around here and all. I should've known Timothy would keep everything in proper working order."

"Cool," I responded distantly, sitting down on the dirt floor and pulling my knees into my chest. Well, as far into my chest as the kickboxer in my nether regions would allow anyway.

Mick sat down next to me and wrapped his wonderfully strong arm around my shoulders once more. I didn't think I'd ever become indifferent to that sensation. "So . . . still want to see a tornado up close and personal?"

"I'm kind of thinking not. Gosh, I hope all the buildings are okay."

"Even the chicken coop?"

"Gosh, I hope the rest of the buildings and the eggs are okay," I amended as the noise from above reached an overwhelming volume, and multiple two-by-fours began creaking from the increased strain. The very air seemed to be sucked away from us as my ears popped from the sudden and dramatic change in the previously-discussed barometric pressure.

"She's overhead now," Mr. Simmons muttered, but I only knew what he'd said by reading his lips. Not a sound could be heard above the hollow howling of vortex and spiraling debris. I clung to Mick and dug my toes into the dirt as if to better anchor us. The tornado demon had officially been exorcised from my wishful thinking.

"The latch!" Mick cried into my ear, somehow making his voice heard above the raucous din.

"What?" I screamed in reply.

He didn't respond, but instead, began crawling toward Mr. Simmons who was crouching in the opposite corner only a few feet away. Mick yelled something to our godsent friend, and I watched as Mr. Simmons jerked his eyes upward. My own gaze followed his, and what we all saw knotted my stomach into more knots than any sailor could've tied. The strip of metal anchoring the latch was slowly, painfully inching free from the soil securing it to the planet. "Shit!" I cried as instinct took over. In what felt like half a second, my legs had transported me up the steps, and my hands were on the wayward strip of metal. I was pushing it deeper into the water-logged mud that used to be dirt, willing it to hold steady for just a few seconds longer. Surely the storm had finished with us by now. I was certainly finished with it!

"Katie, no!" Mick yelled once my recklessness registered with his eyeballs. Then something, some force, pulled me downward just as the tornado decided to take the entire shed and splintering cellar door as souvenirs of its limited lifespan. Rain, mud, and varying pieces of wood, metal, and plant matter slapped my face and ripped through my hair as I crashed back down onto the cellar floor. It seemed that our ghost was a ghost for all seasons.

"This bites!" I screamed in angry, freaked-out tones that almost reached the same decibel level as the departing twister.

Mick held my head to his chest and covered it with his arms. "Just be still, hon, it's leaving now."

"Not before making me thoroughly cranky!" I bellowed in response.

It seemed like hours, but according to Mick's reality, it was only another five minutes before the storm had blown over our location. Now that danger had passed, I felt tremendously guilty for wanting to witness a tornado first-hand all these years and hoped intensely that everyone else was and would be okay. "I need a bath," I whimpered and finally allowed myself to crash into a torrent of stress-relieving tears. Mick just stroked my debris-strewn hair and held me close.

"Either of you hurt?" a much more practical Mr. Simmons asked. "That was pretty bad, but it still wasn't as bad as the mess back in the spring. That was a real doozy!" He slogged his way back to the steps and began to climb, testing each wobbling chunk of wood before putting full weight on it. "Guess we'd best take a look at the damage. Y'all comin'?"

Mr. Simmons didn't mean to be abrupt or uncaring or any of those things. This I knew for a fact . . . in my brain, anyway. However, my emotions had bound and gagged my brain, forcing it into a mental corner and out of commission. As a result, my mouth couldn't seem to force a thought into words. A long series of snotty sniffles were all I could manage.

Mick's brain was never out of commission though, so he promptly replied, "We're fine. She's just . . . "

"She's just suffering from Post-Tornado Stress Disorder," I was finally able to sputter. There. I'd filled my quota of civility for the day.

Mr. Simmons initially frowned in confusion but finally

acknowledged my words with a nod. After this many years of being married, he'd learned that—when in doubt—nodding was generally a safe response. He resumed climbing as Mick pulled me into a standing position. He still clutched me securely as I attempted step after really slow step. "Do you think you can climb up by yourself?"

"I'll manage," I said, still going back and forth between crankiness and crying. I would manage, though. There was no way I was staying down here any longer than necessary, even if there was a ghost rooster waiting to spur me in spirit. It was slow going, but I finally managed to make it up and out of the cellar. Mick followed closely behind just in case stumbling occurred, but all was well. It was a totally different story once we reached topside.

We already knew that the shed was gone. Some of the tools had survived but were scattered haphazardly throughout the yard. A couple of the sharper implements were stabbed through tree trunks, including my gopher-murdering hoe. Weirdly, it was stabbed with the wooden end going through the tree. The trees themselves were stripped of leaves, and only the huge hundred-year-old oak trees were still standing at all. Many of the younger trees had been ripped up and carried off to parts unknown. I had a sick thought of some random pedestrian hundreds of miles away getting one of our trees dropped onto their head while innocently meandering down the street. "I'm sorry," I said aloud, although I didn't realize it was "aloud" at the moment of speaking.

Mick was assessing damage to the house when he heard me apologize. "Sorry for what?" he asked.

"For that tree that got dropped on his head," I responded, pointing to a blank spot in the ground. I knew I sounded insane. "I sound insane," I affirmed just in case there was any confusion.

"Yeah, but the fact that you can acknowledge it probably means you're really not. How about this? It took the shed but not the house."

I stared up at the still-standing structure. It was rather amazing. "It took enough of the shingles though," I observed as we walked the circumference of the building. "Einstein!" I cried as the sweet little guy came careening around a splintered wheel barrow lying in the middle of our front yard. "I can't believe we forgot him," I whispered, hugging him to me. Einstein was filthy but otherwise unharmed, a state of being he immediately started remedying now that he knew he was safe.

"We should probably give him some bathing privacy," Mick said with amusement.

Then smiling happened. I really was going to be fine and set Einstein onto the water-logged grass to go about his sanitary business. "You saw what happened in the cellar, right?"

"Which part?" Mick asked. "There are several instances to pick from."

"When I was climbing up the steps to rescue the door? I didn't just fall, Mick. Something pulled me back down."

"I kind of thought so. I tried to get to you but wasn't fast enough. It's a damn good thing that something or someone was."

"My, but you've come a long way," I observed with a grin.

He grinned back. "By now, I don't really have a choice."

"True. We've really progressed from the Reese's Pieces and tar beer! Now maybe we ought to see if anybody else in town needs help since we know we'll have a place to sleep tonight."

Mick nodded. "Good idea. And after we've all gotten through this particular crisis, I'm focusing my attention on getting us back to the future. My blood pressure can't handle seeing you and Jane or Stephen in another situation like this."

"Aha! So you like my name ideas!"

"At the moment, I wouldn't care if we named the kid Genghis Khan. I'm just happy you're both okay."

Taking him by the hand, we walked throughout the town helping dig people out from beneath crumbled houses and generally helping restore order as best we could. It was still very early in the day, so we had plenty of time to accomplish any Good Samaritan tasks that might arise before dark. True to Mr. Simmons's word, his own cellar had held together—far better than ours, it turned out, despite Timothy's maintenance skills—and Mrs. Simmons was shaken but unharmed. For the most part, it looked as though the storm had only side-swiped our area. Over the next few days we'd hear reports of other sections of Austin that weren't so lucky. Based on the damage done, Mick and I ultimately figured the twister had been somewhere around an EF3. For the immediate moment in time, though, we were mainly concerned with taking care of displaced families by putting down pallets on every available empty spot of our living room, hallway, and bedroom. Under the circumstances, I probably shouldn't have worried about what Eva would think about all these people trampling mud on her new carpet, but I was worried anyway. Even Mrs. Mason gratefully, if not somewhat sheepishly, accepted a spot in a corner of the living room with her miraculously-recovered husband. I pondered offering them a bowl of beans, then repented of my wickedness.

Once Mick and I were finally tucked exhaustedly into bed ourselves, I couldn't help but muse, "You don't see too many storms like this around here in our time. Global warming must have its good points."

****

Our part of town got itself put back together within a week or so thanks to the hard work of each and every citizen. I couldn't help but wonder why it always took extreme disaster for people to pull together like this. Why couldn't such behavior be the norm? These were my philosophical ponderings as I made my way to the store for our very first makeover day. It seemed like appropriate timing to me: the town got a makeover, so why shouldn't the female population do the same?

Mick was already in the field attempting to salvage what cotton was still clinging to boll. He'd waited for the crops to dry out before bothering, and miraculously, there were still salvageable fibers to be bagged. He was borderline gleeful as he set out for a morning of picking. He was almost frolicking his way down the rows, in fact, but only almost. Science and math nerds would never be caught frolicking if they could help it.

At any rate, I'd lugged myself out the door under strict orders not to make all the women in town look like a music video prostitute. "The world wasn't ready for that look in our time, just imagine how people would process such an image right now," he'd said.

"Prostitute lookalikes aren't my goal," I told him. I was leaning more toward Elizabeth Taylor circa 1955.

"Well then, no Egyptian eyes, okay? It always looks like those poor women got attacked by a coal bin."

I sighed at the memory of his creativity-stifling recommendations. Men. They just didn't get it. It was ironic, though, that we only used makeup in the first place to impress those appreciation-less Neanderthals; but as was also the case with leather, our preferences were irrelevant. I did have to admit that, at least in rural 1922, leather pants and bustiers weren't exactly desirable.

The store's front steps now at my feet, I gripped the wooden railing Mr. Simmons had recently erected for my benefit. I felt slightly insulted by said railing when it creaked in agony at having to support my increased weight. "You try carrying around a writhing bowling ball in your gut, Mr. Railing. Then you can complain!" I'd taken to talking to inanimate objects frequently these days, especially when they annoyed me . . . which was also frequently. Yesterday I had repeatedly beaten Eva's biggest and best wooden spoon against her dresser because a.) the wooden spoon had slipped from my grasp and landed way out of reach on the floor at which point I had to bend my huge midsection over to pick it up again (the spoon, that is), and b.) the dresser had the unmitigated gall to leave one of its drawers open just enough for me to trip over it. I was very much afraid that neither spoon nor dresser would ever be quite the same, nor would my shin, which received the brunt of the drawer's wrathful impact. I so hoped my child wouldn't be cursed with his or her mother's clumsiness!

My latest mental aside eventually subsiding, I entered the store to the sight of Mrs. Simmons carefully arranging cheese slices and crackers on a silver-plated tray. "What's this?" I asked with a smile of greeting. "Are we opening a snack bar too?"

Mrs. Simmons looked at me oddly but only for a second. She quickly recovered and replied, "No snack bar, whatever that is, but I did read in a magazine last week about serving cheese and crackers at informal gatherings to add just a hint of class. I can't decide if it's too early in the day for wine though. That's what the article suggested should go along with cheese and crackers, but I thought maybe we should try lemonade in . . . "

Oh, I was all over this one! "Wine, definitely. It's what's being served in the big cities now for meals people call 'brunch.' Brunch is meant to be served between breakfast and lunch, and sparkling wine is traditionally served mixed with orange juice."

Mrs. Simmons listened with rapt attention to each and every word. She was always interested in the latest fashion trends in entertaining. Needless to say, such trends didn't generally make their way out quite this far from the city proper. "So do you think we should mix it with lemonade instead?"

"No, no, I think we should retain the purity of the wine's flavor in this case. It would complement the cheese much better than lemonade would. There's so much acid in lemonade, you know."

Mrs. Simmons nodded sagely as if she had been aware of that very thing and was simply testing me. "Right you are, dear. In that case, I'll finish arranging the horse doovers tray if you'll fetch two or three bottles of wine from the back room. We'll keep them tucked behind the counter here just in case anyone official-like comes nosing around."

I coughed back laughter at Mrs. Simmons's mispronunciation of "hors d'oeuvres" until reaching the back room at which point giggling erupted uncontrollably from within. Nameless Baby reacted with a series of violent kicks. Maybe he or she was joining me in my moment of glee. Locating the semi-hidden stash of classy-ish hooch, I carefully secreted three bottles inside the ample pocket of my canvas work apron. Speaking of which, I needed to find something a tad more feminine for today's protective work covering. You wouldn't catch the Estee Lauder Counter Ladies at Dillard's sporting khaki canvas stained with what I suspected were drops of Mr. Simmons's nocturnal alcoholic labors. I sniffed. Yep, that's what the stains were.

Returning to the shopping area, I noticed that a handful of makeover seekers had already arrived and were sampling the cheese-and-crackers tray. Mrs. Simmons was hovering officiously among them making conversation and retrieving a better grade of glassware for wine-serving purposes. She observed my return and hurried to my side with the glasses. "Very good. Now you go ahead and get started with your introductions, and I'll pour the wine back here." Mrs. Simmons indicated a hidden spot in a corner well behind the counter.

"Gotta stay one step ahead of the revenuers!" I said with a twinkle in my eyes.

Mrs. Simmons was deathly serious as she replied, "You certainly do. I'll serve the drinks shortly!"

My employer and her contraband sneaked into the corner as I made my way to our makeshift makeup counter, cheese on a cracker in hand. The counter was actually an old teacher's table from the original schoolhouse built back in the mid-1800s. The building had been recycled into bits and pieces for local housing years ago, but the table remained. I kind of liked it. No, it didn't scream, "L'Oreal me, baby!", but it had a likeable personality nonetheless. Geez, my mind was wandering way too much these days!

"Good morning, everyone," I began. "My name is Katie McClaren, and if you'd like to gather in closer, I'll give you a quick run-down of what we'll be doing today."

A few more ladies had trickled in, so I had a grand total of eight to educate in the ways of cosmetology today. Eagerness was written on the faces of most, but one or two appeared skeptical. I chomped my cheesy cracker then took a sip of the water—oh crap, it was wine—that Mrs. Simmons had kindly placed in front of me. I'd just have to make sure it lasted the entire session rather than finish it off which, I had no doubt, would encourage refills. "Now how many of you already use some sort of cosmetics, or makeup, as we more commonly call it?"

"I wouldn't be caught dead wearing that stuff . . . whore paint, that," one tall, plain, and surly-looking woman readily volunteered.

Interesting. "I'm sorry, ma'am, what's your name, please?"

"I'm Mrs. Reilly. Mrs. Reverend Christine Reilly," she replied with enough pride to fill the Serengeti.

Consciously infusing each syllable with politeness, I said, "Well, Mrs. Reilly, it's lovely to meet you. But if you aren't interested in learning how to use these products, may I ask why you've come today?"

Her already-thin lips grew even thinner in mute annoyance. Then, "My husband wanted me to come."

"I see," was all I could utter without saying something insulting.

"And I figured Mrs. Simmons would have wine," she added, raising her glass into the air and downing its contents in mere seconds.

Okay, so makeup was evil, but drinking everyone under the table was all well and good. Uh-huh. Hopefully I could do both Rev. Reilly and Mrs. Reilly's liver a service. "Alright, so does anyone else have something to add?"

A small-framed, absolutely adorable young woman tentatively raised her hand then remembered it had a half-eaten cracker in it at which point she lowered it, blushing. "Hello, Mrs. McClaren, my name is Lillian. Well, 'Lillie' for short."

I smiled to reassure her. "Good morning, Lillie, thank you so much for coming. And you all may call me Katie, by the way. I can see that you use a bit of lipstick and possibly . . . face powder, I believe?"

"I do use lipstick, yes, but only a little, of course. But no, I haven't tried face powder before."

My eyes must surely have registered surprise. This girl had flawless skin . . . the wench. "You have beautiful skin, Lillie. You're very lucky!"

"That's what I've been telling her for years," Mrs. Reilly interjected, receiving a quick topping off of her wine glass from their very-pleased hostess. "But she just won't listen. Little sister, I say to her, you could go to Hollywood and be in them new-fangled moving pictures with the looks you got."

Mrs. Reilly was a wild series of contrasts, that was certain. I suspected some quantity of insecurity was at the root of it since the sisters' looks were in as great a contrast as Mrs. Reilly's behavior patterns; but now was not the time to let my analytical brain get the better of my professional, humanitarian activities. I was about to move the conversation forward when Lillie stepped confidently up to bat. "I've told you a hundred times, Chris, that I'm happy here."

"Then you need to get married," Rev. Mrs. Chris said, emptying her glass completely of its contents then glancing around the room for Mrs. Simmons. Making eye contact with the good lady, Chris waved her empty glass at her. Mrs. Simmons frowned ever so slightly but dutifully approached the insistent reverend's wife and half-filled the glass with wine. Chris started to protest but finally shrugged and decided to pout instead.

Lillie's eyes blazed flickering flames as she retorted, "I'll get married when I'm good and ready! And just because you're not happy here or happily married, that's not an excuse to always take it out on me. You live your life. I'm not going to live it for you!"

"Well now, how about we get started?" I asked entirely too loudly. Chris was still pouting but with a face burning in anger to go along with it. Lillie, however, had regained her inimitable look of serenity and was smiling brightly back at me. If I could be as effortlessly beautiful as this one, I'd be serene too! I would've said that she should be in moving pictures too but then remembered the Black Dahlia and any number of Hollywood tragedies since. Lillie was far better off here. "If the rest of you would just introduce yourselves, I'll demonstrate our first product."

The remaining six ladies who had remained sensibly silent thus far introduced themselves one by one. "I'm Callie," said "remaining lady" number one.

"And my name is Abbie," said number two, another young one probably around Lillie's age. She went on to introduce a slightly older number three as well. "This is my cousin Hannah. She's visiting all the way from San Antonio this month . . . chicken pox going around down there, you know."

"Has she never had chicken pox?" I asked

"No," Hannah herself replied. "And I don't intend to."

"Where I'm from, parents try to infect their children on purpose. Chicken pox are much easier to recover from for children than they are for adults," I remarked, waxing a little too know-it-all, even I had to admit.

"And that's why I don't want to get them," Hannah responded practically.

"Point taken," I said somewhat sheepishly. The final two ladies genially and less verbosely presented themselves as Nancy and Anna Grace Potter from "over yonder." I assumed that I was supposed to comprehend geographically where "over yonder" was and did my best to appear knowledgeable. Overall, I was excited to work with this group. All of them had positive facial features that could be accented and enhanced by the products of this decade . . . well, almost all of them. I was very much afraid that Rev. Mrs. Christine's sour expression had been worn for far too many years to be helped or hidden in any way. Still, I'd do the best I could.

"Are we going to learn how to make that new Egyptian eye look?" Anna Grace asked with much anticipation.

"Daddy would turn over in his grave," Nancy told her sister, arms firmly crossed over her chest to emphasize the point.

Friggin' hades. Was I going to have to disregard Mick's advice at the get-go *and* possibly risk waking the dead? "We'll see," I replied. "That look requires some of the more advanced techniques, and we may not be ready for that just yet."

"And just why not, may I ask?" Mrs. Chris demanded, sloshing the remaining contents of her glass onto the floor. "We're just as . . . ad—hiccup!—vanced as whatever fancy schmancy place you come from!"

Oh boy. Here we go. "I have no doubt that you are," I carefully and diplomatically countered. "I just thought we could start with something simpler for now. You know, until you're familiar with the textures and 'feel' of the cosmetics."

Ghosts & Physics

Mrs. Chris hopped her bony backside up onto the makeup "counter" and promptly crossed her legs. For a woman supposedly inexperienced in the more practical applications of whore-ish behavior, she was doing a really good job of faking it. "Texture, schmexture. Lillie, come here, and we'll black up your eyes!"

Lillie looked at me, seemingly for direction or possibly escape. It finally occurred to me that my control of the presentation had already disintegrated thanks to the unhelpful combination of ignorance and booze, so I shrugged and motioned for Lillie to approach the bench. "So we're all agreed? You want to learn how to create the Egyptian eye look?" I asked for clarification purposes and also as a way of delaying the inevitable. They were all going to leave here sporting big, black bullseyes. Mick would never let me live this down.

Every last one of them nodded fervently, and Callie even started bouncing up and down ever so slightly. "The customer's always right," I muttered to myself. Then, more loudly, "Lillie, have a seat in this chair here, and I'll begin the demonstration. Chris, could you hand me that black pencil on the other side of your . . . er, other side of you?"

Chris had chilled out dramatically by now thanks to the introduction of brunch beverage concepts to rural 1922 female-dom. "This black stick thing?" she asked, leaning back on one hand and waving the kohl eye pencil around with the other

"Yes, thank you," I said, taking the black stick thing from her.

"Welcome," she said before tilting her head back and attempting to slurp the last molecules of wine from the glass. When that didn't work, she resorted to licking the glass rim for at least a full minute.

Wow. Bet the Estee Lauder ladies never had to deal with anything like this. "Okay, Lillie, now just relax. I'm going to start by penciling the edge of your lower lids. Hold still." I instructed and commenced to penciling. Lillie was surprisingly still indeed, and her eyes barely watered at all. When I first started using eyeliner, my eyes were streaming waterfalls of liquid saltiness. In seconds, Lillie's lower lids were done. "Now everyone, see what I've done here?"

The ladies were crammed together around me, each straining to absorb my every movement. The end result obviously pleased them because they erupted into enthusiastic applause, Mrs. Chris included. "Now that's what I've been trying to tell you, Lillie girl! You need two black eyes so you can leave this town and make it in Cafilornia!"

"She means 'California,'" Lillie sighed.

"That's what I said. Arizona," Chris retorted, teetering dangerously on her counter perch. "Where's the barkeep?"

"Oh lord," Lillie whispered

"Hey, it's okay. I've worked with far worse, believe me," I told her consolingly

"Really? Were you working in a distillery?"

"Pretty close," I replied, remembering that summer job I had painting faces at the local carnival. You never saw so many redneck drunks in your life except, perhaps, at a NASCAR event. "Alright, everyone, I'm going to do the upper lid now, and this part can get tricky. It's very easy to make the line too thick, so it's a good idea to sketch the outline of the shape then fill it in like this."

Each woman stared in rapt attention as I drew basic outlines of the Egyptian eye on and around Lillie's lids. By the time I began filling in the shapes, Chris was leaning in so far that she did finally tumble off the counter. When she didn't readily get back up again, I decided it would be best to just leave her there until we were finished. "And we're done! What do you all think?" I asked, handing Lillie a small mirror. While the look was obtrusively flamboyant, I had to admit that it inspired a remarkable spark in her delicate features. Upon seeing her altered reflection, her attitude suddenly transformed from that of shy, small-town country girl to one of, "oh, there you are, Lillie!"

"I . . . I don't know what to say," she stuttered.

"Told you so!" came a slurred voice from somewhere floorward.

Still in a state of revelation, Lillie got up so the next lady could have her turn; but she never lost that newfound . . . well, I guess you could call it "etherealness." I had my suspicions about how the girl's future was to unfold, but historical research mode would have to wait until I got internet access again. That might be awhile. "Nancy, it's your turn," I said as a giddy Nancy plopped down onto the chair. Of all the makeover candidates, poor Nancy was the least likely to benefit from this particular eye style. She had practically no eyelid whatsoever and kept breathlessly giggling every time I attempted to put pencil to skin.

"I'm sorry, I'm just so excited," she kept saying over and over . . . and over and over and over.

By the time I was able to finish, she looked like a cross between a raccoon and a Chicago Bear. Luckily everyone else had more tact than I and complimented her appropriately . . . everyone, that is, except Chris who had clawed her way up the wooden counter and back on top of it. "What the hell happened to you?" she asked the bewildered Nancy, still clutching for her empty wine glass. "And what does a girl have to do to get any service around here?"

Mrs. Simmons grabbed the remaining bottle of wine and fled to the back storeroom with it. I had a vivid mental picture of her locking it away in some secret receptacle, hidden from the view of revenuers and the local preacher's wife. When she returned, she was shocked by the sight of Chris attempting to make herself up like Cleopatra. She'd scribbled a swatch of black across her eyes and colored red dots of lipstick onto her cheeks, presumably thinking the lipstick was some sort of rouge-stick. "Hey, who took my rouge-stick?" she yelled, at which point Mrs. Simmons returned to the back storeroom and didn't come out again at all . . . until the mouse found her.

Chris was in the middle of dusting her face with the flour that she'd mistaken for face powder when a blood-chilling scream emanated from the previously mentioned back room. The scream was quickly followed by Mrs. Simmons and a little gray mouse, evidently terrified for its life. "Cheese! It's all the cheese crumbles!" she cried as she jumped up onto a vacant chair. The poor mouse retreated in the opposite direction of Mrs. Simmons which also happened to be our direction.

"Vermin!" Anna Grace squealed and hopped up on the makeup chair. Lillie and Callie had pondered doing likewise but were too slow in their ascent. They resorted to leaping up on a couple of molasses barrels sitting in a nearby corner. Nancy, Abbie, and Hannah were already out the front door and fleeing madly down the street. The odd looks they were receiving from passersby were not unwarranted considering the kohl-blackened eyes and freaked-out demeanors each were displaying.

At this rate, I was very much afraid that I was going to develop a reputation. For what, I wasn't sure, but I knew it couldn't be anything good. "I think we're done for today," I told Mrs. Simmons in exasperation. She shook her head affirmatively but didn't say a word.

I turned around, prepared to return the cosmetics to their appropriate storage bins but witnessed the overly-painted-up Chris capturing the mouse bare-handed instead. Whores of the world would've been appalled. "You're looking kind of pale, my little friend. Let's see if we can't get you gussied up for Sunday service tomorrow!" she told the mouse who was squeaking in desperation and writhing about in an attempt to wrench itself free. The final sight I beheld was that of Chris holding onto the mouse and trying ever so patiently to line its eyelids.

A strong desire to go home and bake the Reverend a condolence cake was forming deep inside my being.

*****

The walk homeward was more eventful than usual. Mr. Mason drove by in the beat-up farm truck Mick had borrowed from him to haul cotton. He started to wave in the typical friendly manner that country folk do which is to nod in the person's general direction and lift two fingers off the steering wheel. That constituted a "country folk" wave. Anyway, he started to wave but paused mid-finger-lift the second he fully realized just who he was about to greet. "Good afternoon, Mr. Mason!" I called, just in case it might spur him to complete his finger-waving action. His head made some sort of movement, so I shrugged and kept walking.

Two cats ambled lazily across my path, but once they caught sight of me, they blitzed off behind a building. Oh no, had the mouse talked? They should be running from that lush in sheep's clothing, Christine, not me! "Hello, Agatha!" I called, somewhat frantically, to the wife of our sort-of next-door-neighbor who had just appeared crossing the street. Okay, so technically she didn't live immediately next door but half a mile or so down the road. She smiled politely in return, appeared to suddenly remember that the Chinese were invading or something, and increased her forward motion by a few mphs. Had word truly spread this quickly? But it wasn't my fault!

At this point, my walking speed increased noticeably too. It had been an interesting morning, sure, but I didn't think it had been that horrible. "They wanted to black up their eyes. Who was I to stop them? It was our very first makeover meeting. Granted, it failed miserably, but I was only doing what the customers wanted done. It's their money, not mine!" I argued heatedly with the back door of our house. The door didn't respond, so I took that as a good sign and opened it. I should've stolen that third bottle of wine! Jane/Stephen could probably have used it as well, bless her or his little heart. The kicking had increased once Rev. Mrs. Chris started downing her second glass, and it was now officially naptime.

Replacing my nicer work dress with something comfortably raggedy, I set about figuring out what to fix for lunch. A sudden craving for taco salad swept over me, but that wasn't going to happen since Tostitos didn't exist yet. "Why aren't there any talented Hispanic women making homemade tortillas around here?" I wondered aloud, finally resorting to a Spanish omelet instead. At least I was keeping our meal in the same seasonings family. Under the circumstances, I had to consider it a "win."

A garden-fresh onion and bell pepper had just been added to my eggs when the back door slammed shut and Mick came running into the kitchen. "I've got it!" he announced between intakes of breath.

"Got what? Milk?" I asked.

"Why would I have milk? No, I've figured out how to help them fix the machine! If they can get candy wrappers through to us, we can get detailed repair instructions through to them! Why didn't I think of it before? An idiot could've figured it out!"

"Well, there's your problem: you're not an idiot," I logically countered, folding the eggs over just so to finish the last several seconds of cooking. Omelets completed, I expertly dumped them onto plates. How I could "expertly" do this, I wasn't sure . . . never made an omelet before in my life. Must be karma or good humidity levels or whatever.

Grasping the glass of tea I'd just placed before him, Mick gulped down the entire thing in less than ten seconds at which point I promptly refilled it. It had become a daily lunch ritual. "That's better," he said, only downing half the glass's contents this time. "Well, I finished picking what was left of the cotton and am taking it to the gin this afternoon."

"Very good news then," I said, finally sitting my tired, child-laden bones down at the table. Hunger had swiftly crept in with a vengeance after this morning's escapades. "Would you like some help?"

Mick's food appreciation was evident as he devoured my culinary creation. He paused mid-chew to answer, "You can ride along if you'd like, but if you're too tired, it would probably be best to rest. You worked this morning, didn't you? That's right! Today was the big day, wasn't it? How many unsuspecting female souls did you infect with Cover Girl Syndrome?"

"Cover Girl doesn't exist yet," I said, crunching on a chunk of green onion. "And to be honest, if I never give makeup tips again, it will be too soon."

"Yikes, that bad, huh?"

"Oh, everything was going well enough. They were all enthusiastic about the idea of beautifying themselves, but then Murphy's Law took over my entire operation, and it all ended with us being chased around the store by a mouse and the Reverend's wife sitting in a drunken stupor on the floor."

Mick was momentarily at a loss for words. Then, "So did you ever get around to making anyone over?"

"Yes, the mouse and the drunk didn't happen until the end. But get this! Every single one of them wanted to learn how to do the Egyptian eye! I didn't think anybody would care about that look pre-Elizabeth Taylor, but it seems to be the all-pervading thought in the minds of the town's female residents."

"Ah, so you disobeyed me," Mick said with a knowing twinkle in his eyes.

"I wish I could've obeyed you but didn't have a choice in the matter. They stampeded me."

He laughed. "Could any of them pull off Liz's signature look? I mean, I can't imagine any of the ladies around here looking anything but ridiculous sporting 'the Cleopatra.'"

"One of them looked amazing. You know Rev. Reilly's wife, right?"

Mick spat out a sip of tea. "She looked good in black eyeliner?"

"Hell no, she was the drunk on the floor trying to make over the mouse."

"Oh. That makes more sense. Who was it, then?"

"Her little sister, Lillie. I didn't even know she had a little sister and would never have guessed that Lillie was her sister had she not said so herself. Actually, it was kind of sad. Christine kept insisting that Lillie get a makeover and move to Hollywood to become a movie star."

"Yeah, they haven't heard about the Black Dahlia yet."

"I know, that's what I thought! I wasn't about to encourage Lillie who is a total sweetheart in no need of corruption. But Christine kept pushing the matter despite Lillie's attempt to make her shut up."

"Lillie likes it here, huh?"

"She said she did at which point Christine told her she needed to get married then."

"Sounds like a typical mentality for this time period. Go on."

"Anyway, Lillie told Christine to live her own life and stop trying to live hers which pretty much did shut Christine up. The sad part is that Christine really does seem to want to be Lillie, but at the same time, I don't think she's jealous of her at all. It's a paradox . . . a paradox within a paradox, even. It's a paradoxical paradox!"

"If a paradox was paradoxical, wouldn't that cancel out the paradoxicalness completely?"

"I think so," I finally said, my mind and tongue weary from expending all that mental and oral energy at the same time. "But when Lillie saw herself in the mirror, you know, after I'd finished the eyeliner? She seemed to completely rethink her entire existence right there in those few seconds."

"You think she'll go to California then?"

"I got that distinct impression."

Mick scooted his chair back from the table and rose to place his dirty dishes in the sink for me. He even proceeded to wash them again. What a guy! "In that case, when we get back to our own time, we'll have to look her up online."

"It's one of the first things on my to-do list," I said, handing my own dirty dishes to him. He scrubbed them down without complaint, and I gave his bottom an affectionate squeeze.

His head jerked up, and his eyes achieved their mischievous state. "Wow, really?" he asked eagerly.

"Yeah, why not? It's been awhile, and this will just make the cotton hauling that much more enjoyable . . . something fun to think about."

Mick had already grabbed my hand and was leading me to the bedroom. "Something to think about and expound upon later!"

CHAPTER TWENTY

The cotton sold, and for an unexpectedly good price too, considering that it had nearly been tornado-ed out of existence. "So here's our dilemma," Mick announced on the drive home. "Do we keep shoving all this cash under the mattress, or do we go crazy and open a bank account?"

I didn't answer immediately, taking time to consider the opinion of those in whose house we were squatting. "My first instinct," I began, "would be to say let's stick it in the bank. But since we know what's on the financial horizon in about seven more years, maybe we should deposit it now and leave instructions for them to withdraw it sometime in the summer of 1929."

Mick rubbed his chin, looking entirely too much like Commander Riker. Geez, I missed my *Star Trek*! "Of course by now they probably know what will happen in 1929 and can make that decision for themselves. Alright, it's settled: we'll deposit the cash first thing in the morning.

"That's true, you're a man of leisure now that the cotton is harvested."

Mick was incredulous. "Leisure? You call having to plow those fields with nothing more than a plow and a . . . oh yeah, we don't have a horse. You call having to plow those fields with nothing but a plow 'leisurely?'"

I smiled. "You could hitch the plow up to me."

"Maybe if you weren't pregnant, but under the circumstances . . . " he teased. "No, I'll talk to Mr. Simmons when I walk you to work tomorrow. If anyone has any idea where I could find a horse or a mule or maybe several sled dogs, he would. Then I'll run the money over to the bank."

But when we got back home and entered the bedroom, we quickly deduced that our money-depositing plan wasn't the preferred plan. "Poltergeist activity is annoying," I said, hands firmly planted on my hips. Einstein was behind me, hissing away at some unseen entity and clawing a hole in Eva's carpet rug. I asked to thin, empty air, "So are you ticked off because of the bank idea or because the cat is ripping up the carpet?"

"Whoa!" Mick shouted, jumping back as a wad of cash leapt up from the floor then floated slowly back downward. "I don't think they want it in the bank."

"Do you think they haven't heard about the whole stock market crash then?"

"Well even if they hadn't heard about it yet in our time, they certainly would've heard about it by now. They'd have lived through it."

"Maybe that's the confusion then. Maybe they didn't consider taking the money back out just before the crash," I contemplated.

Mick shrugged. "Or maybe they just know something else that we don't. Either way, we should probably nix the bank idea."

"Boo. You always want to do something else when I want to do something else."

He kissed the top of my disheveled head. "It's not my call, babe. Now how about I stash all this money while you start dinner?"

My mind was already assembling the evening's menu. I grabbed an apron from the stack of clean clothes lying on a chair and clumsily tied it on over my ever-expanding abdomen. "Good idea. Right now it looks like we just robbed a bank and probably shot up the town with tommy guns just because."

"What are we having?" Mick asked, piling the scattered bills into less suspicious-looking stacks.

"Soft tacos."

"Really? Where did you find the tortillas?"

"I didn't. I'm going to flatten and semi-fry a few slices of white bread."

"Creative."

"I thought so."

And so it was that we had what basically turned out to be taco sandwiches with a side of grease. This town really needed to import some nice, tortilla-making Mexican ladies, and pronto! Ruminating on both that thought and my fried Wonder bread, it occurred to me that my brilliant husband had been working on repair instructions to send into the future before being waylaid by ghost-vandalized wads of dinero. "Any luck writing up instructions on fixing The Time Traveler? Or rather, any luck writing up instructions on fixing The Time Traveler that mere mortals can actually comprehend?"

Mick grinned and soaked up a drop of taco-seasoned grease with the last of his faux tortilla. "I'm not that bad . . . am I?"

I patted his hand in mock sympathy. "Oh honey, if you'll recall, you told me college physics was going to be, and I quote, 'a total blast, you'll understand it in no time!' "

He blushed. "I did, didn't I? Well, I may have to let you read over the how-to list before we try to send it . . . which brings up another issue: I'm not entirely sure just how we're going to make this work."

My brain immediately shifted into "Ghost Hunting Theory and Methodologies 101." "Well, we may not have to make it work at all. We already know there's a higher concentration of electromagnetic energy in this area, right? So maybe you could build—they don't have batteries yet, do they?—maybe you could build some voltaic cells, or whatever, and we can create our own early-20th-century version of your localized and focused electromagnetic force-field thingy. Yes?"

"Interesting," Mick commented, now deep in practically-applied scientific thought. "You may have something there. It would be relatively simple to recreate voltaic cells with materials available now, although finding some of them could get a little tricky. It's doubtful that they have science supply warehouses around here. I'd have to make lots of cells in order to get a strong enough field to do anything significant, but since all we're trying to do is shift a couple of pieces of paper . . . "

"Yay! I have knowledge! Okay, just give me a list of the stuff you need, and I'll get whatever I can from the store tomorrow before coming home."

"We won't be able to get everything here. This may require a trip into Austin for the more specialized items."

"That's awesome! I haven't been shopping in ages," I said with much anticipation.

Mick sighed, accepting the inevitable. "At least there won't be any bras made out of leather to distract you."

I frowned. "And probably no Vietnamese people with foot-massaging bubble baths either. I could really use a pedicure."

I ignored the absence of beauty-aiding devices and trotted off to the bedroom for a blank sheet of paper and a pencil. I'd look stupid in hot pink nail polish right now anyway. Upon returning, I discovered Mick holding a tasty bottle of full-bodied Simmons contraband. "To celebrate," he said, obviously proud of himself. "I tried to get something sparkling, but all Mr. Simmons could suggest was adding seltzer water."

"Yeah, no," I said, gratefully grasping a glass of liquid bliss. Hey, French women drink when they're pregnant, so don't judge me! At least I think they drink. They do in books, anyway. "Here's paper," I remembered and handed the writing accoutrements to him.

"Okay, so first we'll need glass bottles, at least ten, probably. Then we'll need to get sulphuric acid, zinc plates, copper plates . . ."

My wine and I hung over Mick's shoulder while he finished composing. I could see "conducting wires, clips, and hydrogen peroxide solution" rounding out the list. "So how will all this work?" The second I asked, I knew I shouldn't have.

Mick had that irrepressible sparkle in his eyes again, the kind that generally didn't appear without a calculator in the vicinity. "Well, in its simplest form, a voltaic cell is made up of a solid metal called an electrode that's submerged in a solution; the solution contains cations of the electrode metal and anions to balance the charge of the cations. And a half-cell contains a metal in two oxidation states; inside an isolated half-cell, there is an oxidation-reduction reaction that is in chemical equilibrium."

"What?"

"In other words, the metal atoms of one half-cell are able to induce reduction of the metal cations of the other half-cell. This reaction between the metals can be controlled in a way that allows us to do something useful with it like producing an electric current that can be harnessed . . ."

"Never mind," I said, cutting his dissertation short. My brain couldn't get any more numb than it already was without ceasing to function completely, and I really didn't think my child would like that much. "Just build the things," I told him, kissing his mega-intelligent head before heading off to heat water for a bath in which I'd lounge lazily and sip my wine. Mick would be forgetting that I existed for at least an hour now anyway. Before giving myself over completely to the hot, steamy, sudsy water, I yelled, "And don't forget to ask about the horse!"

Mick murmured something along the lines of "remind me again in the morning."

*****

The next day turned out to be one of those days where the sky can't seem to decide if it wants to actually rain or simply look drearily depressing for the next twenty-four hours. "It looks like

November," I remarked as Mick and I descended the front steps and headed in the direction of the store.

"But it definitely feels like September . . . still too hot and humid out here."

"Try being pregnant in the heat and humidity."

"I'd really rather not."

"Oh, and don't forget to ask Mr. Simmons about the horse."

"You had to remind me."

"You asked me to."

"No, I didn't."

"You did, but you were also operating under the influence of higher math at the time which, justifiably, shorted out your memory neurons."

"Oh. Yeah, probably so. Well, I can think through the finer points of how we're going to accomplish this while the horse and I plow."

"I know I can get the glass jars, hydrogen peroxide, and possibly the sulfuric acid at the store. They carry some drug store items since your average country person doesn't like to go into 'the city' for much of anything. But it might seem kind of strange if I start asking for the other stuff like copper and whatever other 'soluble metals' you were talking about."

"Not a problem. We can go into 'the city' tomorrow morning and probably have some manner of power percolating by dark."

I batted my eyelashes and grinned goofily at him. "That's my knight, always ready to protect with his massive mental muscles."

"Hey, only mental muscles? I've developed nice sets of biceps and triceps hauling all this cotton around, you know."

I kissed his much larger right bicep. "I know. You're just cute when you beg for compliments." At which point he swatted my butt, as he so often enjoyed doing to the point of overkill, and traipsed off to locate Mr. Simmons and horse knowledge, flexing his manly arms and winking in my general direction.

"Men," I muttered as I ascended the wooden step and prepared to face any forthcoming make-up counter antics. I nearly decided to turn around and descend the steps once Mrs. Simmons rushed at me in an apparent frenzy of confusion.

"Katie! Thank goodness you're here!" she gasped, grabbing me by the elbow and dragging me to our makeshift make-up table thingy. There awaiting my arrival with unexpected anticipation were five husbands and one boyfriend, one of those husbands being the Reverend Reilly himself. "These gentlemen were wondering what you might suggest as gifts for their wives."

"I don't have a wife yet," the youngest of the men said, cheeks flushing with embarrassment.

Mrs. Simmons smiled and gave the young man an encouraging pat on the back. "Well, it won't be long though, will it? It's high time you were married, Albert."

"I'm only seventeen," he remarked.

"Exactly!" a much older man added. "He has plenty of time yet! Don't want to settle for any old broad, do you, m'boy? Give it time, give it time. Otherwise you'll be in my shoes thirty-odd years from now and buyin' high-fallutin' color in a tube tryin' to make the missus look like she did those thirty-odd years ago."

I refrained—with much effort!—from smashing a nearby bag of granulated sugar into his unenlightened cranium. Albert just stood there looking more sheepish than ever and attempting to hide himself behind the lipstick display along with Mrs. Simmons who had retreated there the second I took control of the situation. I imagined that she'd make an escape to the back room as quickly as possible. "Now then, Mr . . . ?" I began, addressing the misogynistic idiot who dared insult my gender.

"Reverend," he corrected, holding out a far larger and more weathered hand than I would have ever anticipated. "Reverend Reilly, ma'am."

I gawked wordlessly which only inspired a more amused grin on the good reverend's already-grinning face.

"Don't look much like a reverend, do I?"

Recovering my powers of speech, I replied, "Well, I must confess that you don't exactly, no."

Reverend Reilly nodded in apparent understanding. "I'm also a farmer . . . not enough sins in this town to employ a full-time preacher, so they only pay me for half-time. I got ten or so acres outside of town that my daddy left to me when he died."

"Oh," I said quickly, suddenly worried that we hadn't been near the church enough to recognize the local preacher. People were going to talk! "I'm sorry to hear about your father, Reverend," I said by way of making up for our heathenism.

"No matter. He died years ago, you know. My mama always told him the drink would kill him, and one day it finally did."

"That's terrible," I added with as much sympathy as possible. "Did he have a bad liver?"

"No ma'am, a barrel of whiskey fell out the back of a wagon while he was trying to fix a broken wheel. Hit him square in the head, it did."

"Oh my," I responded. Seriously, what's the proper response to something like that?

The reverend held his hat in hand and nodded somberly for several seconds. The other men squirmed, obviously unsure if they should mimic the gesture or just look somber along with their bereaved preacher. Finally returning the hat to its resting place, Reverend Reilly continued, "At least he didn't suffer. From then on I figured it was my duty to run the farm and take care of my mama. Mama thought I should try and make up for my daddy's sins by becoming a preacher...guess you could say I'm taking care of both duties now."

"And you have a wife? Christine, I believe?"

Reverend Reilly slapped an emphasizing hand onto the make-up counter which made me jump, Albert nearly run away, and Mrs. Simmons knock down that old hat rack she kept in the back room. He followed up the previous emphasis with, "And that's what brings me—and likely all of us—here today." The other men nodded their agreement

"And what is that?"

"We want to buy some of that face paint," an as-yet anonymous townsperson replied.

"But we need you to show us how to use it first," Albert added timidly, creeping slowly from behind the lipstick. "See, our women don't want to come back here to learn because . . . well, because . . . "

"Aw, forget about it, Albert. You won't offend me none by tellin' the truth. They don't want to be within a mouse's throw of my Chris."

The men shuffled around some more but ultimately had to agree with the Reverend Farmer's assessment. "I see," I said, and I really did see. She was a fiasco waiting to happen. "So how would you like me to demonstrate? Would you like to watch me apply the make-up to myself?"

"No, no, I figure the best way for us to learn is by doing it our own selves," Reverend Reilly continued. "Only we don't want none of that black stuff around the eyes. The women seemed to take to it, but we all think it made 'em look like a herd of raccoons."

More agreement from the men as I remarked, "Well, Reverend, I can't help but agree with you there. I tried to tell them, but . . ."

"Now, ma'am, you know you can't tell a woman nothin' unless she already agrees with it herself," he sagely commented.

My first instinct was to be insulted by this mass assumption but had to finally admit that the man had a relatively good take on the situation. His declaration certainly rang true in my own life, and I was woman enough to admit it . . . just not out loud or in front of so many witnesses. "In that case, Reverend Reilly, would you like to have a seat?"

He did so, politely removing his hat to reveal a surprisingly thick and healthy head of hair for a farmer. I was so impressed that I had to ask, "You have an excellent head of hair. What do you use to keep it so healthy and shiny?" Heck, I might invest in whatever he was using too.

"Oh, I been usin' that constipation medicine on it. Works miracles, it does!"

Or I might not. Mrs. Simmons educated me on that particular medicine and said that it had its uses, just not the use for which it was primarily intended. "Well, it certainly works for you. Alright, first I'm going to show you how to apply the face powder. It's going to be the foundation for everything else you'll be using."

And for the next two hours, I applied foundation, rouge, eyeliner, eye shadow, lipstick, and mascara to each and every one of those men. I had to admit, I was very impressed with the fact that they took such a hands-on interest in their wives and girlfriends, even if that interest was selfishly motivated. Still, knowing that the ladies themselves wanted to learn the correct way of applying cosmetics overrode any of that selfishness. Mick could learn a thing or two from these guys, although at the moment, they were looking very un-guy-like.

Mick entered the store just as my painted entourage was leaving, bags of brand new cosmetics in hand. I couldn't blame him for staring so shamelessly. Clearly in shock, he approached me very slowly and asked, "What have you done to them?"

"They wanted educating, so I educated them."

"On what? Paving the way for RuPaul?"

"No, you silly man," I replied, kissing his cheek. "Their wives were afraid to come back here after the whole Christine-with-the-mouse incident, and I honestly can't blame them. But the men were also interested in their womenfolk learning how to use cosmetics. Sure, their reasons weren't necessarily of the purest intent, but regardless, now both genders will be happy. The husbands can pass along my instructions and advice, and yeah. Everybody will be happy."

Mick was still staring at the now-vacant front door space. "It's like a disease you spread."

"It's a calling," I said "So did you get the horse? Oh, and I need to get the other ingredients! Hang on while I get it all together."

Mick "held on" in the literal sense, clutching the edge of a countertop. Evidently sheer disbelief wasn't going anywhere anytime soon. I handed him some chocolate. "Here. It helps."

That brought him out of his coma. "I wasn't the victim of a dementor attack," he said, taking the chocolate nonetheless. I well-knew his greatest weaknesses, and this was one of them.

"No, but you needed to be brought back to reality."

"Reality? With a Harry Potter reference?"

"Hogwarts is real."

"Uh-huh, and Dumbledore lives," he remarked, chewing contentedly on his sweet and creamy candy. "So yeah, the horse. He knows someone—actually, it's Reverend Reilly—who has a couple of draft horses. But now I'm half-scared to go ask him about borrowing one."

"Why?" I asked, bagging the last of our voltaic cell-making necessities

"Because I might leave looking like he just did."

I threw my head back and howled. "We can only hope! But I'll go along with you and protect the integrity of your manhood, if you like."

"You up to it? I mean, you've been busy spreading the Gospel of Maybelline all morning and must be exhausted."

"Not at all, my good man," I replied, looping my arm through his. "Lead on!"

We exited the store and began making our way to the outskirts of "town" where Rev. Reilly and Christine lived. Several women pointed and stared as we walked along the road, whispering to one another now and then. I quickly noted that none of them had attended my Cosmetics Summit Meeting and must therefore be scandalized at the reports they'd heard in the past couple of days about our drunken in-store escapades. You'd think that they could be less obvious and more publicly polite about it though. "We're being watched."

"I'm guessing that you've officially been labeled 'infamous.' "

"We may have to leave town sooner rather than later."

Mick patted my hand. "That's the plan, babe. Now . . . what the . . . ? What are they doing?"

I looked in the direction he pointed and was much amused by the sight of Rev. Reilly sitting beside his wife on the front porch instructing her on how to properly apply rouge. "You don't want two big red spots on your cheeks like a confounded Raggedy Ann doll. You want to blend. No, watch me now." He dabbed his finger in the rouge and began blending it into the skin of her cheek. She was watching, seemingly enraptured, as he demonstrated.

"Are we really seeing this?" Mick asked, disbelief returning once more.

"Oh stop it," I said, punching him playfully in the arm. "They're having fun."

"That's not the part that freaks me out. It's the fact that they're taking it so seriously that may induce cardiac arrest."

Mick got over his fear and managed to convey his horse request to the reverend. Christine offered me some lemonade, but I only accepted because there was no way that all lemonades could possibly be created equal, even in such a small town. After the first sip, it was obvious that, while sugar was added appropriately, the adventurous woman had also added her own magical mystery libation to the mix. I suspected moonshine and tipped my glass onto the nearby lawn anytime Christine wasn't looking, which was often. She was too absorbed by her colorfully made-up reflection in the mirror to notice much else, and I really didn't want my child to be born a confirmed alcoholic. "We have a new shipment of eye color arriving next week, if you'd be interested in trying some of it," I mentioned.

"I just might," she replied, carefully plucking a stray eyebrow hair. "But only if you'll teach me. I really do appreciate my husband's attention, but quite frankly, it's somewhat unnerving to have the town preacher giving these sorts of lessons."

"No doubt," I said with a grin. "I'll talk to Mrs. Simmons about arranging another class and let you know. But here come the boys. Time to head home and start thinking about suppertime."

Christine nodded vaguely, intent upon the eyeliner she was carefully applying. "Have a nice time," she murmured.

Mick was leading a massive horse and looking somewhat nervous about it. He was even more nervous about it once I was in close proximity to the hooved animal. "Not too close now," he said, holding up a hand to stop me from coming closer.

"It's a horse, Mick, not a charging rhino."

"Not too sure about that fact just yet," he countered.

We thanked Reverend and Mrs. Reverend then turned in the direction of home, or at least, home for now. A sudden mid-afternoon thunderstorm was looming on the horizon as we neared the back porch. "This better not be a repeat of the last weather event!" I said in worried tones. "And we'd better get horsie tightly tied up in the shed before it hits too. He might get scared and bolt or something."

Mick was already thinking the same thing. "This coming from a confirmed tornado chaser!"

"That was before a tornado chased me," I reminded him. "I'm going to light some candles in case the power goes out then get the battery ingredients sorted."

"I'll be back momentarily," Mick said, leading a surprisingly calm Belgian behemoth to the shed.

The power did go out, but the horse remained calm throughout what proved to be another nasty summertime tempest. There was no tornadic interference, but plenty of lightning, thunder, wind, and hail did their level best to peel the paint off the boards of our humble abode. We munched away on a comparatively uncreative—but easily-prepared by candlelight—dinner of cheese, crackers, and assorted sliced garden veggies. I suddenly missed the availability of ranch dressing, hip-expanding calories and all. Otherwise the evening passed pleasantly, the cool—albeit sandblasting—wind whooshing in through the open windows. I was now deathly afraid of low pressure systems and insisted that windows be opened in all rooms of the house during storms so the building wouldn't explode. Mick conveyed a different point of view. "The whole practice of opening windows during thunderstorms is a weather misconception. And personally, I think you should be more afraid of what Eva is going to say about the water damage to her new carpet."

CHAPTER TWENTY-ONE

Plowing was delayed thanks to the rain, so the next morning we instead headed into the absence of urban sprawl that was then the Austin city limits. I had harbored overly-grandiose ideas of just how much shopping I'd be allowed to do and was therefore understandably deflated when we departed only an hour after setting foot inside one store. Mick was maneuvering the borrowed vehicle back toward Eva and Timothy's immediately thereafter. "But there were no impractical clothing distractions. Why the mad dash to get back home?" I asked, pouting ever so slightly.

"Because I want to get back *home* home as quickly as we can."

He had a point. "Okay, but be prepared to endure some serious shopping excursions once we're back where we belong. I'm being cruelly deprived of such distractions these days."

"But you have a captive make-up audience. That's not enough?"

"Not hardly. Maybe if we could stage some fashion shows or something, it would help. But can you imagine Christine striking a pose on the catwalk?"

"Only if the pose involved a little brown jug. Even then, I think she'd just fall off the catwalk."

"At least it wouldn't be the wagon," I added with amusement

"Her wagon fell, crashed, and burned many brown jugs ago, I'd bet."

"Not to change the subject, but changing the subject, do you think you'll be able to squish some plowing into the schedule tomorrow? I'd really, really like to watch!"

Mick was immediately skeptical. "Why? Are you hoping to witness an impressive display of my manliness, or were you just hoping for a good laugh?"

"The second part. But seriously, you might need some help wrangling that critter into the plow leather strap whatchamacallits."

"That critter is the most easy-going, laid-back animal I've ever been around."

"What other animals have you ever been around?"

"Besides the rooster that escaped from Dante's Inferno?"

I shuddered. "Yeah, besides that thing."

"We went to the zoo when we were twelve."

"And the elephant stole your cotton candy. Yeah, that's what I thought. Well, as a more experienced animal-handling person, I insist on accompanying you to and assisting you in the fields tomorrow...at least until I start having contractions from the laughing part."

"Fine, but only because you need a good laugh. It's certainly not because I need the help . . . probably."

The rest of the evening proceeded lazily on my part and industriously on the part of that genius husband of mine. Okay, so your average third grader probably knew how to build one of these crude voltaic cells, but I'd bet a hundred shots from the famed brown jug that said third grader's life wasn't dependent upon creating it. Okay, so our lives weren't likely to be dependent upon it either, but there was an epidural in my not-so-distant future that desperately needed me there in order for it to be of any use. I'm pretty sure I annoyed Mick by repeatedly indicating that we should take some of this cheap copper back to the future with us and make our fortune, but I was absolutely certain I was annoying him when I drizzled one of the acids on top of the snack salad I was about to eat. At that point, I safely assumed it was time for me to go to bed and that he'd join me whenever he was good and ready.

I woke up the following morning at the usual time, forced myself out of bed with the usual difficulty, and wrapped Eva's fuzzy and comforting robe around myself. I stopped by the icebox for several eggs and the last of our latest slab of bacon then ambled into the kitchen where a still-sleeping Mick lay sprawling across the table, and Einstein lay sprawling across Mick's back. The square footage of table unoccupied by my sleeping sweeties supported several completed jars of cell-ness. Several voltaic goodies sat upon the floor as well and sparked a friendly good morning in my direction. No, they didn't actually spark, but I liked to imagine that they did because it would mean they worked and could help get all of us into our right times and spaces.

I rubbed Einstein's back for several seconds as he sank his little claws into Mick's back. Mick awoke with a cry of, "Ouch! I thought he liked to sleep with you."

"And a lovely morning to you too. No, I move around too much for him . . . always manage to kick the poor kitty off the bed."

"You've nearly managed to kick poor Mickey off the bed a few times too. Is it that time already?"

"Yep," I replied, cracking eggs into Eva's cast iron skillet. "And I've got a hearty breakfast in the works for you too. Something tells me that you'll need extra energy with all the plowing to do today."

"More than likely," Mick commented, rising slowly to a standing position and working the kinks out of his joints. "I'm going to go throw some cold water on my face and change. Back shortly." He kissed my ear and retreated to tend his morning toilette. I scrambled the eggs like a pro and slid a pan of tasty biscuits into the stove. "Just when I get the hang of this, we're leaving . . . hopefully," I said to myself.

"There are still ovens in the future!" Mick called from the bedroom. "And I expect you to be even more brilliant with the improved technology. There's got to be . . . "

He didn't have his scientific treatises on hand, so why would he suddenly stop talking? "Babe? Mick, are you okay?" I asked, wiping my hands on a dish towel, and making my way back to the bedroom.

Upon brushing past the semi-closed door, I saw Mick staring silently at the mirror atop Eva's dresser. "Well Katie . . . looks like the horsie will be Timothy's problem."

My gaze moved from Mick's pallor-stricken face to the mirror upon which was uniformly written (in my new "hooker" shade of lipstick): "Tonight."

"So much for the detailed instructions," I whispered.

"Andy came through after all. Well, my sweet, we'd best get those voltaic cells online then."

"How do you get jars of metal and liquid 'online' anyway?"

He just shook his head and shifted rapidly into time-transcending math nerd mode. I knew we wouldn't be chatting again until we'd reached the other side.

CHAPTER TWENTY-TWO

Eva raced to the employee restroom, rushing for a free sink. She'd just sliced her hand open for the third time this hour attempting to filet today's shipment of halibut and was vehemently declaring to her reflection in the mirror that, "I will not get blood on Katie's shirt! Wouldn't you know it: the one day I put off running the clothes washer and borrow one of her shirts instead, that's the day I let nerves get the best of me." She ran cold water over her wounded hand yet again and noticed that the skin had become decidedly pruny from moisture overexposure. "You must get a grip, if not on yourself, then at least on the knife!" she stated with resolve. Hopefully her inner self was paying close attention.

Josh knocked tentatively on the door and asked, "You okay in there? Need me to get you a transfusion or two?"

Transfusion, transfusion, Eva pondered. She wasn't sure what that was, but he sounded like he was only joking, so she answered cooly, "Ha, ha, ha. No, not right now, I think. I'll be back out shortly to finish the halibut."

"Sounds good. Just don't bleed all over the fish anymore. If it was a shark, it would've bitten you."

Eva lifted an eyebrow then shook her head. There were entirely too many—what did they call them?—pop culture references to keep up with. Wrapping and taping her hand up in another bandage from what they called a "first aid kit," Eva returned to her fishly duties. She was understandably flustered considering she'd just gotten very exuberant permission that morning for them to use the garbage truck that same evening, ostensibly to haul off the extra store garbage. Since Andy had commanded them to remain silent no matter what, she couldn't get word to Timothy or Andy until her shift was finished . . . which was in another fifteen minutes, assuming she could finish fileting the damn fish without cutting off a hand. Picking up her knife and resuming her work as quickly and safely as possible, she whispered, "I sure hope Andy has had more luck than I have today."

*****

At that very moment, Andy was careening as clandestinely as possible through the back alleys and side streets of the college campus on his discreetly pathetic silver Vespa. He couldn't believe what he'd just done and successfully, too! There was no way he'd be graduating in the next few months barring legal intervention of some sort. Do secret government agencies have authority to confer PhD degrees? He really hoped so. Either way, he would, at least, be protecting peoplekind from further government exploitation: the entire file his Professor/Evil Mastermind had on Mick's project—including its location—was hidden safely in his backpack inside the brown horsie Trapper Keeper from third grade that he kept for sentimental reasons. Thank goodness Evil Masterminds got bladder infections too and had to pee frequently, even in the middle of a doctoral thesis presentation!

Andy was shaking like a rotten, crispy leaf as he turned out of the campus and onto one of Austin's main thoroughfares. He really wanted to call Eva and Timothy but remembered that he'd sworn them all to phone silence. Normally self-chastisement would've taken precedence over such conspiratorial thinking, but considering who the Prof was obviously in bed with, Andy figured that even Agent Scully would've forgiven him just this once.

A police siren blared obnoxiously from behind him, and Andy's heart ceased beating, or at least he thought it did. He assumed it hadn't when he didn't fall off the Vespa from acute onset of death. He slowed his vehicle and pulled to the side of the street, prepared to face the government's wrath, but the police car drove right past him, ostensibly on its way to keep either downtown Austin or the local Starbuck's safe. "That doesn't need to happen again," he declared to himself over the noise of his pounding heartbeat. Blood rushed loudly in and around his ears which had a kind of reassuring effect since it meant he still wasn't dead. But he had to get to their clandestine meeting location in one piece too, so focusing on driving was probably a better way of spending mental energy than was fearfully imagining the layout of his solitary confinement cell at Guantanamo Bay.

As luck and the city's layout would have it, Eva's job was only another ten or so minutes away, minutes that passed quickly once the police sirens and visions of Navy Seals midnight-raiding his apartment ceased. He wasn't sure why he pictured Navy Seals. He was nowhere near the ocean. The important fact was that he was now pulling into a parking space and sprinting into the automatic sliding glass front doors of his destination, quite literally, because the door was broken, closed, and Andy had just rammed into it. Timothy, keeping lookout for the past half-hour, rushed to his comrade-in-time's side. "Are you alive? Can you hear me?"

"You're supposed to ask me how many fingers you're holding up," Andy slurred dazedly.

"That must mean you're alive," Timothy said with relief, slowly helping Andy to a shaky standing position. "Eva will be finished in a couple more minutes. Did you find out what we need to know?"

Andy reached back and patted his battered backpack. "It's all here, but do you think we could find the Tylenol aisle before hooking up with Eva?"

Hooking up, hooking up, Timothy thought. He had a long mental list of phrases, terms, and concepts he meant to ask Mick and Katie about once they saw each other again . . . *if* they saw each other again. "Um, yes. It's this way."

The boys embarked upon their pain-killing mission just as Eva finished washing blood—the fish's this time, not hers—from her fingers and ditching the filthy guts-covered apron. She waved a quick "good night" to Josh and headed for the front door where Timothy and Andy were to meet her. Before making it that far, she caught sight of Timothy guiding a disheveled Andy in her direction, Andy being focused on the medicine bottle and soda he held in hand. "What happened?" Eva asked.

"The door hates me," Andy replied before downing several Extra-Strength Tylenols

"He ran into the door when it was closed," Timothy more thoroughly explained.

"I did that yesterday. It's still broken."

"I figured that out," Andy responded. "At least I do have good news. All the information we need to locate and repair Mick's invention is right here in my backpack. You have the truck ready?"

Eva nodded nervously, but not without enthusiasm. "It's out back, loaded, and ready to go. Josh said his friend said we could use it for as long as we need to use it. Just leave it at the waste management plant once we're finished."

"Easy enough, at least in theory," Andy observed, his confidence gradually building. "But you said it was loaded?"

"Well, we had to take some trash to maintain the ruse. Josh had a couple of the guys from the warehouse stack some of it in there," Eva explained.

"Valid point. Alright, you two, ready to go? I have no idea how long this will take, so we'd best get moving. Oh, and do you have any undercover clothes?"

Timothy displayed a blank expression, and Eva's wasn't much better. "Undercover? You mean are we wearing underthings? I don't see how that's any of your business, but . . . "

Andy grinned for the first time since falling asleep the night before watching some random Will Farrell movie. "No, no, y'all. I mean do you have any clothing that can make you look less obvious and more hidden?"

"Oh!" Eva said with a laugh. "No we probably don't, but Josh mentioned that there were uniforms in the garbage truck we were supposed to wear . . . city rules, or something like that."

"Even better!" Andy said with much relief. As the three of them made their way through the hubbub that is a post-workday shopping experience and finally reached the back loading dock, they immediately realized that a certain potential issue was indeed an issue.

"Well. This could be a problem," Timothy declared, arms now crossed across his chest. There in front of them was the truck, but instead of it containing only "some" trash, it was loaded down with all manner of haul-able refuse. He even discovered a couple of bags sitting in the passenger seat.

"Eva, I don't suppose Josh mentioned where the trash is supposed to be taken?"

"He said it all goes to the waste management plant," Eva replied, turning and addressing Andy. "Do you happen to know where that is, I hope?"

"Nope, but thanks to these handy little devices, I can look up the address then program it into the phone. It has a special app that will talk to you and give turn-by-turn directions."

"We sure could've used that last year when we went to visit your uncle in Little Rock."

"We got there okay, didn't we?"

"Yes we did, but first we had to find our way out of Omaha."

"I told you I was a bad map-reader," Eva frowned.

It had taken Andy the length of their brief discourse to locate the needed destination. "Here it is. It's something of a drive, though, so let's get changed and on the road."

Timothy retrieved three respectably-fitting coveralls from behind the driver's seat and distributed them. While shoving in a leg, he asked, "Do you think anyone will still be at the plant? I mean, won't they expect us to leave the truck once we've unloaded it? It might seem peculiar if we drove off in it again."

"Possibly," Andy replied, fighting to get his arm into a sleeve. "I suppose we could always tell someone we have to go pick up another load, get our equipment, and then drop the truck off for the night."

"Sounds believable, not that I honestly know what would sound believable at a time like this," Eva commented, zipping her coveralls up to the neckline. "As long as nobody asks too many questions, we might just be able to pull this off."

"A zillion things could still go wrong," Andy reminded her, climbing up into the driver's seat. Timothy rearranged the bags of trash still sitting in the passenger seat then helped Eva and himself up into the cab. "We'll just have to hope for the best."

"Or a miracle," Eva added.

"That would fit the definition of 'the best,' now, wouldn't it?" Andy said, shifting the gear into drive and moving them forward into some manner of undetermined destiny.

*****

Their route was reasonably clear of traffic until Andy took a wrong turn and ended up on a packed downtown street during the early throes of an Austin rush hour. Half an hour and innumerable pedestrian-hurled insults later, they were finally able to inch forward at a consistent rate of speed. "We should've gotten a pizza or something. Who knows when we'll get to eat tonight, and I'm starving."

Timothy concurred. "I'd eat anything about now. Well, almost anything."

"Ugh, food sounds terrible. How can you even think about eating at a time like this?"

"We'll need energy for everything that has to be accomplished tonight," Andy reminded her, carefully making a left turn into a diner parking lot. "I'll make it quick and just order three burgers. What do you like on yours? Lettuce, tomato, pickle, onion, ketchup, mustard, cheese?"

"Will it be anything like the fast food burger?" Timothy asked cautiously.

"Yes, but with mustard and ketchup instead of that nasty orange sauce."

"Everything you said sounds good."

"The works it is, then," Andy said, disembarking from their cumbersome-but-necessary conveyance. "Coke to drink?"

"Ooo, yes, please!" Eva said with increased interest. Timothy only nodded.

"So be honest, Eva," Timothy said, once Andy had entered the diner. "Do you really think we can do this?"

"Oh, I don't know. I think we can, but I'm not entirely sure that we will. That is, someone could very easily stop us. It's the government we're going up against, after all."

"But we don't have a choice. Mick and Katie need to get back home, and so do we . . . just like the strange looking talking animal that flew away in the space airplane."

"That's right, he was always talking about home and how he wanted to phone it. I wonder where home was?" Eva pondered.

"Probably Africa. The National Geographic says there are lots of animals there that scientists haven't found and classified yet."

Eva nodded her agreement and grasped Timothy's hand. "I think we're going to be just fine. We'll find the machine, and Andy will know how to fix it. After everything that's happened, though, I don't regret anything that's happened . . . except the salmon. Do you? Regret anything, I mean?"

"Not at all, except for the couple of food disasters you mention," Timothy began. "If nothing else, I think I figured out how to build you one of the clothes-washing machines. I took it apart one night when I couldn't sleep."

"Was I snoring again?"

"Yep. But I didn't mind because it gave me a chance to write down what parts go where."

"Aha! So my snoring served a purpose after all!"

"It has," Timothy replied, kissing my cheek. "Now if we can just teach you how to read a map."

Eva smacked his shoulder just as Andy was returning to the truck with dinner. "I think I'm hungry after all," Eva said, tearing into the paper wrappings encasing her burger. A look of ecstasy appeared immediately after her first bite. "Why would anyone think this needed a special sauce?"

"Probably to disguise the fact that the meat it really from a horse," Andy replied with a smirk. "You both take your time with that, but I've got to mix eating with driving."

Timothy was already finished and shoving the burger wrappings into the paper bag-turned-waste-receptacle. "Handy that we're already in the garbage truck," he observed to no one in particular.

Tummies full, the rest of their journey to the drop-off point passed uneventfully. Traffic cooperated which, in itself, signified a miraculous intervention on some deity's part. Upon reaching the facility and backing into the unloading position, Andy's confidence was cautiously on the rise. After unloading half of the truck's smelly load, Andy realized that his body temperature was strangely on the rise as well. An unanticipated intestinal gurgling began followed by several waves of nausea. He let the Hefty bag he was hefting fall to the ground before doing the same himself. "Uh, guys . . . I think we have another problem."

Both Eva and Timothy recognized this particular sitting position all too well after their recent negative digestive experiences. "Oh dear," Eva said, laying a sympathetic hand on Andy's shoulder. "It must be catching. Maybe you should go hang over the edge of the giant trash-squashing gadget there. I have a feeling I know where this is going."

Andy dutifully and pathetically did as she suggested and abruptly emptied the contents of his recently-filled stomach. By now he was pale and sweaty and very ready to crawl into the nearest corner to die. "At least we were mostly done. There's no way I'm going to be able to drive though. One of you think you can handle the wheel, at least until my vision un-blurs?"

Timothy nodded in the affirmative while Eva shook her head vehemently back and forth. "I'd rather be chopping cotton dressed in dead cow skin on an August midafternoon than try to maneuver this thing through the outrageous number of automobiles moving at hurricane speeds down the road. I'd rather go grocery shopping with one hand tied behind my back on the day before Thanksgiving than even think about having to . . . "

"I can do it, Eva," Timothy interrupted, feeling it best to calm her down before she fell completely apart to the point they couldn't put

her back together again.
She took a deep breath. "Okay. I'm alright now. Help me get Andy back in the truck, will you? Now we have extra reason to do this as quickly as we can."

Andy reluctantly stood, greatly assisted by his partners in well-intentioned crime. Getting him up and into the truck seat proved to be far more challenging this time around considering their invalid was mostly dead weight. Eva climbed into the truck and pulled while Timothy pushed from his solid position on the ground. Eventually Andy was acceptably situated, the window rolled down in case he had a resurgence of vomit. He did, of course.

Timothy noticed several plant workers meandering around them, but none approached to ask for identification or a garbage bag quota or if they were in the process of subverting the government. He took this as a positive and climbed into the truck, feeling for the very first time that he was finally contributing something valuable to their cause. Eva had the quick and practical wit that helped squeeze them out of tight situations, Andy had the high levels of intelligence to help him fix Mick's magical mystery machine, but Timothy? Timothy was the agriculture guy. The crop-and-cow guy. Figuring out how many pounds of cotton were in the canvas sacks and what price he should be able to get for them was about as scientific as his brain could get. But now there was a task he could perform and perform . . . reasonably well, he hoped. He'd driven automobiles many times but not in such close and constant proximity to hundreds of other automobiles operating at—as Eva just observed—hurricane speeds. He very carefully turned onto the access road that would land them on the raceway known as an interstate.

"You're doing just fine," Andy said weakly, but sincerely.

"Yes you are, dear," Eva added, both her voice and reassuring hand passing along extra encouragement. "If I had to drive, we'd either wind up in the hospital or in the vicinity of Des Moines."

Timothy allowed himself a relaxing chuckle, suddenly infused with a realization that he could indeed do this. Then he remembered that he had no idea where they were going. "So where to now, Andy? How do I get us to the secret location?"

"Oh yeah," Andy replied, pulling his head out of the window and fully back into the truck. "We need to head out to the airport. First get into the far-right lane; then when the interstate splits up ahead, take the road to the left . . . highway 70 East."

"This is just ridiculous," Eva remarked, taking in the vastness that became Austin in the years since the early twentieth century. Unlike her wonderful new domestic appliance experiences, Eva didn't care much for the roadways soaring high overhead nor did she care for being the one actually doing the soaring. What if someone ran into them, and they soared right over the edge? And why did everything have to move so quickly? "At least if we fly off the edge and die, it will happen fast," she noted aloud.

"We won't fly off the edge, honey," Timothy promised her. "I think I've got the hang of this. You just have to pay attention and not lose patience. It's not that much different than driving in our time, after all."

Eva stared in stark disbelief. "We've been gone too long, in that case! Your memory is starting to go. I can deal with deveining shrimp, and I completely enjoy the machine improvements where dishwashers and clothes washers and re-fri-ger-a-tors are concerned, but . . . but doesn't it seem like we've lost something important at the same time? Like humanity has gone backwards in some ways?"

"There's the Eva I married," Timothy said with a grin. "Completely losing me after the first sentence."

Eva smiled and blushed ever so slightly. She often wondered why it had taken her so long to say "yes" to the idea of marrying her now-husband, and this moment of wonder was no different. They truly were an excellent team which was a good thing, especially right now. Following her own personal train of thought but entirely shifting the verbal subject, Eva turned to Andy and asked common-sensically, "Do you know what sort of guard they'll have protecting the equipment?"

Feeling somewhat better—or, at least, not so dizzy—Andy answered, "There was nothing in the file about what type or amount of security would be in and around the building. I'll bet it's top notch, though, based on what I saw the night they took the equipment from the house. There could be actual people, an electronic security system, or maybe even both."

"Okay," Eva began, deep in analytical thought. "Then we'll need a diversion if there are guards around . . . a really long diversion, with so much stuff to load. And what about guns? Ideas, gentlemen?"

"Guns are our biggest concern, yes," Andy said with a sigh.

"They'll have the highest caliber weapons and lots of them. We have exactly zilch."

"I saw something on the television several nights ago about a bomb threat at the airport. They evacuated everybody, workers included. Is there a way we could make a bomb threat at whatever building we're going to?"

"But how would they know we were threatening?" Timothy asked logically. "We'd have to walk right up and tell them face to face."

"Or write a note, make it into a paper airplane, and fly the thing in," Andy said hopelessly.

"Well, it is an airport," Eva said with mock seriousness.

"Could we phone it in?" Timothy asked with real seriousness.

Here Andy paused to dry-heave out the window and to consider Timothy's suggestion. "You know, that's generally how this particular felony is done these days . . . call in a bomb threat. And they have to take it seriously just in case, even though it rarely is serious."

"Can you find the airport phone number using that thing too?" Eva asked, pointing at Andy's smartphone.

"Easily. Oh, and I can even change the sound of my voice! I downloaded this awesome app last week that lets me sound like a robot or an alien or even like I just sucked helium!" Andy replied excitedly. He'd been wanting to prank-call Mick, but since the Verizon service area had yet to reach into the future, he figured he'd just have to wait. But this would be so much better than annoying Mick, especially considering that Mick was on his final doctoral thesis review panel.

"Then we'd better do it if we're going to. The exit sign for the airport is just ahead," Timothy informed them.

Andy quickly found the airport's main line, called it, and asked for the security office once someone answered. As far as Eva and Timothy were concerned, Andy's app whatever wasn't doing anything to disguise his voice at all. "Nothing's happening," Eva said. "You sound the same."

"Not to anyone on the other end of the line. I'm on hold . . . still on hold . . . horrible hold music…why would anyone record elevator-music versions of KISS songs? It . . . oh, hello! Yes, I'd like to report a bomb in the main hanger area. Actually, there are two bombs. One is mixed in with the luggage from Ft. Lauderdale, and the other is on one of the SkyChef delivery trucks. Yeah, that's right, mixed in with the pretzels."

Eva had no idea how to call in a proper bomb threat, but she suspected that this wasn't it. If one was going to commit a felony, one may as well do it right. Grabbing the phone away from Andy who was growing more flustered by the second, she demanded forcefully into the tiny receiver hole, "Look, enough small talk. You have exactly one hour to locate the bombs before they detonate, and you damn well better know we mean business. This is a terrorist speaking. Hey, how do you turn this thing off?"

Andy grabbed the phone away from her and disconnected the call. "This is a terrorist speaking?"

"Last week I watched a documentary about all the terrorist attacks. It's all really horrible, what's been happening. I can't believe anybody would do things like that to so many innocent people, but then again, I can't believe that a second world war is coming either. Do you think they heard that last thing I asked you?"

Andy sighed, and Timothy's knuckles tightened their grip on the steering wheel. "They probably didn't, but overall, that entire call was a fiasco. I don't know if they'll believe it's for real or not."

"Can we call them back?"

"Do you really want to go through that again?"

"No...we should've written everything out before we called them," Eva said, mentally smacking her head against the dashboard.

"There wasn't time," Timothy reminded her, his demeanor relaxing under the influence of his very practical nature.

"On the plus side, we really did sound crazy. Crazy people are capable of planting bombs, so maybe it will all work in our favor, I don't know," Andy said, trying to maintain optimism. This entire attempt was crazy, so why should the threat have been anything else? If they got out of this at all, time-travelling machine successfully loaded into the truck or not, it would be phenomenal.

"We're here . . . and just in time, from the looks of it. If they took the machine away on an airplane, we'd never get it back," Timothy announced, exiting onto the access road for maintenance workers and deliveries. "What building do we need to find? That must be in the file somewhere."

Andy thumbed through the small stack of specs and

miscellaneous documents, finally locating one specific photograph. "This is it," he said, tapping a finger against the black and white surveillance shot. "Now, we just need to drive around until we find . . . ."

Timothy took this as his cue to continue driving around while Eva and Andy looked analytically at building after building. Ultimately it was Timothy who asked, "Could that be it? That one over there on the left?" He pointed to one of the utility hangars used for plane repairs.

"I think so!" Andy exclaimed. "It looks like it's used for smaller planes too. That's a good thing since it means a smaller space to search."

"And a shorter distance to carry everything," Eva added, starting to feel the nervousness more acutely. Suddenly her stomach wasn't feeling so great either . . . stupid burgers mixed with intrigues!

The sun had mostly set, leaving only a few lingering colorful bands of burnt orange and deep purple. Cover of darkness would be helpful, Timothy thought as he turned the truck toward its destination. "No turning back now," he said aloud. A line of several police cars whizzed down the road now behind them, presumably headed for the main hangar. "Guess they're looking for the bomb then."

"Yep, they fell for it," Eva said, her eyes following the forward progress of the police cars lest they suddenly decide to turn around.

"Look there!" Andy half-yelled, staring open-mouthed as heavily-armed soldiers quickly piled into two black vans. "They must be responding to our phone call too. This is awesome! There's probably only a few of them left behind to stand guard."

"We hope, we hope," Eva pleaded to whatever Fate happened to be listening to her.

Timothy slowed the truck to a stop behind the hangar, searching for an obvious entrance into the building. "So do we just walk in?"

"What do we say if we run into someone?" Eva anxiously asked.

"Yeah, we haven't talked about that yet, have we?" Andy mumbled, trying his hardest to think quickly. "Well, we're in a garbage truck, right? So we tell them we're here to pick up the garbage."

"It couldn't possibly be that simple," Eva said, then, "Oh no! Here comes someone! Get out of the truck, hurry!"

The trio did their best to nonchalantly disembark from the

vehicle. Andy, still weak from being sick and calling in bomb threats, stumbled on the lowest step and crashed onto the pavement. Timothy slammed the sleeve of his coveralls in the driver's side door as he closed it and was fighting to disentangle the material from the latch's inner workings. Eva surveyed this train wreck in the process of happening and took charge. "Hello there!" she called to the approaching guard . . . the approaching very-armed guard. "What's going on around here? It's usually so quiet when we swing by on our rounds." She hoped with all her might that this guy was an "import" and had no clue how often they swung by on their supposed rounds.

"I dunno," the guard began intelligently. "We heard something about a bomb threat called in by a psycho Betty Boop. That's what the security office said she sounded like anyway. So what's in the back of the truck?"

"Nothing yet. That's why we're here: to fill up the back of the truck with whatever garbage needs to be hauled to the waste management plant." She was very proud of herself for remembering the proper term of the business for whom she was supposedly working. "So can we get to work?"

The guard leaned around Eva and surveyed her two helpers. Andy was hobbling pitifully along, bleeding from both knees and one elbow. Timothy was still fighting to free his arm from the devil door. "You got any ID?" G.I. Joe finally asked.

"ID?" Eva began. "Any idea about what?"

"I have our identification here, sir," Andy announced, coming to Eva's rescue and placing three small cards into the guard's hand.

After a couple of minutes examining the oh-so-very fake ID cards manufactured on a demo printer in the superstore's office supply department, he handed them back to Andy. "Looks okay. 'Course I don't know what garbage collector ID cards are supposed to look like." He seemed to hold his gun a bit more tightly as he made this observation.

Andy clammed up much as he had on the phone, but Eva made a quick comeback after the whole ID/idea thing. Squaring her shoulders and assuming a more haughty air, much like head garbage man's three-piece-suited wife, she said, "We prefer to be called 'waste collection technicians.' Being called garbage collectors undermines the dignity of our profession, not to mention the validity of the place of garbage within society."

Huh? Andy thought. Something about this woman reminded him so much of Katie . . . had to be the overgrown vocabulary and irresistible need to wield it like a big, obnoxious, dam-busting weapon. Maybe it was overcompensation for him beating her on the SAT verbal section.

High-powered military dude had the very same "huh" expression on his face but finally murmured, "They said Austin was weird."

Fearing the gig was up and Eva might need protecting, Timothy had thrown nonchalance to the wind and simply ripped his sleeve from the door. Bare-armed from the shoulder down, he rushed as calmly as possible to Eva's side. "Hello," he said to the guard with what he hoped would look like an unobtrusive wave.

"Go on inside then," gun-toting guard said. "But load up quick. I've got to get to baggage claim in, like, five minutes."

Timothy returned to the truck and backed it up to the entrance for easier loading. How the hell were they going to get rid of this guy? Andy considered. They had to get him to baggage claim now, not in five minutes. "His name is Harwell," Eva whispered, covertly appearing at Andy's side. "I read the name on his duffel bag."

"Where did you see his duffel bag?" Andy asked, amazed at her powers of observation.

"It's lying against the wall over there," Eva replied, pointing to a dark lump to their left. It was conveniently positioned directly beneath the flood lights and clearly illuminated. "Call the security office and pretend you're some captain or general or something and tell them they need Harwell in baggage claim right away."

Andy shrugged. He had no better scheme in mind. Ducking quickly inside the hangar entrance, the security office was almost instantly having an unpleasant conversation with a Major Burns demanding to see Lieutenant Harwell at once. Tapping his phone to off, Eva asked, "How did you know he was a Lieutenant?"

"Doesn't matter. Airport security wouldn't know a lieutenant uniform from a chief petty officer's. They're all dressed in black."

Eva watched in carefully-disguised awe as Harwell received an urgent call on his walkie-talkie device. He silently mouthed several rather obscene words then answered, "Right away, sir," to the voice at the other end of his walkie-talkie.

" 'Now we find out if that code is worth the price we paid,' " Andy whispered

"What?" Eva asked, completely lost
"Forget it. *Star Wars*."
"You really need to get over that."
"There's no getting over *Star Wars*."

Harwell was packing his armaments into the tattle-telling duffel bag and safety-ing the pistol hanging from his hip. Giving Andy and Eva a dangerously lethal look, he ordered, "And you will take care of business quickly, yes?"

Eva gulped. "Of course, of course. We'll be out of here within half an hour."

"Make it fifteen minutes," Harwell demanded. "And I'd appreciate it if you didn't tell anyone I left you here alone," he added while climbing into his black .007 van and speeding out of the lot.

"Can we even do this in fifteen minutes?" Eva asked, tension oozing from every syllable.

"If the equipment is sitting just inside the door there and we don't have to dig around for it? There's no way in hell," Andy replied.

They ran into Timothy exiting the entrance, a look of relieved elation on his face. "Is he gone? It's all just inside here, and it's been fixed!"

Andy grinned goofily. "They figured out the specs then! I knew that was a possibility in the event of NASA-level intervention but really didn't want to count on it. Then all we have to do is load everything up and take it to a secure location of our own. Still, no easy task, but it's a crapload of a lot easier than it would've been with everything in pieces."

Timothy and Eva were already carrying the first ion disperser/charger contraptions to the truck. "And that secure location would be?" she asked.

Andy picked up a stack of electrical cords and followed them. "Wherever we take this stuff, it won't be long before the CIA lackeys are right behind us. The most logical place for them to look first is Mick's place or mine."

"What about Eva's?" Timothy asked, pushing the already-loaded equipment further back into the truck so more could be loaded. They were making terrific time. "Nobody would think about looking there because of the shape that house is in."

"True," Andy considered. "The lack of security might be our best security. Plus they already looked there."

"Hey, boys, if you can't talk and work at the same time, then please just work!" Eva called, squatting down so she could get underneath the next ionic tower. They were at her side in seconds. In mere minutes, Andy was in full control once more and closing the back of the truck. This would never happen in real life," he remarked, shaking his head in disbelief as he climbed up into the cab.

Seated inside the cab themselves, Timothy asked, "What would never happen?"

"This!" Andy replied, waving his hands around in the air around them. "What are the odds that our crackpot bomb threat scheme would work and that each and every security person would be needed in the main hangar? No government agency is dumb enough to leave equipment like this unguarded."

"Apparently they are, Andy," Eva said. "Besides, they never considered the possibility that you'd turn traitor and try to steal it all back. Keeping a significant airport from being blown up probably took precedence."

"I guess," Andy replied, putting the truck into gear and mashing down on the gas pedal. Nice and smooth, don't floor it right away. He kept checking the rear-view mirror for any sudden tails, but the space between them and the airport proper was nothing but black space. Somehow they really had pulled it off with only the most minor of hitches. "So the burned-up house it is. Then we've gotta get this truck back to the plant."

*****

An hour later, the machine was unloaded, and the garbage conveyance was safely parked in the appropriate parking lot. The three would-be felons surreally found themselves cruising in a taxi back to Andy's pharmacy. He'd completely forgotten that all three of them wouldn't fit on his Vespa. Eva wondered why they were going to the store, but Timothy very reasonably replied with, "People would probably think it was strange if we asked the driver to take us back to a blown-up house."

"Oh. Yeah, probably. I'm really tired right now," Eva sighed, resting her head on her hand propped up against the taxi cab door.

Timothy patted her knee. "We all are, but it seems we have even more work ahead of us tonight."

Once they got to their destination, Andy bought several energy drinks and bags of Doritos, hoping desperately that it would be enough to keep them awake long enough to figure out how to operate Mick's creation before the federal powers-that-be found them. Unused to ingesting so much caffeine compacted into an aluminum can, both Eva and Timothy were bouncing off what was left of the walls. Or rather, in Timothy's case, he merely became more talkative. Eva zipped around what was left of her rooms, trying to straighten up the debris. Maneuvering her way in and around dead cockroaches and rat droppings, she chattered, "I used to keep my broom right here . . . and my mop went over here. I wonder if there's any way I could locate a bucket and some clean water?" She stood surveying the wrecked room with arms tightly crossed, a frown deeply creasing her forehead.

Andy glanced up from the plug he was shoving into a power strip. Once again they were ripping off electricity from his place of employment. "Hey, Eva? What good would straightening up this place do, anyway?"

"I don't know," she responded in a despondent fashion. "When one has company over, one simply cleans up, that's all. Oh no, and I forgot to get that dead mouse out of Mick's bathroom cabinet!"

"Well, they're not really 'company,' " Timothy interjected, absorbing the meaning behind Andy's every technical move. "They've been living in my—our—house for the last few months just like we've been living in theirs."

"I guess that does negate the meaning behind the term 'company,' then, yes," Eva conceded. "Still, I can't stand seeing this place in such a state."

"You put it in that state," Timothy bravely said with the hint of a smirk.

"Damn moonshine," Eva muttered as she kicked a sizeable chunk of charred wood across the room and out a windowless window space.

"Okay, I think I've gotten everything assembled and connected and plugged in, and . . . we just might be ready to start this process. I just need to find the switch or whatever," Andy announced, running his hands over the equipment in search of said switch.

"Mick was carrying something that looked like that television gadget thing you use for making the sound louder or quieter and changing channels, that . . . remote control! That's it," Timothy said.

"And he was making adjustments on a sort of knob-thing in the middle of the remote control. He would turn it, and that's when the room would start getting fuzzy. I had a headache for hours after we switched times. Gosh, I hope that doesn't happen again unless Mick and Katie went to the store. We're out of aspirin!" Eva said, downcast at the prospect of aspirinlessness.

Andy hurried to the giant black bag that had contained various and assorted remaining parts that weren't used for repairs, for whatever reasons. He semi-frantically dug through the mish-mash of metal and plastic components but found nothing even close to resembling what Eva and Timothy were describing. He grabbed the plans and speed-read each page, finally hitting upon what he was looking for on the very last page . . . of course. "Here's the schematic for constructing it, but . . ."

"You mean they didn't build it?" Eva asked in disbelief. "Can you? I'll go get the remote from Mick's apartment if it would help."

"Yeah, it would help, alright, if all I needed was HBO, but this . . . geez, this is a complicated piece of electronics. Well naturally it is, Mick built it.

"But we're out of time," Timothy observed simply

"Literally," Eva muttered.

"The government so-and-sos could be here any time."

"That's pretty much our dilemma, yes," Andy sighed, flopping down onto a stack of boards that appeared capable of supporting such a dramatic action.

Eva went back to her attempt at straightening up the room. When stressed, she resorted to cleaning something, and luckily, there was almost always something that needed cleaning. Brushing aside several dead bug carcasses, she spied something quite out of place for her blasted-out, pre-circuit boards abode: an object that looked surprisingly like a remote control. "Hey, look at this!" she shouted, snatching up the object and tossing it in Andy's direction.

Even as it soared through empty space, he knew she'd found it. "This is it! Great job! Now if I can just figure out how to operate it.

"I must've accidentally kicked it over there looking for a broom," Eva mused.

"You really thought there'd be a broom?" Timothy asked.

"You never know what some kid might leave lying around," she answered, blushing.

"Or some old train hobo, I hear they're way more interested in cleanliness these days," Timothy continued to jibe.

"Oh hush," Eva said, smacking Timothy's arm and hurrying over to see what Andy was accomplishing.

Moving his eyes back and forth between Mick's schematics and the device itself, Andy appeared to be making progress. "So the trick is to power it up slowly. There's already increased electromagnetic energy in this area anyway, so we don't want to overload."

"Yeah, that's what they said. Because of limestone and water and stuff," Eva added.

"And stuff, right" Andy continued. "Okay, I think I can do this now. Everybody get into the center of the circle or semi-circle or whatever."

They all moved into a wad an equal distance from each magical electromagnetic tower. Timothy, ever the practical one, voiced a pertinently practical thought. "Andy, what about the machine itself?"

"What about it?"

"Well, even if we're gone or Mick and Katie are back, the equipment will be here for the government to find. And if we all get stuck in the past, they could take it with no problem."

"Yeah, because when we swapped times with them, we could see the machine, but the machine didn't travel with them—or us—or whatever," Eva said.

"That's a good observation, actually. I wonder if there's a way I could safely expand the EM field beyond the towers. Dammit, I need a calculator!" And without another word, Andy ran across the street to the pharmacy, returning in a few minutes with a small package in hand, plastic and cardboard flying in multiple directions as he tore the calculator from its wrappings. "Alright, give me a couple of minutes here," he panted and sent his fingers flying over the keys, pausing only to scribble down solutions to whatever calculations he was calculating.

Eva peered over his shoulder and shivered involuntarily. "I don't know how you can drown yourself in numbers and equal signs and cosines and, and . . . I'd rather be chopping weeds out of the cotton patch!"

"And that's saying something," Timothy contributed. "Speaking of cotton, I wonder how Mick and Katie did with the picking this year? It was shaping up to be a good crop, if bad weather didn't get to it first."

"They would've had to harvest at least some of it by now. The money you hid all over the bedroom wouldn't have lasted this long. I don't understand why you don't just put cash in the bank."

"Now Eva, we've talked about this before. I don't trust banks, and after that program I watched last month on The History Channel, it's a good thing I don't."

"I know, the crash of the stock market whatever-it-is," Eva replied, then added with a wink, "Maybe we should wait a few more years to go back, huh?"

"Oh, I'm sure Mick and Katie would appreciate that, even if they do know it's coming. No, we'll make it just fine because we know it's coming . . . "

" . . . and we have time to hide still more money under the mattress. We're going to need a bigger mattress, honey," Eva observed.

"Got it! Got it!" Andy cried, running elatedly from tower to tower making more adjustments by punching numbers into electronic gadgets on each of them. It was a dizzying sight. "It was so simple. All I had to do was extend the peripheral equation to include a few more minor variables then reduce the centrifugal equation to balance out the extension, and voila!"

"Speak English!" Eva insisted.

"I am. Okay, so some of it was French," Andy replied with a frown.

"Then speak American!" Eva added, exasperated. She softened at the semi-hurt expression on Andy's well-meaning face and said, "Think of that, Timothy. Reducing the central fungal equation was all he had to do."

"I'm at a loss myself, Eva."

"Okay, you two, ha, ha," Andy commented, relaxing with the levity. "Now get back into the center here. I'm switching on the machine and getting ready to start adjusting the field."

"Do you think we'll see pieces of history when everything starts shifting?" Eva mused aloud.

"Well, we didn't see anything when we were shifted here, but maybe it's different every time," Timothy answered.

"And I think we have it! Hang onto each other, now. This will probably be a bit disorienting," Andy warned.

"What about China?" Eva asked as her quizzically raised

213

eyebrow started phasing in and out of focus with the rest of her body.
   "What?" Timothy asked
   "He said something about the Orient!"

CHAPTER TWENTY-THREE

"This looks bizarre," I observed, brow furrowed and hand on hip. I was staring dubiously at the conglomeration of liquid-and-metal-filled containers wired together and connected to . . . honestly I wasn't quite sure what the contraption was that Mick had it all connected to.

"Well, it would," Mick explained, carefully twisting still more wire into makeshift cable. "We're not exactly working with state of the art components in this day and age. They haven't even invented light beer yet."

"Fortunately for them! As for your electrically/gadgety components, I know. I just had the set-up all laid out visually in my head. I think I'll go rearrange it now," I announced, semi-waddling back into the kitchen to make sure everything was situated neatly and cleanly. Einstein rubbed against my bare leg then collapsed onto my foot as was his wont when in need of attention. I didn't have the heart to move plus my feet were too sore to bother anyway. "I know, buddy. I want you to come with us too, but cats might not do well with time travel and space warping. Eva will probably love having you around to catch mice and nibble any stray dollar bills that waft out from underneath their mattress though."

Someone giggled. It was a faint, barely perceptible sound, but I well knew what I'd just heard after the quantum freak show we'd been living in for the past several months. As chills raced up and down my arms, I felt a gentle pressure on my shoulder then what seemed like a couple of pats in the same spot. "Well, Einstein, I think you've officially been accepted into their family. I'm gonna miss you though," I told him, my eyes getting weepy and leaky.

"Hey, I think I've got it!" Mick called from the living room floor. Disentangling himself from the countless strands of wires and jerry-rigged fuses, he had an unignorable grin of pride and accomplishment smeared across his face. "And I must give props where personal props are due! I think I did a kick-ass job here."

I smiled and kissed his elbow. "No doubt you did, babe. And although I might regret it five minutes from now, would you care to explain how all of this will work, theoretically? And without speaking in Voltaic?"

"Sure!" he replied, as excitedly giddy as ever I'd seen him. "First I had to build enough of the cells in order to create a concentrated enough current to feed the primary centrifugal equation. Wiring those babies together was a job of work, let me tell you. Now, if there wasn't enough power to support the tiniest variable, then the peripheral equation would have to . . . "

"Never mind," I said.

"You always do that," Mick said, not without a modicum of amusement.

"I know I do, but at least I'm trying to give you 100% support even if I haven't a clue what you're talking about, and my brain turns to protoplasm after the first mention of an equation."

"You're a very supportive and helpful wife," he confirmed, kissing me atop the head as he so often did. "And I don't hold your love of words against you either. You can write a novel about this once we get back. Make us rich."

"Me make us rich? Honey, after what you've just managed to do with Gerber baby food jars, wiring probably left over from Ft. Sumter, and an unnaturally massive amount of twisty ties, it's you who's going to make us rich!"

Mick looked momentarily disconcerted in his almost-moment of triumph which disconcerted me. "Yeah, well, I'm still debating whether or not I'll go public with this just yet."

"Really?"

"I can't help but wonder what the government would use it for . . . probably turn it into a bomb carrier that can travel through time then blow up Bavaria before Hitler was born."

"I always wanted to go back in time and take a machine gun to the Alamo, but you have a much more humanitarian point," I agreed. "So can you at least start writing the scientific paper or treatise or whatever so I can edit? I feel the need to edit after all my non-contributions to this project."

Mick laughed outright, hugging me as tightly as my expansive belly would allow. "And edit you shall, my dear. Edit you shall! We should probably get this thing up and functioning. I don't know exactly what time beyond 'tonight' we're supposed to be ready, but . . ."

" . . . but we'd better be ready," I finished. "Right, then. I've got what few things we have bagged up and ready for transport. I left a note"

"More like a hand-written documentary."

"..." on the kitchen table explaining what I could, but do you think we'll be able to actually talk to them at all? I'd so love to know how they liked the future, and I'm dying to ask Eva what she thought of a modern kitchen! And don't think your snide remark went unnoticed, bucko."

Mick grinned. "I think it would be safest for all involved if we just made the swap. If we stop for a chit chat, as fascinating as that would be, we might all get stuck in one place or the other."

"Well, it would be great to get back to my waterproof mascara as soon as possible. The stuff they have nowadays streaks all over my face every time I so much as sneeze."

"So that was you creeping into bed last night and not Zorro?"

"Hardy, har," I replied and hit him squarely in the gut. Wow. His gut actually felt like a gut. "Didn't you used to have at least a four-pack going on there? All this outdoor work is supposed to help maintain abs."

"No, that would be a gym membership. Here we only have a cotton *gin* membership."

"Yeah, not the fun kind. It will be nice to get back to my Tanqueray too!"

"Alright, ya lush, I'm switching everything on. Just act natural."

I watched Mick move amongst the forest of wiring and pureed carrot jars with unabashed amazement. I mean, it was awesome the first time he made all this happen, but the crudeness of his equipment for the second attempt had me all the more impressed . . . and not a little turned on! His ridiculous amount of intelligence combined with that smarty-pants sense of humor was such a turn-on. I lovingly patted my tummy as little Jane or Stephen kicked. "Almost time to go home, sweetie, where epidurals and post-natal painkillers await," I mumbled to our future novel-writing physicist. He or she would be a second Jules Verne but with a much cooler name.

"Hey, how are you going to do this without a garage door opener?" I asked.

"I have it. I was able to make the original one work by plugging it into . . . okay, by plugging it into one of the jars, basically.

"There were a few potatoes that could've worked."

"They had gopher infection."

"Nice," I commended and let my eyes wander into the kitchen

while he finagled his mathematical magic with manually-scribbled calculations and modified time travel remote in hand. On the kitchen table next to my overly informative note, I'd also left a lovely vase of freshly picked wildflowers for Eva as a small "welcome home" token of our appreciation and an apology for anything about their lives we'd royally screwed up. But the flowers were no longer on the table. Instead, they were meticulously arranged on the kitchen floor to spell out the word "now." "Hey Mick?"

"Yep?"

"I think you'd better get that thing going right now," I announced, pointing a finger at the unusual floral arrangement.

Mick stared in frantic disbelief then raced from jar to jar adjusting fluid levels, metal rods, and wads of wire. Did I mention that this was all really bizarre? "It's too soon. I don't think we have enough power to boost the electromagnetic field to a high enough level!"

"Get in the center, babe, hurry!" I cried, suddenly terrified that he wasn't standing next to me. What if I made it, and he didn't? What if he splinched?

"I'm coming," he replied, tweaking several mechanisms one last time before tightly grabbing my hand.

"Oh my . . . Mick, look!" I directed, pointing my free hand toward a still-blurry sight just now coming into view.

"How the hell . . . they did it! They repaired the machine! Andy must be around here somewhere."

My heart pounding with elation, I watched with overwhelming excitement as the grinning forms of Eva and Timothy materialized directly in front of us. Just as they were about to come into clear, sharp focus—just before we could reach out and hug them—they began fading away again. The twenty-first century version of the farmhouse raced into clear view, as did Andy, who was literally bouncing up and down in his Doc Martens and waving to us like a five-year-old. "Really, Andy? Gone on any dates lately?" I asked before giggling and throwing my arms around his neck in vast amounts of gratitude.

"Lately, no. I've been too busy trying to right the time/space continuum after the two of you blew it to pieces. Doc Brown would be disappointed!"

It was Mick's turn to asphyxiate Andy with one of his bear hugs.

Ghosts & Physics

"At least we didn't break the Delorean. It's great to see you, man! I can't believe you worked it all out in such a short period of, although come to think of it, how long did it take you to work it all out?"

Andy was already rushing about the room and disassembling Mick's miraculous invention. "Tell you what: help me get this thing packed up and back on the road to 'hidden,' and I'd love to fill you in."

My brow creased as I crossed nervous arms across my belly. "Why do I suddenly have a bad feeling about this?"

"Because any second now the secret forces or possibly Imperial Stormtroopers will be here to lock us away forever."

"Oh geez, what was that you were saying about the government, Mick? And just how did the government find out about his project?" I demanded of Andy.

"Can we please talk about this later?" Andy asked, joyful triumph rapidly being replaced by tangible fear.

Mick gave me his "let's wait until later" look, I shrugged, then he and I both began helping Andy disassemble the multiple machine parts. "Where are we supposed to take everything once it's all separated?" I logically asked.

Andy had his head fully inserted into a space between several broken floorboards. His voice echoed as his reply began. "There's a cavern down here. It's not too deep but deep enough to hide everything."

I looked questioningly at Mick who was already assessing the feasibility of what seemed to be our only possibility. "If we replace the boards, it should be okay for the short term. Are you sure all of this will fit in there?"

"Oh yeah. I haven't crawled down inside it, but I used sonar waves to measure the expanse. There's room."

"What?" I asked disbelievingly. "Sonar? Do smartphones have a sonar app now, or did you just kidnap a bat?"

"The first thing you said."

"Seriously? They invented a sonar app?"

"For locating fish, or at least that's how it's marketed. I doubt they're allowed to market it as a 'hide stuff from the government' app."

"Not bad," Mick commented, helping Andy lower each tower thingy gently down into the space.

"I don't suppose you put down any throw pillows first, hmm?" I asked, assuming a spectator's stance at this point. My tummy kept getting in the way of any attempt to "lower."

Andy missed the humor, not that there was much to miss. "No, but I found a bunch of bubble wrap in the dumpster behind the pharmacy."

"Way to recycle, dude," I said. The lowering of the equipment into the conveniently-located cavern didn't take nearly as long as I'd thought it would. My manly man was flexing his beautifully toned arms non-stop which made me want to tackle him onto the moldy old boards right then and there (what was it with pregnancy that inspired such nymphomania?). Andy, heaven bless him, never took advantage of what hoeing and picking cotton for several months can do for the biceps. Still, he was panting his way through the process admirably.

"And I think we're done," Mick announced, breathing in deeply and stretching out his stiffening but gorgeous arms. He glanced around what was left of the room to make sure they hadn't missed anything. "Let's get these boards back where they came from and get the hell out of here. It's been way too long since I've had a Guinness, and I intend to imbibe as soon as we can find an open bar!"

"No fair," I pouted. "One good thing about the 1920s was that they didn't accuse you of child abuse for having a glass of wine."

"Or a bottle."

"Yes, darling, thank you. Or a bottle." I swatted his butt with a stray board.

Andy gave me the post-2000 accusatory look. "You're pregnant, and you drank an entire bottle of wine?"

I sighed. "In my defense, I didn't know I was pregnant yet. And don't think I've forgotten about the whole government conspiracy thing either because I haven't. You've got some explaining to do, and no amount of alcohol-related jibes shall distract me!"

"Calm down, Katie, he's on our side . . . now, anyway," Mick reminded me and he smushed the last board into place.

"It's mostly the pregnancy talking, but it's also the 'I can't have any Tanqueray' talking with a slight hint of 'I don't know if we can trust Fox Mulder over here.' Ya know?"

Both guys stared at me for a moment then exchanged glances you'd need a "y" chromosome to comprehend. "See?" I said half-maniacally. "Guys do it too! I don't know what you just said to each other without saying anything to each other, but you said something!" And with that, I plopped my baby-filled self onto a stack of boards . . . that had a nail sticking out the top.

My predicament registered with Mick even before it registered with my nerve endings, but once it finally did, "Shit. Now I have tetanus. Can babies be vaccinated in the womb?"

"Haven't you been vaccinated before?" Andy asked with much concern

"Well yeah, when I was born."

"No boosters?"

"No health insurance."

"Oh," Andy replied. "I think we have some in the store's pharmacy."

"Health insurance?"

"Boosters."

"Do you know how to give someone a shot?" I asked dubiously

"Well, no, but..."

I smiled. He really was just trying to help even if he was a back-stabbing, two-faced, brilliant invention-stealing government conspirator. "It's okay. I'll be just fine once the stab wound is all nice and disinfected. There's first aid stuff at Mick's place. We can go there."

"Want beer," Mick sighed resignedly. "Guess it will have to wait until tomorrow."

"Unless you want a wife and kid with lockjaw," I reminded him, allowing the boys to lead me outside and slowly down the sidewalk toward Mick's apartment.

"Come to think of it, that idea has merit," Mick mumbled.

"Shut up."

We made it surprisingly quickly considering the hobbling state of my walk, and by the time Mick had made a thorough inspection of my bleeding backside (unable to wait until tomorrow, Andy was sent to buy beer), relief finally managed to settle in. "It's not deep at all . . . not nearly as bad as I thought it would be," he informed me, gently cleaning the wound with rubbing alcohol and hydrogen peroxide then applying triple antibiotic ointment and multiple thicknesses of bandages.

"Shove a nail into your butt cheek, and then tell me how bad you think it is," I commented, rising carefully to my feet and gingerly patting the excellently applied dressing. "Good job though. There's enough cotton here to fill one of those cotton-hauling sack receptacles, but I think I'll live."

The front door opened and closed. I heard the deadbolt slide into place as Andy noisily entered the kitchen. Mick and I made our way to his location and were greeted by two gorgeous sights: a six-pack of ice-cold Guinness and a miniature bottle of Tanqueray. "For me?" I cried, hugging Andy for the second time that night.

"Well, considering your injury, I thought it might kill any germs that happened to make their way into your bloodstream," Andy blushingly replied.

"I don't suppose you happened to get any . . . "

Andy set a cold bottle of tonic water—diet tonic water, no less—on the counter before me. "If Mick and I weren't married, I might have to ask you out," I said giddily, reaching for the freezer and ice cubes

Andy was briefly stunned. "Wait, you're married too?"

Mick grinned. "Well, yeah. You don't think I run around knocking girls up without proposing to them, do you?"

Andy laughed and pulled a six-pack of his Heineken out of another sack. "Not hardly. I just can't believe it took you so long to do it. I forgot to ask: how far along are you anyway, Katie?"

I'd just taken my first glorious sip of the happy juniper-flavored liquid and was relishing this beautiful snippet of time. The snippet passed, and I responded, "Well, as far as I can tell, it's about six months. I really need to get checked out by a doctor though . . . you know, to make sure the baby is developing properly."

"And to find out if it's a boy or a girl?" Andy asked.

I looked at Mick, head tilted back in an intense state of guzzling, and raised my eyebrows in a questioning way. Once his head became level again, he shrugged and said, "If you want to know now, that's fine, but I kind of like the idea of being surprised."

"That's the right answer. I want to wait too," I said, pausing between tiny sips to open-mouth kiss the crap out of him.

"I can go if you two want to be alone."

Mick and I disengaged lips but kept hands locked together. Our drinks were in our free hands. "Not yet. We really do have a lot we need to talk about," Mick said. "Let's take this party into the living room. I've missed my overstuffed leather couch."

"I haven't. The leather always sticks to my legs when I wear shorts," was my practical observation.

"Well, honey, you don't have to wear shorts," was Mick's equally practical observation.

For the next few hours we swapped time-and-space stories, marveling and cringing in the appropriate places. It was genuinely terrifying that the government—THE GOVERNMENT!—could potentially be after us. I mean, can you imagine achieving "top 10" status on the FBI's Most Wanted list? We just might rank right up there with Hannibal Lecter! Mick was amazingly calm as Andy explained the reasons for his involvement in the whole scenario, calm probably because Mick was working on his third Guinness. I was tempted to get angry but remembered my Tanqueray and remained silent. After all, he did the right thing in the end, and who wouldn't be tempted by getting a perfect grade on their thesis and getting a big chunk of cash from the powers that be? Wait a minute, maybe I should rethink this whole "what's best for humanity" thing myself . . .

"But they don't know you're back," Andy was reminding Mick as I came out of my reverie "They'll be looking for me, Eva, and Timothy. If you two could change your names and relocate, it's entirely possible that no one will ever find you."

"We'd have to do it, like, right now, though," I added. "We can't even use our debit or credit cards without them being able to track us."

"Or our phones. Or our e-mail," Mick reminded me. "There's GPS tracking in them now, and what's private about a free e-mail account?"

"We can turn off the GPS," I suggested.

"Which might look suspicious in itself."

"Your cards could've been stolen," Andy offered after a moment's consideration.

"But we would have to be here to report them," I said with a frown.

"No, we actually wouldn't," Mick said, brightening at the idea. "If we reported them stolen, they'd be cancelled and become unusable. If they were simply stolen unannounced and without comment, we could still use them long enough to get cash to live on."

I was getting nervous, but it still made sense in yet another weird sort of "is this really happening?" sort of way. Another green mini-bottle would've been helpful about now. "And then we could leave the cards lying around on a street corner somewhere next to an empty wallet making it look like Joe Wallet-Stealer took it from us. So what, do we stage a break-in?" I asked for clarification's sake.

Andy, in full "thinking" mode, rose from the couch and began pacing around the room. "Exactly, stage a break-in! It would be simple to do since anyone who might look for you believes you to be in the past. Anyone who isn't looking for you could've been staking out your empty apartment and, knowing that it's empty, might break in and take whatever valuables they could find."

Mick nodded and reached for a fourth bottle. "Good thing I never got around to buying that new computer. Awesome. Now let's tear this place apart!" he said with uncharacteristic enthusiasm. He stood up, swayed momentarily, then fell back onto the couch. "But maybe we should eat something first."

"Awesome! Pizza delivery!" I half-yelled, clapping my hands together like a kid on Christmas morning. I'd really missed the fresh 'n hot grilled chicken jalapeno pizza that the nice people delivered right to my door for a reasonable tip.

Andy dug around in his back pocket. "Yeah, I still have some cash."

I ran for my purse then realized that all the cash I had would be antique by now, the realization of which gave me a great fund-raising idea. "Hey! Let's hock the rare, pre-Depression-era currency!"

"You didn't leave it at Eva and Timothy's house?" Mick asked.

"I forgot. We kind of had to leave in a hurry 'n stuff," I replied, feeling rather bad about practically stealing from them. But I got over it. "E-Bay, anyone?"

"Wait, my 'new computer' fund! It's stashed in the junk drawer over there," Mick said, pointing in his old desk's direction.

"Umm, well, not anymore," Andy informed them. "You may have had to 'steal' from Eva and Timothy, but they had to do the same to you, initially, at least."

"That's fair," Mick remarked, head laid back and eyes closed. "Everybody needs to eat and drink and buy laundry detergent . . . toilet paper . . . pool cleaner . . . "

"What would you know about buying laundry detergent?" I

demanded of Mick, seeing as how I was the only one who ever did any laundry around here and was in the process of picking up his dirty socks from the middle of the living room floor at that very moment.

But he was already out, snoring away as his body slowly processed the fizzy dark tar-beer coursing through his digestive and circulatory systems. I smiled sympathetically and covered him with the afghan his grandmother had crocheted for him when he was five.

"Poor baby," I whispered. "It's been a long day . . . or days, since we just covered about ninety years in a matter of seconds."

"It's true, though, you really will need to disappear as soon as possible. I have a few friends—well, family members, I wouldn't exactly call them friends—that work in the social security office and hall of records," Andy informed me.

"Really? What are the odds of that?" I exclaimed in ongoing disbelief, my face instantly lit by the aforementioned disbelief combined with relief. "And they wouldn't mind doing a federally-offensive favor for a family member who really isn't their friend?"

Andy grinned. "Well, they won't exactly know they're doing it. While conducting recent nefarious investigations, I stole their logins, passwords, and access codes. You know, in case I had to flee the country."

"Oh my gosh!" I cried, hugging Andy yet again. "Who'd have thought that your brief life of crime could be so redeemingly beneficial?"

"Not me, that's for sure."

The doorbell rang, and I ran to retrieve our beautiful pizza. I didn't even wait to sit down again before I had the box open and half of one piece in my mouth. But it was really hot, so I spit it back out again. "Wow. Hot. That's my spit-tained lump of pizza. You can get a piece from the other side of the box."

"Yeah, didn't really need to be told, but thanks anyway," Andy said, grabbing his own wedge of deliciousness. "And once we're finished, we'll destroy the apartment."

I considered the décor and couldn't help but admit, "I'd like to request full and exclusive access to ripping apart those drapes. They were hideous in 1963 and are still hideous today."

"They're all yours."

*****

Mick woke from his alcoholic stupor to the sight of a royally decimated apartment. I was passed out on the bed while Andy lay sprawling on the living room floor, empty pizza box for a pillow. "There better be some leftovers in the fridge," Mick mumbled and he slowly rose from the couch, rubbed his throbbing head, and investigated his refrigerator's contents.

"I saved you two pieces," I said, shuffling sleepily down the hall and into the kitchen. Planting a dazed kiss somewhere in the vicinity of his shoulder blade, I opened the pantry door and reached for the happy, sugary cereal that wasn't in existence where/when we'd just been. "And there's a dead mouse in your bathroom cabinet. Hey, did you notice how practically no one was overweight back in the day? The absence of stuff like this is probably the reason why. Farm labor might have contributed too," I said, crunching madly on a handful of my favorite breakfast vice.

"Pizza . . . ," was Mick's comment contribution, his words muffled by the fact that his mouth was full of cheese-slathered crust. "So you two had fun last night? Wait, dead mouse? What?"

"Yep, dead rodent."

Andy appeared next to Mick and edged him away from the refrigerator. Completely ignoring breakfast etiquette, he reached for his last remaining Heineken. "It's brunch time somewhere," he announced and popped the top. "Ah, that's nice," he said after the first sip.

"Ick," I said, immediately dropping the cereal and grabbing my pregnancy-affected stomach. "Not the best thing for Baby Jane right now."

"How's your butt today?" Mick asked, gently patting the body part in question.

"It's good. I re-medicated and stuck a new bandage on it just in case."

"You think you'll be able to travel comfortably then?"

"Oh yeah, butt injuries are the least of my concerns," I replied as the baby kicked the crap out of my bladder. "I'm actually starting to worry about baby-induced incontinence."

"I'll start working on your new identities," Andy announced, whipping out his phone and tapping like there was no tomorrow.

"You can do it from that thing? What about the GPS?" I asked, somewhat alarmed.

"I disconnected it. I'm now as under-the-radar as one can be in the internet age."

Verbally observing the obvious, I asked Mick, "I know I've already said this, but doesn't it seem kinda weird that we're really having to do this? These things only happen in books or . . . "

"Bad made-for-cable movies," Andy added, still swiping and tapping on his phone.

The father of my child smiled. "Babe, everything we've been doing for the past six months has seemed kinda weird. I'm actually getting used to it. If something normal happened, it might freak me out beyond recovery."

I nodded. "I see your point. Well, let me go pack some things—again—and we can take off as soon as Andy is done working his government-sabotaging magic."

"Pack light, okay? And please toss any dead animals lying around the apartment."

"Well poo. And I thought the desiccated carcass might add something to the ambience. There goes interior decorator school," I replied whilst disappearing into the bedroom. As I tossed the few fashionable yet utilitarian articles of clothing into a bag, Mick and Andy discussed various logistics of disappearing. I still couldn't believe this was happening. It all felt like we were stuck in a poorly-written adventure movie that probably would've starred Elizabeth Shue or Matthew Broderick before he got all Broadway on us. As if the concept hadn't been reiterated enough, this sort of drama didn't happen in real life to real people. Then again, we were warned back in 1985 how time travel could screw up one's mundane existence. As I was marveling at humanity's inability to learn from film history, Mick walked into the bedroom and handed me a little blue card. "Here ya go, Rachel."

"For real?" I asked, taking the card from him. "So is this me now? What name did you get?"

Mick showed me his own fake social security card. He was grinning at his cleverness as he replied, "Ross."

"Oh geez," I said with an eye roll. "Can we at least have a different last name?"

"Yes. We are now officially Ross and Rachel Aniston."

"This is getting worse by the second," I sighed, plopping down onto the bed and clutching a pillow to my chest. "Hey, how did you get the card to look so authentic anyway?"

"Andy has an app."

"There's an app for forging social security cards?"

"There's an app for everything."

"Well, I'm glad you had ink in your printer for a change. Otherwise, I think I have everything packed that we'll need right away. And get this: I found a huge wad of cash under the mattress!"

Mick laughed as he took the money I held out to him. "How much?"

"There's almost $500 there."

"That's exactly what I had saved in my computer fund. I'm impressed."

"It should last us awhile if we're careful and until we get jobs. Speaking of which, I don't suppose Andy forged us some college degrees that might procure lucrative, baby-supporting employment?"

"Actually, that's what he's working on right now."

"So he can hack into the college's system too?"

"Apparently. His questionable integrity aside, I seem to have been underestimating the guy for years."

"Hey, you ought to be grateful for that questionable integrity about now," Andy advised, making his grand entrance into the bedroom and clutching official-looking pieces of paper. "Besides, the feds deserve it, and you're my friends. I always take care of my friends."

"Just not your family," I added.

"Exactly. Here are your educational credentials, if you will."

I took the papers from him and found myself quite pleased to be holding the most inexpensive and easily-acquired Master of English degree in the history of English degrees. "Crap, does this mean I have to teach?"

"You could teach college online . . . better anonymity that way anyhow. And Mick, with that piece of paper and your practical experience, you can get a job wherever you want. I also threw some rather glowing professorial recommendations into your file just in case."

Mick eyed his PhD with equanimity. "Well, it's not like I wouldn't have earned it eventually anyway."

"So we're good?" I asked, ready to embark upon our new and unexpected life together. Baby Jane—by now I was convinced she would be a little girl—was digging what had to be her elbow into my backbone, apparently as ready as I was to get out of here.

Mick touched my cheek and smiled. "Almost."

*****

We walked, hand in hand, through swishing grass and rows of monumental stone in various stages of weathering. I clutched two bouquets of the best flowers the local convenience store had to offer—hey, we were on a budget!—as a small "thank you" gesture to our time-transcending cohorts. My heart was pounding with the excitement of coming full circle . . . a very fantastic full circle. "They would have to be towards the back with the older grave stones."

Mick nodded and squeezed my hand. "Andy said they're in this section to the right, and I think . . . wow. Here they are."

We were completely silent, my blood pressure the only sound registering with my ears. There in front of us were the graves of our space-swapping counterparts and friends, Eva and Timothy. My eyes overflowed with tears, and I even noticed Mick wiping something from his own cheek. "1965 and 1966," I whispered. "They got to see a lot."

"Mmmhmmm," Mick acknowledged. "And look at this!" he directed, helping me kneel on the ground.

Tears still flowing freely, I also doubled over with laughter upon reading Eva's epitaph, "'Dog hair makes me sneeze.' That explains the flying cup! What does Timothy's say?"

"Let's see," Mick began, brushing grass from in front of the weathered stone. "It says, 'Thanks for getting rid of the gophers.'"

I rolled on the ground like a silly kid, giggling maniacally. Mick was leaned up against Timothy's grave stone doing precisely the same thing. "Obviously they did okay," he said between gasps for air.

"And they must not have minded that we murdered their rooster. I still feel kind of bad about that, but only 'kind of.' I wonder if they kept farming."

"I'm sure," Mick replied, rising from the grass and helping me to my feet. "But I also like to imagine that they were able to apply some of their futuristic experiences as well."

"It's a shame we can't take care of their graves or something," I said, carefully laying the flowers against both headstones. "Maybe one day we can come back here to live and raise the kid. And maybe when we die, we can go back in time and helpfully haunt them like they did us!"

Mick dug my digital camera out of our communal bag and snapped several pictures of Eva's and Timothy's plots. While snapping several shots, he noticed a much smaller, slightly crumbling gravestone to the right of Eva's. "Hey, Katie, take a look at this."

I halted my retreat the car and returned to kneel beside him. "It looks like a baby's grave marker. 'Katherine Mildred Reed, born 1925, died...' It doesn't say when she died."

"A daughter, then?" Mick asked.

"It has to be, but why would there be a grave here if she hasn't died yet?"

"Maybe Eva and Timothy were simply planning ahead?"

I frowned in concentration as I considered the whys and wherefores presented to us. This was a new kind of mystery, one that I fully intended to get to the bottom of as soon as I could. "They could have. This sort of thing is typical for husbands and wives but not so much for children still living."

"I share your curiosity, but for now, we've got new identities to assume. The longer we stick around, the more dangerous the situation becomes. You ready?"

Forcing my attention from the three unassuming graves, I rose and brushed dirt from my jeans. "Yessir, I'm ready."

Baby Jane kicked her agreement as we climbed into my car. Andy had sold Mick's car to a chop shop he knew of and handed us the cash. A guy with such a variety of dubious connections like his would be able to evade any government capture, I had no doubt. As Mick shifted the car into drive and accelerated us out of the Austin city limits and into parts unknown, I noticed one particular eatery/seafood market for the very first time: "Eva's Fish and Sea Sundries." She'd done it! She'd gotten all progressive! Pointing the business out to Mick, I couldn't help but ask, "Hey, do we have time for lunch? You know, before we become all nomadic 'n stuff and have to live on Vienna sausages and Ramen noodles?"

Mick took his foot off the accelerator while his mind considered the possibility of sudden capture and incarceration should we pause to enjoy food that didn't come prepackaged. He and his growling tummy eventually nodded their approval. "A burger does sound good.

"A burger??"

ABOUT THE AUTHOR

April Arnold, a daughter of the rural Texas farming and ranching culture, has been writing since before she could spell. Inspired by her grandmother's bedtime storytelling and a love for all fiction genres, April's own word-weaving incorporates a healthy dose of romance, mystery, adventure, sci-fi, and fantasy. When she is not writing, she spends her time in indulging her passion for singing and music in general. After living in Nashville, Tennessee for several years, she resides once more in the Central Texas area, where she works at a grocery and foodservice distribution company in Temple, TX.